The One,
the Only,
the Amazing...

The One, the Only, the Amazing...

Bonnie Shiloh

About the author
The author grew up in a small county in Texas where there were more cows than people. In romance novels, cowboys are the stuff of dreams, but in real life, cowboying is hard work and real cowboys aren't easy to live with. After riding in pick-up trucks with most of the local opposite sex, the author decamped to the big city to find free love and the swinging singles life-styles of the 1970's. Bonnie didn't marry and settle down until she was 44 years old, so there was plenty of time to sow her wild oats. After all the great and terrifying sexual experiences over 26 years of being a single adult, a touch of imagination was the only ingredient required to create The One, the Only, the Amazing...

Published in the United States of America by
O•Zone Press, El Paso, Texas

ISBN-13 978-0-9976760-1-3
ISBN-10 0-9976760-1-9

Published 2018

To my family and my real friends, thanks for sticking with me. It was a long road.

Contents

Contents Continued

Contents Continued

Chapter 1

The Revelation

It was an affliction or maybe a blessing, a curse or a gift, the boy couldn't tell. All he knew was that the onset was sudden, first becoming aware of it when he was fourteen years old in the fall of 1967.

Growing up in a conservative small town deep in the piney woods of east Texas, not much ever seemed to change. Hippies were a group of people the town folk ridiculed even though they had never met one or even seen one. The Vietnam War was a patriotic duty and church on Sunday was pretty much compulsory no matter what kind of debauchery one engaged in the night before.

The boy was on the tall side for his age but skinny like all 14-year-old boys back then. He was considered to be good looking and not just by his grandmother. The girls were starting to notice. Hormones were racing through him and at the slightest provocation, an erection would occur.

He had just discovered the joys of masturbation and finding a place to do it was always a challenge. Sometimes he would do it in the small family bathroom and every time he took two seconds longer than his mother thought was necessary, she posed the question, "What are you doing in there?" He was certain she knew what he was doing especially in light of the number of crusty socks she found under his bed in the morning. That was part of the game of life, young boys and girls masturbated, thinking they invented sex while their parents pretended not to notice. But no matter how many times he did it, he still sprouted a horn at the mere thought of a chance to do it again.

He was good at math and invariably the teacher would call upon him to solve a problem in the front of the class at the most inopportune time. One day while daydreaming about the new freshman cheerleader, he was called to the blackboard to work a story problem concerning a farmer's need to determine the number of trucks required to haul bushels of apples and oranges. It was a simple math problem for the "smarter" kids but the chore was to get to the blackboard without anyone noticing his penis predicament, he was hard as could be. This was no easy task because in those days kids were required to wear slacks, not jeans, to school. Slacks were made of thin, loose fitting cloth, designed for aesthetics and not for holding in one's raging knob.

Dropping a pencil on the way up to the chalk board, he bent down to pick it up while walking forward. He rose up just before reaching the wall and stood with his nose pressed to the black slate. Only, Lisa Davis, a cute girl on the front left seat on the first row had a view and it was nearly a perfect profile. There you have it, his nose up against the board breathing chalk dust and a tent sticking out of his crotch just as close to the wall as his nose was to the blackboard.

His only thought was to solve the damn problem quickly, throw his pencil on the floor again and retreat back to his seat. But Lisa laughed at him and his condition manifested for the very first time. Even embarrassed as he was, a particularly prurient thought flashed through his mind. Lisa looked him in the eyes, began to turn a little blotchy around the edges and slid down in her seat. Her legs pinched together and she turned away looking toward the windows. No one noticed until she grunted as if she had just picked up a heavy object. The class stared but she stayed facing away from the students, slumped at her seat. The teacher asked if she was okay but the only response was a lesser grunt. The teacher went to see what was wrong but Lisa got up, hurriedly fled the class, and ran down to the bathroom.

Everyone was focused on Lisa's exit so the boy rushed back to his seat completely unnoticed. The teacher told the class to study the book as she left to go check on the girl. The room was abuzz with speculation about what just happened. The unofficial consensus and the opinion that received the boy's vote, was that Lisa accidentally and abruptly went number two in her pants.

What actually happened was she had her first orgasm and the boy gave it to her just by looking into her eyes.

Chapter 2

Football Practice

As a freshman, he accomplished his dream of playing on the varsity football team. He was quicker than all of the other players for the first few steps, going forward, backward or sideways but after those steps, almost anyone could overtake him. He only weighed a buck and a quarter but could catch the ball if thrown to him. With those qualifications, he was suited for only two positions, middle linebacker because he could fill an inside hole quickly or he could play tight end whose job it was to run down the field, turn around rapidly and catch the ball. Both of these tasks didn't require a run of more than five yards and he could do that faster than anybody.

During one particularly grueling September afternoon practice, the offense ran fifty plays. Of those fifty plays, the boy was on the ground for forty-eight. He was knocked down, blocked down, tackled down, shoved down, tripped, and once he just fell down. No matter how hard he tried, he never seemed to get into shape. He was sore after every practice and even worse after every game. At some point in time during football season, he thought it was supposed to get easier, but it never did. Getting face planted on the first day of football season hurt just as badly as the last day.

Practice finally ended after ten wind sprints and he was carrying his helmet and shoulder pads up to the field house. He ran into Prissy Walker, a junior, one of the varsity cheerleaders. She had her hands on her hips looking all sassy wearing her team sweatshirt, short-shorts, and tennis shoes. "Dog, you look like a dead dog."

In 1967, people hadn't yet started calling each other Dawg. However, the boy's name was David Gideon. His mother, having a Master's Degree in English, gave her son Othello as a middle moniker. It didn't take a higher-level education in anything to figure out that the boy's initials were DOG. He'd been called Dog ever since the sixth grade.

David looked at Prissy, wanting to say something witty but trying to muster any sort of dignity proved to be too much. He had a semi-black eye, he was bleeding from the crown of his nose, dirt covered his face, his whole body smelled like feet, and he was exhausted. He had nothing left. He just stared at her with her perfect hair, clean white shorts, and tennis shoes with a megaphone charm in the laces.

She kept looking at him, waiting for a response. He couldn't say a word but he managed two conflicting thoughts: *I think I'm going to fall over.* And *this girl is gorgeous.*

As soon as he had formulated the second thought, Prissy grabbed her lower abdomen, made a strange sound, turned, and ran in a serpentine drunken sailor pattern to the field house. He couldn't quite grasp what had just happened. Of course, David's brain wasn't working well, maybe due to possible multiple concussions which were completely disregarded in 1967. As he walked to the field house, longing for a shower, he realized that Prissy probably had to go to the bathroom to poop or vomit. He was convinced that the sight of him was too disgusting for her to take.

As he trudged to the showers, he was thinking of the girl from class. What are the chances of two girls getting sick at the mere sight of him? It was a heavy weight for the boy to carry.

Chapter 3

The Victory Dance

The Homecoming game was about to start. The victory dance would follow later in the evening. David sat in the locker room going over his game plan: *don't get killed*. The team was terrible. They had lost three out of four games with the tough part of the schedule yet to come.

Out on the field, the team introductions were just starting. All the players lined up underneath the goalpost and when their names were called, they ran through a gauntlet of cheerleaders, pep squad girls, band members, and assorted other persons of the student body who had wrangled their way on to the field. It was time for the boy to be introduced. "And now, number 55, playing middle linebacker, freshman, Mad Dog Gideon!" The fans in the stands laughed and he could hear the announcers in the press booth snickering over the loud speaker. With his 125-pound frame draped in an oversized uniform, he was anything but "mad dog" in appearance.

The game started and he played. He got knocked down, a lot. He got dragged by bigger boys he was trying to tackle. He ran into brick walls of human flesh charging at him. Most of the game consisted of futile expenditures of energy and opportunities to get hurt. However, in one magic moment in the first half, he fell on a fumble becoming a hero for about ten seconds. Once again in the second half, he swatted down a pass that was sure to be completed for a touchdown that would have given the opposing team a score of over fifty points. The game ended with the Yellow Jackets beating the boy's Broncos by a score of 48 to 7.

On to the victory dance. One would think the dance was named inappropriately but for the boy, it was a victory, he didn't get killed. He was wearing his slacks, button down collar shirt, and a tie. All athletes had to wear ties on game day. The dance was being held at the VFW. The music was provided, for free, by DJ Bobby Soul. Bobby Soul was really Robert Jarnigan from the 10th grade who happened to have a big stereo on which he could play the latest 45's. Bobby played whatever he felt like playing, but if you gave him a quarter he would play the song you wanted. Bobby Soul was not dumb.

Scouting out the single girls, David spotted Claudia Wilson sitting in the corner. Claudia was a freshman also. David searched his pocket and found two quarters. The choice needed to be made, did he spend a quarter for Bobby Soul to play a "slow" song or did he keep the money for a couple of chocolate sodas at the Rexall Drug Store the next day. With two quarters, the decision made itself, a quarter for a song and a quarter for a chocolate soda tomorrow.

He went up to Bobby, clandestinely flashed him a quarter as if it were an illegal substance, and asked him to play the summer's big smash song, *Whiter Shade of Pale* by Procol Harum. *Satisfaction* by the Rolling Stones just ended, Bobby expertly flipped the 45's, and within a second, the first chords of *Whiter Shade of Pale* were blaring through the speakers. Bobby and David looked at each other and nodded as if to say, "Job well done Bobby Soul".

David turned to find Claudia and ask her to dance, but across the room, he could see Jimmy Anderson with his hand stuck out saying,

"May I have this dance?" She accepted. David didn't curse a lot back then but, "Damn!"

There were two girls left in the wings, the chaperone's eleven-year-old daughter and Big Cindy Griffin, the sophomore, founder, and president of Cindy's Scents. As far as anyone knew, she had only made four scented candles and gave those away last year as Christmas presents to the teachers.

He practiced his line as he walked over to Big Cindy. "Would you care to dance? Would you like to dance with me? May I have this dance?" He approached. "Wanna Dance?" came out of his mouth.

Not so debonair and definitely not what he practiced but effective. Big Cindy stood up, put down her drink and half eaten, third piece of cake, and took his hand. They walked to the center of the dance floor and fell into an awkward rhythm. She was not ugly but she sure was big. Her hands felt big, her back felt big, and her legs felt big as she slowly tried to push one of her legs between his as they danced. He found himself nearly dancing bow legged around her thigh.

Being fourteen and laced with natural hormones, the boy's body began to involuntarily respond. Big Cindy was not what one would consider to be an instant turn-on, although not bad looking for a big girl, but just the pressure of her thigh on his groin was enough to stir things up. He pulled his head back and looked up slightly because she was a smidge taller than him if you call four inches a smidge. He started to ask what she was doing but he realized what was going on. He wasn't sure how it was going to end but he knew she was having her way with him.

Their eyes met and she made that now familiar grunt and squeezed him tighter. All he could think was *Oh my God, Big Cindy is going to be sick.* He tried to pull away but she grabbed him in a full-on bear hug, a half-Nelson, arm-bar kind of thing, and he was hers for the taking.

She panted heavy rasping breaths into his ear and clutched him tighter. During the thirty seconds she was in this state, he was completely trapped, immobilized, and nearly choked unconscious. He just kept thinking, *what is going on?* All the while he was afraid that he made her sick like the other girls and, at any moment, she might projectile vomit her dinner, three pieces of red velvet cake and four glasses of coon-dog punch, down the back of his button-down collar shirt.

Chapter 4

Outside the VFW

Big Cindy regained some composure and let go of David enough where he could right himself and look as if he were dancing again instead of being strangled by a luchador.

"What happened?" he asked her.

"You made me cum," she said.

"What do you mean?" he asked completely ignorant.

"I mean I came, don't you cum?"

"I'm not sure," the boy responded. He full well knew what "cumming" was, because he had been masturbating for months, he was just not familiar with the terminology.

"Follow me," she said, leading him out the side door of the VFW hall.

They were standing where the food servers went to smoke. It was dirty and the trash cans smelled like dead fish. "This is no good," she said and led him into the trees and slightly up the hill from the building. They were only twenty feet into the woods but they were isolated from view.

"Okay and be quick about it, c'mon, c'mon," she said as she snapped her fingers and held her hand out.

He wasn't very experienced but he was pretty sure what was about to happen next. And he was right, she didn't wait for him to make the first move. She reached down with her extra-large fingers, expertly unzipped his fly, pulled out his soft dick, and began kneading it with skill that was way beyond her years. This was not Big Cindy's first hand job. However, it was David's.

After an incredible orgasm, a short explanation about how he made her cum just by looking at her, and exchanging sad stories, Big Cindy and David Othello Gideon agreed to create a mutually beneficial semi-permanent sexual relationship. He would give her no strings attached orgasms at any time of her choosing just by looking at her and she would give him hand jobs at convenient opportunities.

Back in the VFW hall, he was sitting on a bench, eating a finger sandwich contemplating the series of recent events. The ability to give girls orgasms just by looking at them seemed so extremely peculiar that he could hardly fathom it. He wanted some advice but he really didn't have anyone with whom to discuss the matter. It was not exactly a problem for a coach, certainly the school counselor was the wrong choice, his parents were the worst choice, his older brother would do nothing but ridicule him, so by process of elimination, Big Cindy was his new confidant and conspirator.

After thinking a little more about it, he realized that he caused what happened to Lisa in class and Prissy on the practice field. Had he been just a little bit more astute, he could have had endless hand jobs from Lisa, the quintessential girl next door or Prissy the hot cheerleader or maybe even both. Instead….Big Cindy.

Chapter 5

Revenge and Regret

Football season was long gone as was the memory of the abysmal one win and nine loss record. David was in history class taught by Mrs. Edgemere. They were discussing her favorite subject, the Great War. The reason she liked talking about it so much was because she was born in 1911 and actually lived through the conflict. She was only fifty-six years old but the students thought she should either retire or just go ahead and die because fifty-six to a fourteen-year-old seemed ancient.

Being bored and not really caring what happened in Sarajevo Austria nearly forty years before he was born, he decided to experiment. He gave Mrs. Edgemere the look. She didn't notice. He was the only one actually paying attention to her besides brainiac Candy Schiller. She always paid attention in class.

He upped the ante by sliding his desk-chair across the floor a few inches making a screech that hurt most peoples' teeth. Everyone looked in his direction and Mrs. Edgemere caught his eyes to give him the "you better settle down" look, but it backfired.

Mrs. Edgemere sitting behind her desk, put her head down in her folded arms and began to shake and cry. One student flew out the door and went racing down to the principal's office to get help. Before the shock wore off, the vice-principal was hovering over Mrs. Edgemere trying to ascertain what could have possibly happened. David heard her say in a low, muffled voice, "Get me out of here".

She stood with the vice-principal's help and slowly walked to the door. She was wearing a blouse buttoned up to the neck, light grey wool slacks and clunky black shiny shoes. Her light grey slacks were wet and discolored from the crotch to the knee from urine.

The old woman couldn't handle the intensity of the instant and unexpected orgasm. All he wanted to do was have a little fun. It was not fun. It was degrading to both of them. The gravity of his power settled in and he immediately felt remorse. He decided then and there to keep his head down and never unexpectedly look a girl in the eyes. He would be, from now on and forever, labeled shy.

Chapter 6

The Big Cindy Years

Gossip flourished about the strange relationship that had formed between David and Big Cindy. They met almost every day for lunch and were frequently seen "going off" with each other to undisclosed locations. They never had any public displays of affection so the kids thought they were doing drugs, especially that insidious marijuana.

David and Big Cindy enjoyed a hot and heavy platonic sexual relationship, if there could be such a thing. Big Cindy would scout out the hidden locations and tell David where to meet her. They had four primary spots, the woods by the school, the groundskeeper's shed, the boys vocational shop, and the top row of the football stands.

David experimented with Big Cindy trying to find ways to cope with his ability. He wore sun glasses but they didn't work. While in the vocational shop, he put on a welder's mask and looked at her hoping that whatever he had couldn't penetrate the almost opaque glass. She still had an orgasm. Obviously, the trigger was his looking at a girl and not the girl actually seeing his eyes. It was a minor distinction but a major reinforcement for him to keep his head down and appear to be shy.

As the years went on, Big Cindy and David became friends. There was a real closeness between them. He didn't know if it was because she jacked him off nearly three times a week or if something was really blossoming. He was way too young to determine if he was in love.

She would sometimes play games with him. If they hadn't seen each other over the weekend, she would take him to one of their spots and say that he had to cum in two minutes or she would quit and leave him hanging. He never got to find out if she would really leave a guy in the lurch because he never failed to cum within the two minutes. She was an expert masturbator.

Sometimes she would talk about her candle business, Cindy's Scents, while she stroked him. David loved to listen while she massaged him. When she finished talking she would concentrate on him for about twenty seconds and he would have a tremendous orgasm. On those days, he would give her the look until she begged him to quit.

He had finally gotten over the fact that Big Cindy was... big. He learned to see through the outside layer. Granted that the entire relationship was their secret meetings. He never dated her but he thought he wouldn't mind it so much if she wanted to go out. The only thing to do in town was go to the drive-in theater and they both knew what would happen, the same thing that happened no less than three times a week at school. So, they never went out.

In May, a day before the seniors were to graduate, David, a junior, and Big Cindy, a senior, planned a final rendezvous. They met on the bleachers of the football stadium sitting on the top row as they had done dozens of times before. The usual routine was to chat a few minutes and then get down to business but today was different. Big Cindy wanted to tell him something.

She told him how much she appreciated his gift, his loyalty and his silence. She said she really enjoyed the conversations mainly because he was the only boy who ever talked to her. She said after she graduated tomorrow she would never contact him again. She said that he should make his own way in the world and use his wonderful gift wisely. She told him he could be a great man and all she wanted to do was make candles. There was no place for her in his life. Her eyes filled with tears as she said she would love him forever. "I will, you know," she said. "Love you forever."

He listened, feeling some sort of sorrow while waiting for her to give him the signal that she wanted her orgasm, but she didn't signal. Then she did something that she had never done before. She wet kissed him for a long time and then lumbered down the bleachers wiping the tears off her cheeks. She was out of his life, but not his heart.

Climbing down the bleachers, David's legs nearly gave way due to some sort of total body anguish. He knew pain from the outside. He had been beat up in football enough to know about scrapes, cuts, and bruises but he never knew that something could hurt so badly from the inside out.

Time passed, the Texas summer burst forth, and he nearly suffered heat exhaustion every day working at the filling station, changing oil, fixing flats, and pumping gas. He worked eleven hours a day and made eight bucks. That's about seventy-three cents an hour. However, no matter how hard he worked, that forty dollars at the end of the week seemed like a lot.

He took his money every weekend and went looking for a good time, something to fill the hole in his life that Big Cindy left. He asked many girls to go to the movies or out for a hamburger but none would take him up on it. Their universal response was that he had been with Big Cindy and they didn't want to play second fiddle. He did not like those girls.

He started driving to Endicott, the next little town over to try to find a date but the boys in that town were extremist when it came to protecting their women. He surmised that there were about four or five good looking girls in the town and all of them were dating super studs and he had no choice but to back off. It was a long summer.

He began his last year of high school with hopes of playing sports and finding hot dates to homecoming, the Christmas Pageant, and the prom. Now weighing 160 pounds, he was not quite the punching bag in football he had been in the past years. He did really well during the season and earned an All-District recognition. Being a football hero still didn't get him a date to Homecoming because the ghost of Big Cindy haunted him.

He played basketball and had the privilege of being on the team when they raised the district champion trophy over their heads. But he failed to get a date to the Christmas Pageant.

In the spring, playing baseball, he had a streak of eleven hits in a row. In the on-deck circle waiting for a chance for a twelfth hit in a row, a junior twirler put her face up to the fence and said, "Hey Dog, bash one out of the park for me, will ya?"

"What's in it for me?" he asked.

"You hit a home run and I'll let you take me to the prom."
David went to the plate with a man on first base, two outs, and the Broncos were behind by one. It was a perfect chance to be a hero. The pitcher served up a fast ball on the first pitch. Here it was, an eighty-four mile an hour "tater" coming straight over the plate. David swung and hit the ball but he didn't get all of it. The ball flew towards the right field fence. Everything went into motion and David was hauling ass around the bases as fast he could go. He was really quick half way to first base but his natural inclination was to labor after a few yards. David ran for all he was worth; a prom date was at stake. He decided he was running home no matter where the ball was. The player ahead of him scored, tying the game, which took the pressure off. He rounded third and realized that the ball had gone over the far-right corner of the fence. His twelfth hit was a home run and he was going to the prom!

Chapter 7

The Prom

He was driving his mother's Dodge Dart to pick up Susan McVey, the junior twirler who challenged him at the baseball game. He was more than excited. He had a corsage that cost half a week's pay from working at the filling station. He was wearing a rented white tux, going for the James Bond look and he didn't totally fail. Susan appeared at her door looking like an angel. She walked down the steps swaying a little more than she should to let the dress speak for itself.

He opened the car door for her and helped her shove the dress in behind her. As he was running around the front of the car he was thinking, *I'm gonna get some tonight.* He opened the driver's door and basically jumped in behind the wheel. He looked at her and their eyes locked. Her legs spread, her feet went up on the dash, and she was in the throes of an orgasm in broad daylight right there in front of her parents' house. He started the car and drove off at a high rate of speed with Susan grunting like a rutting pig in the passenger seat.

Three miles out of town on a dirt road near cemetery hill, he pulled the car over. "What did you do to me?" she asked gaining composure.

"Did you release some kind of Spanish Fly sex gas in the car as soon as I got in so I'd start cumming?"

"No," he said. "I don't know what happened," lying through his teeth.

"Well, I'm so sorry you had to see that," she said. "Do you want go on to the dance now?"

"Yeah, let's go to the prom." And then he looked at her and she smiled back. He started to pull away but within three seconds, she was at it again. This time it appeared to be even more powerful than the first time. He just spun the car around in a circle and parked in the original position and waited it out.

When she was back to her normal self, she looked like she had been dancing at the prom for several hours. Her hair was sweaty and her face was flushed. The make up she spent two hours putting "on" was now "off". Most of it had been wiped on the sleeve of her dress.

"Do you have anything to drink?" she asked. He didn't and offered to drive her to the Dairy D'Lite and buy her a cherry coke. On the way into town she tried straightening up her face and he tried to keep his thoughts as pure as freshly fallen snow and his eyes on the road.

"I don't know what's wrong with me," she said. He did, but couldn't tell her.

At the Dairy D'Lite they sat across from each other in a booth in complete silence, each one trying to not think about the previous thirty minutes. When she finished about half of her drink she suggested they go on to the prom. They got back in the car and headed for the high school gymnasium. Three blocks away, he couldn't help himself and mentally pictured what would happen after the prom. They locked eyes again. "Oh No!" she said as she succumbed for a third time in less than forty-five minutes. This one seemed almost painful. It was certainly painful to watch.

As she was going at it and then recovering, he drove back out to cemetery hill and parked. When she finally finished, she sat up in the car seat and tried to clean her face. She started to cry a little bit and then she wanted to talk... a lot.

"I don't know what's wrong with me. I guess I've been thinking about going to the prom with you too much. I have been planning for weeks to lose my virginity to you. I really wasn't sure if I was ready for it because you have such a big one."

"A big one?" he asked.

"Yeah, everyone knows that you and Big Cindy have been going at it for years and she is ginormous so you must be bigger than usual to be able to satisfy her. At least that's what everybody says. I knew you were experienced and hung, so you're the guy I picked to pop my cherry and look at me now. I'm like a baby and can't seem to hold it long enough for you to even touch me. Every time I turn around I start cumming all over myself. Now I really don't want to screw you. One, because I feel stupid and two, I don't want it anymore because I just had three of the best cums I ever had in my life, believe me, I know about cumming. I have been practicing bunches. Every night as a matter of fact. I've used a hair dryer, the water out of the bath tub faucet, a magazine, my fingers... I was ready, I thought." She went on and on.

When she stopped jabbering he asked her what she wanted to do and she told him to take her home. After the short and silent drive, he walked her to the door and was thinking about a kiss when her father stepped out. Her old man asked him what the hell he was doing bringing her home three hours early and looking like she'd been crying. He didn't have an immediate answer but Susan bailed him out. She told her Dad that she had gotten violently ill and threw up a hundred times and wanted to come home to go to bed. Her mother, who was standing right around the corner, rushed out to comfort her baby. David was off the hook but still didn't have a date for prom. He too, went home.

Chapter 8

College

Monday morning after David's miserable date, Susan started spreading a vicious rumor. She said she didn't make it to the prom because David took her out to cemetery hill and tried to have his way with her, refusing to take her to the dance. All of her friends and their friends either gave David the cold shoulder or worse, spoke their minds. He was not the most popular guy around to begin with but now, he was certainly ruined and had no choice but to leave town and go to a college a long way away.

One of the schools on his short list was Texas Tech University in Lubbock, almost 500 miles away from home. Only one other kid he knew was going there and she was in a different socio-economic class. She never spoke to him in a town of twelve hundred people, why would she speak to him in a school of twenty-three thousand?

On a September Monday morning, he found himself in class, English Literature 101. He sat in the back of the room as the students waited on the professor. At five minutes after the hour, the age-old argument began about how long one waited for the teacher. Most of the students agreed that a full professor got fifteen minutes and any other instructor only got ten minutes. At nine minutes after the hour, Professor Emily Crews, PhD, walked through the door apologizing for being late.

She was a young forty something, brown haired, and about five-foot, five-inches tall. She was not a classic beauty, but she was someone who commanded attention by her presence. David made a point not to look at her for fear of causing her to have an orgasm. She seemed pleasant, obviously smart, and, of course, well read. He looked forward to attending her class.

By the third week, the class had broken down into book review groups. His group chose *Jonathan Livingston Seagull*. The book was not exactly David's cup of tea, but he read it and participated in the discussion. Professor Crews joined the little circle of chairs in the back of the classroom and started listening to the group argue about the book. David watched her out of the corner of his eye and saw her smile a few times at some of the more ludicrous arguments being made. The professor leaned back in her chair and her dress slid up to around mid-thigh, then she crossed her legs and David was forced by ancient instinct to look. She caught him looking, their eyes met, "boom!". And he was trying so hard to be careful.

She slowly stood, straining to remain composed, said "Excuse me please," and walked very deliberately out the door. He was super impressed with her ability to pull that off. In maybe five minutes, she reappeared in the classroom as if nothing had happened.

Two minutes before the class was to end, she instructed everyone to put the chairs back in neat rows and take a seat. One minute before the hour was up, she said "At the next class, have another book in mind that your group wants to read and... I would like to see Cassie Armstrong and David Gideon after class."

He didn't know what to think, but he and Cassie were standing in front of her desk after everyone else had left. She handed Cassie a sheet of paper that had several assignments on it and told her to complete them when she was home while her mother was recuperating from the upcoming hip surgery. Cassie thanked her and left the classroom.

Professor Crews was then alone with David. "I want to know how you did it?" she asked.

"Did what?"

"Don't play dumb, tell me how you did it."

"You won't believe me," he said.

"Try me. I know what happened. I just don't know how."

She was just like Big Cindy. She figured it out the first time. "I can make a girl have an orgasm just by looking at her and thinking about it. Lately, I haven't really needed to even think about it."

She got up, locked the classroom door and sat back down in the chair behind her desk and said, "Prove it."

"If you insist," and he looked at her with the nastiest notion he could imagine.

She exploded without any hint of trying to show restraint this time. She said the "F" word twice while she was cumming. He'd never heard a woman over forty say anything like that before.

When she got her senses back, she opened the desk drawer, pulled out a pen and paper, and wrote down an address. "You have a special assignment this semester. You must attend the Women's Book Club. They meet the second Tuesday of every month at this address at 6:00 pm sharp. You must be at every meeting. Your first meeting is tomorrow night." She handed him the paper. "Go on out of here now."

While in the dorm that night he was thinking about the Women's Book Club. He couldn't tell if it was punishment or a reward. He wasn't a fast reader, so reading an extra three or four books during the semester was more than he really wanted to do. Besides, it being a *woman's* book club sounded dangerous.

Chapter 9

Book Club

The next day, the second Tuesday of the month, David was waiting at exactly 5:59 pm outside the address that was written on the paper. He was in front of a residence in a nice neighborhood near the university. Although really wanting to chicken out, he approached the front door and meekly knocked. To his surprise, Professor Emily Crews opened the door and invited him in.

There were five other women in the living room, all sitting on various chairs and couches, each with a book in her lap. Professor Crews introduced David to the ladies. There were three other professors. All three were more matronly looking than Professor Crews. Another woman was in her mid-thirties and was not an employee of the university. She seemed rich and he figured she just married well because she didn't look like she worked a day in her life. The last woman was the university librarian. She was kind of mousy but if she took off her glasses and let her hair down, she would transform very well.

Professor Crews, had them all sit and she began the session. "We will not discuss our assignments tonight. Instead, we will have a magic show. David has a special talent that he is going to share with us." Professor Crews wouldn't look at him because she knew what would happen. The other women were clueless.

"David," she said. "Please allow the ladies to experience your magic." She leaned back in the lounge chair and kicked off her shoes.

David stood, looking down. "I'm not sure I want to do this," he said quietly.

"Of course you do, David." Professor Crews was being coy. "Now, do your magic."

David turned his back on the group and began to speak. "Ladies, what you are about to witness must be kept secret. It is an ancient art, practiced only by those chosen by destiny. No one can explain it and once witnessed, one will never forget it. Are you ready for what will change your life?" He heard Professor Crews giggle a little. "Are you ready ladies because here he is, the one, the only, the amazing Mister Orgasm!" And with that self-introduction, he spun around quickly catching the eye of every woman and the carnal thought was transferred immediately.

The women, without exception, went straight from mature collegiate faculty types to writhing, wiggling, wailing sirens. Professor Crews was turned sideways in her lounger trying to get through it with some dignity. The three other professors were looking straight at each other screaming at the top of their lungs. They sounded like they were going down the big drop on a roller coaster. The rich lady was doing some kind of splits and the librarian was on the floor on her hands and knees, face on the floor, with her butt up in the air.

David stood with his arms crossed surveying his work. The work of Mister Orgasm.

Chapter 10

Book Club Burden

On the second Tuesday of the next month, he found himself at the Book Club thirty minutes early. Professor Crews told him she had a surprise for him. It was a cape, top hat, and cane. "If we are going to call you a magician, you need to look like one."

One by one the ladies began to arrive. He had met them all before except the last one through the door. Each month they would invite a guest for a onetime meeting with the Women's Book Club. A book discussion with the foremost minds in literature, at least in Lubbock, Texas, was a real honor. The rich woman from the last meeting was the guest that month. This time it was Lilly Flores, the local baker's wife. She brought *pan dulce* with her.

They sat in their usual places knowing what was in store for them. Only Lilly was oblivious. David slipped out to the kitchen to put on his new costume. Professor Crews began her speech, "Ladies we are excited to have back with us tonight the greatest magician alive. What you will experience must be kept secret and only discussed in this sanctum. Without further ado, I'd like to introduce, the one, the only, the amazing..... Mister Orgasm!"

David stepped out of the kitchen and took his place in the circle. The ladies giggled at his appearance but Lilly asked, "What is this?"

"This, is magic," David said and he gave them all the look. The librarian melted to her knees, face on the floor, butt up in the air just like before. The three middle aged professors fell together in a pile and started dry hunching on each other. Lilly, the new woman, leaned over with her head in her lap, hands around her ankles. Professor Crews slipped into the kitchen and was absent during the whole ordeal. She never participated after the first meeting.

David stood with his arms crossed, as before, lord of the carnal carnage.

Chapter 11

The College Years

David reconciled himself to going to class and attending the monthly Women's Book Club. As the years rolled by, he became the dorm Resident Assistant and found it comforting that he had a "job" that didn't involve working around women. However, his "job" mostly consisted of calling the "Kampus Kops" when things got out of hand and putting in work orders to repair the building when the residents tore off the wallpaper or blocked the drains to flood the halls and play slip and slide at four in the morning. He was destined to live in the dorm for all four years at the university.

In early November of his senior year, he was returning from chemistry class when he caught sight of a young woman sitting on the steps of the Baptist Student Union building. She was wearing a white dress, had flaming red hair, and literally looked like an angel. He sat down beside her and struck up a conversation. She was as shy as he pretended to be and avoided his eyes even when he looked directly at her. Also, she seemed uninterested in sex. She was his opposite.

The angel's name was Claire. She was an intense student but found time to go out with him on Saturday nights. She went to church all day on Sundays, had a study group on Mondays, left Tuesday nights for washing clothes, shopping, studying, and catching up on reading. Wednesdays were reserved for choir, Thursdays were taken up with volunteering at a nursing home and Fridays she had Bible study with a group of at-risk teenagers.

David always looked forward to his Saturday nights. He and Claire did something different every week. They went out for hamburgers, had ice cream, and went to the movies as long as they were rated G or PG. He didn't know if it was love, but it sure was comfortable. She liked his shyness and he was safe with hers.

They spent a lot of time together during the Thanksgiving and Christmas holidays. They held hands and almost kissed a few times. However, when the spring semester started, the relationship returned to seeing each other only on Saturday nights. She was too busy for anything else.

In February of that year, 1975, Valentines Day was on Friday. Claire agreed to go out with him on Friday instead of Saturday because they both wanted to make Valentine's Day special. He bought a ring, not an engagement ring, but something impressive that he was sure would eventually become a treasured heirloom. On the Saturday before Valentines, they just kept smiling and giggling, knowing something big was coming that might change their relationship. He was, after all, planning on telling her he loved her.

On February 11th, he started walking toward Professor Crews' house for the Women's Book Club meeting. Because there was a new guest every month, he didn't want the guest to see him before the show, so he started slipping in through the back door and changing into his costume, which had taken on a fairly professional look. He had purchased a second-hand tux, with top hat and tails. He actually looked the part of a magician.

At 5:55 pm, David was standing around the corner in the kitchen waiting for his cue. Professor Crews was in the bathroom. He heard the librarian say, "It's time, girls!" The three professors ripped off their blouses and wriggled out of the slacks. Within seconds the librarian and the three professors were naked. This was the new ritual that had evolved. The guest sat in the chair near the fireplace shocked at what was taking place. "Oh dear God," she said. "What kind of sinful place is this?"

David stepped through the door with his back turned to the group. He spread his arms out wide holding his cane. "The man that you have all been waiting for has arrived, the one, the only, the amazing Mister Orgasm!" He turned around and let them all have it full force. At the last second and unable to stop himself, he realized that the guest was, Claire, his sweetheart, his angel, his new love, but there was no taking it back once it started.

The three professors started rolling all over each other in the floor screaming like school girls in a funhouse. The librarian assumed her position, face on the floor and butt up in the air. Claire, always the lady, crossed her legs at the ankles, put her hands in her lap, and pressed between her legs. Her face turned as dark red as her hair.

Two of the three professors were scissor fucking each other while the third was on her knees masturbating with a huge black dildo she'd brought from home. This was the norm for the Women's Book Club after four years of "magic" but for someone like Claire, it was a glimpse into Dante's Inferno. David didn't know what to do, so he just stood looking pathetic. After a few minutes when all the action had subsided, Claire got up, straightened her clothes, holding the book in her hand that they were supposed to be reviewing. She walked over to him and nearly knocked him unconscious with *To Kill a Mocking Bird*. She hit him square across the jaw, cheek, nose and eye with one fell swing. Without saying a word, she walked out of his life forever.

He was bleeding from the eyebrow and nose. The women ran to him and had him recline in the lounge chair while they went to get ice and band-aids. After the room quit spinning, he felt the women leaning over him. They were all still naked.

The librarian had her face very close to his. She was trying to wipe the blood away from his brow when her tit brushed against his chest. They looked at each other and she collapsed across him having another orgasm. The three professors, still naked, rolled the librarian on to the floor and started tearing away David's tux. When they were through, he was naked except for his socks.

Professor Emily Crews came out from the kitchen, naked, and fell on his hard cock with her mouth. His whole body stiffened and he locked eyes with the three professors, two of whom were trying to guide his hands to their dripping mounds. All three professors went off again. One was on either side of the lounge chair hunching on his fingers and the third professor was behind Professor Crews banging on her from behind as if she had man parts.

He couldn't last much longer and announced to everybody that he was about to cum. All of the women encircled the chair as Professor Crews finished him up by hand. They were impressed at the load he was carrying. Little did they know, it was his first blowjob. Professor Crews looked at him and he gave her a wink. She was on her knees at the end of the lounge chair having what appeared to be a serious orgasm. The other women comforted her by squeezing her nipples and stroking her crotch.

When she was done, David said, "I think that's enough for the night," and they all got dressed. The women went home leaving Professor Crews and David alone. David was dressed in his street clothes, holding what was left of his ripped tux in his hands.

"Sorry about ruining your tux," she said.

"Yeah," was all he said while he rolled the remains around in his hands.

"I am also really, really sorry about Claire. She sought me out and asked if she could attend. She knew you went to the Women's Book Club every month and she wanted to surprise you. She said you guys had been dating for some time now. I thought she knew about you and what went on."

"Nope," he said. "She didn't have a clue."

"I am so sorry."

After a dramatically long pause, he said, "You know this is my last time, right?"

"I don't blame you. It's getting out of hand. My husband would kill me if he got caught me doing this. The university would censure me for sure."

"I didn't even know you had a husband," he said.

"He's overseas. He's a lieutenant colonel, a Special Forces commander in Southeast Asia."

"Well, I hope he doesn't find out either. I'm sure he's trained well enough to kill me with nothing but a spoon. But what I want to know is why after four long years did you decide to join us in the living room now. You were there the first meeting but always absent thereafter?"

"I think I knew this was it, the last one. You have given the group so many orgasms over the years, I thought it was time for yours."

"It was my first time with a mouth. Plenty of hand jobs, but never a mouth or ..."

"You're kidding," she interrupted. "With a gift like yours I thought you would have had your way with all the girls."

"No. It's just confusing most of the time." He moved to the front door.

"Good Bye, David." Closing her eyes, she kissed him on the cheek.

He walked out into the West Texas night throwing the tux in a garbage can by the street.

Chapter 12

College Twilight

In April, David had the realization that in a few months, he would need to face the real world, find a real job and somehow learn to deal with his affliction in society. This was more than he could handle. Even though he would have an accounting degree, he went down to the local Army recruiting station and signed up for the delayed entry program (DEP). DEP just meant that you joined now but didn't actually have to go basic training until an agreed upon later date. In his case, he signed the papers on April 23rd with a sixty-day delay, meaning he would be shipped off to Basic Training on June 23rd. He felt better after making the commitment.

On the way back from chemistry class, he saw a solitary young lady standing on the lawn in front of the Fine Arts Building. She seemed nearly catatonic. He watched her for a few minutes as she just stood there. After a moment, a girlfriend came over and the two girls walked arm in arm into the building. She had dark curly hair and was tomboy attractive.

This girl was so intriguing that he waited at the same spot several days in a row until he saw her again. He approached and realized that she was blind. He spoke to her and she picked up the conversation easily. She was wearing sunglasses and he couldn't see her eyes. When he thought she was looking at him, he gave her a long look but absolutely nothing happened. After all the experiments with Big Cindy, he never once thought of blindfolding the girl to see if his magic would penetrate.

He began meeting this girl, Margaret, regularly at the cafeteria for lunch. Then they went out to a concert, then dinner and then she invited him over to her place. When he arrived, he was introduced to her roommate, Jill, who had prepared a gourmet meal. David had to be extremely careful to keep Jill in his peripheral vision.

Margaret and David became close but still had not had a real sexual encounter. They were going to take a road trip after David graduated in May and he was hoping it would be his breakthrough opportunity. Jill, the roommate, was hired as a companion for Margaret during the school year but after finals, her obligation was over and she would go back to Indiana for the summer. Margaret and David would finally be alone.

Margaret was starting to press David for his plan after he graduated. She was just a junior and wanted to know if he was going to get a local job and wait for her to graduate or leave her all by herself for her senior year. He kept putting her off and said he would let her know his plan during the trip when they had time to talk. That satisfied her for the time being.

The night after graduation, they were in her bedroom packing all of her stuff. The last stop on their road trip was her home in San Angelo, Texas, because she was going to spend the summer months with her family. The left half of her double bed was covered in clothes. She was feeling around in her chest of drawers not wanting to leave any of her garments behind, talking the whole time.

David completely disrobed and laid down on the half of the bed not covered in suitcases and female unmentionables. He began to masturbate. She kept talking for a minute and then she became quiet and listened. "What are you doing?" she asked.

"Come over here and find out," he said. She listened a little while longer and then made her way to him. David was flat on his back with his testicles stuffed between his legs causing his shaft to stick straight up in the air. Using her hands, she felt her way over to him. She first found his thigh and then moved up to find his little pole. She explored every part of what was usually covered up. After familiarizing herself with his manliness and before she started really working on him she set some ground rules. "I'm not ready to go all the way, but I'll keep my clothes on until you are finished and then you can put yours on and I'll take mine off." It wasn't a negotiation.

She went to work on him with a rote hand job that felt somewhat like she was pumping up a bicycle tire. It was completely passionless and he had a hard time reaching completion. When finished, he got dressed, she undressed and they switched positions. She had a great body with small breasts and the hairiest bush he could imagination. It was good. He tried to go down on her but she pushed his head away instructing him to manually stimulate her. He rubbed her where he thought her clit was buried in the bush and he must have hit the nail on the head because in less than thirty seconds, she gave an understated whimper and was done.

The morning of the trip arrived and the rental car was packed to the gills. The first stop was going to be Albuquerque, New Mexico for an Indian Pow Wow. She couldn't see the beautiful costumes but she could hear the drums, singing, shells and rattles. They were no more than five miles outside of Lubbock city limits when she said, "You promised me you'd tell me your plans now that you have graduated?"

He felt like he had just been ambushed. Women remember everything. "I've done something that I don't think you will appreciate," he said. "I've joined the Army."

"What do you mean?"

He thought it was a simple understandable statement. "I joined the Army," he said again. "I leave in about a month."

"Take me home," she said.

"Back to Lubbock?" he asked.

"No, take me home to San Angelo right now."

Again, it wasn't a negotiation. He turned the car around and drove two-hundred miles in complete silence to her home in San Angelo. Her parents rushed out to greet her along with her monster size brother who played right guard for the University of Texas Longhorn football team. Her brother grabbed all of her suitcases at the same time and carried them into the house. Each suitcase probably weighed fifty pounds and there were four of them. Her entourage closed the front door behind them and David made a quick exit giving her no chance to tell her family, especially her brother, how much she was hurt.

He was not proud of running away but judging from her reaction to his news, there was no sense in trying to remain friends or confronting her brother. Timing in life was everything.

Chapter 13

You're In the Army Now

On June 22nd, David took a bus to Houston and caught a plane to St. Louis. From there he took another bus to Fort Leonard Wood, Missouri. After completing a stack of paperwork, his sergeant doubled-timed him over to the barracks in the Reception Company area. There he waited for nine days until enough personnel arrived to make up a basic training class. While he was waiting, he white-washed the rocks lining the driveways in the senior officers' quarters, he scrubbed about a million pots and pans in the mess hall and he cut grass with a hand scythe.

On day ten, an eighteen-wheel tractor trailer came to the Reception Company and all of the recruits were herded into the cattle car and driven to Basic Training. The Drill Sergeants were waiting with baseball bats and began banging on the sides of the cattle car. "You've got thirty seconds to get out of that car and twenty-nine are already gone!" The soldiers wildly stampeded out of the trailer and stood with their boots on yellow footprints painted on the concrete. After a screaming lecture and eighty push-ups the recruits were finally allowed to enter the barracks. From that moment, his mind was on nothing but learning army regulations, drill and ceremony, marching, weapons training and most of all, not thinking about women.

His plan was good and working well until he and two buddies got an overnight pass. They decided to take a bus to St. Louis and chasing women was inevitably on the agenda. The bus station was only a few blocks away from a dubious hotel called the Excelsior. As run down as it looked, a doorman stood out front. When they went to check-in, Tommy asked the doorman where they could get some girls. The doorman told them to go inside and pay for a two-room suite and he would send up a girl with a six pack of beer.

The three of them waited nervously in the living room of the suite, speculating what the girl would look like. They didn't have to wait long. Within thirty minutes, there was a knock on the door. Tommy opened the door, "Hello boys," and she had two six packs of beer, one in each hand. She was a little tall, a decade older than the boys and she definitely had that bored housewife look about her.

The boys quickly played rock, paper, scissors to see who would go first. The woman seemed amused. Tommy won the cherry, Red Bone got sloppy seconds and Mad Dog David Gideon got clean up. Red Bone and Mad Dog stayed in the living room while Tommy and the woman went into the bedroom. Red Bone broke into a six pack and the boys discussed the situation. There was great anxiety about the price and the etiquette. About five minutes into the conversation the boys could hear Tommy grunting like a water buffalo and then complete silence.

The silence was broken by a muffled conversation from the bedroom then Tommy emerged with a giant shit eatin' grin. Before Tommy could even sit on the couch Red Bone asked "How much?"

Tommy responded, "Eighty bucks, but that's because I was first." Red Bone and Mad Dog both groaned. After a minute more of discussion, Red Bone decided he would offer $60.00 for sloppy seconds.

Within moments of making his decision, the woman hollered "Next!" and Red Bone entered with trepidation. Tommy began to tell Mad Dog how he damn near wore her out as he popped a top on one of the "free" beers. Within a few minutes Red Bone belched out an animal-like vocalization and all fell silent in the bedroom. Tommy started giggling. Red Bone stumbled out on wobbly legs and said "Seventy-five." Red Bone grabbed a beer, "Go get her Mad Dog, I've slowed her down enough for you to handle." Mad Dog David Gideon got up and headed to the bedroom to do something he had never done before, get a piece of ass.

David walked into the bedroom, slowly closing the door behind him. There was a $155 on the top of the night stand. She was sitting up in bed with her lower body under the covers. "What do you want?" she asked.

David wasn't really sure what the correct answer was supposed to be so he responded, "Just regular, I guess."

"Seventy dollars on the night stand before we start." She finally looked up and smiled at him and that was all it took. Her legs came out from underneath the covers and she grasped her knees like she was trying to do a "cannon ball" off a high dive. She started verbalizing something that could only be described as barking. That went on until she completed her orgasm.

"What is wrong with me?" she asked rhetorically.

David answered anyway, "Nothing."

She wiped the hair away from her forehead and said, "That's never happened to me before."

David said, "Well get ready because it's about to happen again." She looked at him and went up on her knees in the middle of the bed with her arms outstretched up over her head. She vibrated and let out one long, low guttural tone for the duration of her orgasm. David thought she might pass out because there was no way that anyone could expel that much air without a breath. She sputtered after nearly a minute and fell forward with her head now at the foot of the bed.

"How do you do that?" she asked with her face still buried in the bedspread. "I don't know," he answered. She rolled over and jokingly said, "I think I love you." She winked at him and off to the races she went. She tried to spin around to get her head to the top of the bed but only made it half way, with her face and arms hanging off one side of the bed and her feet hanging off the other. This time she just repeated "Oh No" over and over again until her body was no longer overwhelmed with the orgasm. She was deathly quiet. David stood waiting for her to make the next move, and she then she made it, "I've had it. Take forty bucks off the night stand and leave please."

"You want me to take money from you?" he asked a little confused.

"Please," she said. "I'm paying you to stop now, okay? I've had it."

David grabbed two twenties, shoved them into his pocket and stepped out of the room. At once, Red Bone asked "How much?"

"Forty, going third gets you a special discount I guess," answered David. He never told the guys that she paid him. The fellas peeked into the bedroom and saw the woman still lying across the bed, hanging off both sides. She was asleep, passed out or in a state of transcendental bliss. They praised themselves for wearing her out. Grabbing beers, they went to get something to eat. Mad Dog was going to buy. It was a hell of an experience, but in the end, Mad Dog David Gideon was still a virgin.

Chapter 14

Serving in Alaska

After a couple of months of training, Private First Class David Gideon was shipped off to Alaska to serve in the Quartermaster Branch. Several weeks of cold weather training completed, he was assigned to a warehouse at Fort Wainwright, Fairbanks. This was a good assignment because he could avoid almost all women. Men outnumbered women nearly ten to one in Alaska, and the ratio was even higher in the Army and no women were assigned to the warehouse. David claimed an abandoned office area in the back of the warehouse and made it his living quarters. The sergeant didn't mind because David would permanently pull nightly warehouse security duty. It worked out well for everyone except it was very boring. He could only watch so much stupid TV and he read too slowly for it to be enjoyable.

By the second month, David had organized the weekly Saturday night warehouse poker game. It was a friendly game of quarter ante and dollar limit. To buy-in, it took twenty bucks. David did not play poker, he just ran the game. Every player paid a dollar to get in the game and David cut a quarter from the pot for every hand. He provided the first beer free but they had to pay a premium for every beer after that. He had sandwiches, chips and dips, cookies and sodas for a nominal price. David was easily making $75 to $100 each Saturday. Considering that a private first class made less than $400 a month, the poker game doubled his income. He didn't go anywhere or do anything socially and had very few expenses, so his "bank account" started to grow rapidly.

After six months, he had nearly $3,000 in a box under his bunk. The game became so popular that he decided to expand the operating days from Thursday through Sunday, doubled the entrance fee and made the stakes a dollar ante with a five-dollar maximum bet. He cut the pot accordingly and sold the merchandise at convenience store prices. At the end of twelve months he had $18,000 in the box under his bunk.

He was promoted to Specialist Four and offered a job in the battalion headquarters which he immediately turned down. He was then offered a two week leave which he also turned down. When asked why he didn't want to take a leave, he simply expressed that he didn't have anywhere that he wanted to go. Then the sergeant major asked, "Could it be because you don't want to lose the profits from the poker game for two weeks?" Busted!

Specialist Gideon was given two choices: receive battalion level punishment, lose a stripe, forfeit pay and get transferred from the warehouse or share the proceeds from the game. The solution was obvious but expensive. The warehouse sergeant received $50 a week, the first sergeant received $75 and the sergeant major got $100, cutting his profits considerably but it was better than being put out of business.

The unintended benefit was, with the protection of the chain of command, the most popular and lucrative past-time on post got even more popular and more lucrative.

Chapter 15

Las Vegas

At the end of his Alaskan tour, David was given another choice: re-enlist and be promoted to sergeant or be discharged and put on a plane to go home. As a sergeant, his assignment would change and he would probably be sent to another post. He chose to be discharged. Within a week, he had his paperwork completed and he would fly to Seattle and take a bus to San Antonio, Texas.

He turned in or otherwise disposed of all his army gear and actually sold the rights to the poker game to the warehouse sergeant for $1,000. On a fine Wednesday morning, he boarded a plane to Seattle. The airport security rent-a-cop was clueless but David had $42,000 in his duffle bag.

He spent the night at an airport hotel in Seattle and then boarded a bus to San Antonio. What he didn't know, was the bus passed through Las Vegas on the way to Texas. Late Thursday night, the bus pulled into the Plaza Station Hotel and Casino in downtown Las Vegas. He was surprised that the bus stop was at a casino. He got out, grabbed his duffle bag and decided that Vegas was going to be his new home.

He got a room at the Plaza, stored his duffle bag and hit the streets. After wondering around downtown for a little while he found himself at the Golden Gate Hotel and Casino. He was at the bar and had a beer in one hand and what he thought was a free shrimp cocktail in the other. He didn't know if it was free or not because he tipped the waitress fifty-cents for bringing it and she never brought him a bill.

Sometime about sunrise, a woman sat down two bar stools away from him. She looked like she had been up all night. She, in her younger years, was probably quite attractive but the Vegas sun, night life and substance abuse had turned her old for her age and a little leathery around the edges. She was super suntanned and dark skinned to begin with so David guessed she was Mediterranean or Armenian or part of some other dark swarthy culture.

She lit up a cigarette and shot a glance his way. She wasn't really a hooker but she had been known to do whatever she needed to do to pay the rent, get a little sustenance and keep her flush in alcohol and cigarettes. He turned his head away or stared at her boobs every time she looked at him. He hadn't had to deal with the auto-orgasm in a long time and he didn't want to start with this woman in the morning light at a casino bar.

She picked up her drink, pack of cigarettes and lighter and moved over two bar stools and sat right next to him. She was wearing an evening dress looking a little on the Saturday Night Fever side.

 "What's your deal?" she asked. He told her he was fresh off a bus and was looking a for a situation that might sustain him. "You got a place to stay?" was her next question.

He didn't really want to have a discussion with her, so he said, "Look, I'm really not in the mood to....." When he said "look," she did. They looked at each other and she responded instantaneously. He could not recall, reset or undo his look. Once he did it, it was done forever and in a hurry.

It hit her like ton of bricks and she slumped over on the countertop with her face between the drink and the cigarettes. She looked like she was in pain but she didn't make a sound. David waited for her to complete. When done, she sat upright, brushed her hair back a little, lit a cigarette and asked, "How did you do that? Was it hypnosis?"

"Do what?" he responded.

"Don't be a dick. How did you do it?" Her countenance told him he shouldn't try to bullshit her.

"Believe it or not, I can make women have an orgasm just by looking at them. I can do it every time or at least it has never failed in the last ten years."

"OK stud, do it again." He shrugged his shoulders and gave her the look. She reacted almost the same way she did the first time but this one seemed to be a little stronger or maybe she was a little weaker.

When she was mostly recovered, she lit another cigarette even though there was already one burning in the ashtray. "Alright," she said. "Do you need money because we are about to make a shit load of it?"

"I don't even know your name," he said.

"It's Janice, Janice Goldberg. J-Gold to my friends and believe me Honey, we're going to be friends".

She downed her drink, crushed out her cigarette, stood up and said, "Come with me." It wasn't a request.

Chapter 16

The New Career

They walked three blocks out behind the Golden Gate Casino to a slummy looking motel/apartment complex that made him really want to turn around and go the other way. She led him through the warren for a couple of turns and then she reached above the door jamb to get a key. She opened the apartment door and they entered.

It was an efficiency apartment with the living room, bedroom and kitchen all in the same area. The bathroom was the only separate room. She said that she had to go out and buy some things and told him to lie down and get some rest because he looked like shit. He thought, *I look like shit?* He had been up all night and just got off a bus but she had been up all night, was a dozen years older and had been doing who knows what. "Don't leave," she said, never looking at him directly. David didn't respond as she stood in the doorway with her head down. And then she finally said, "Please," and stepped out into the very bright morning sun.

David was left alone in the apartment and there was no way he was going to even touch the messed-up bed let alone lie down in it. Every inch of the apartment was covered with some kind of refuse, newspapers, soiled clothes, dirty dishes, old mail and a few unpacked boxes scattered around. He decided to snoop and try to figure out who this woman was. He started with the mail pile. Most of the mail appeared to be bills and advertisements. No help there. He went to the chest of drawers and pulled each one open revealing a few clean clothes but nothing else. He looked in the refrigerator but only saw a pitcher of something that may have once been tea, a ball of tin foil that he knew had a disgusting content and one can of beer. He looked in the bathroom and found nothing out of the ordinary except a tub that hadn't been cleaned in months and the expected "girl" things on the sink. There were no family pictures anywhere and nothing that remotely looked personal except the dead plant in the window sill. His search had turned up no clues.

David sat down at the tiny table and began shuffling through some of the old newspapers when he discovered the want ads. She had circled several waitress jobs in the help wanted section. *Okay*, he thought. *She's unemployed, obviously not doing very well, but at least looking for a legitimate job.* After reading an article about a new hotel going up on the Strip, he found he couldn't hold his eyes open any longer. He moved some days old dishes out of the way and dozed off with his head on his arms on the nasty table.

An hour or so later he heard Janice coming through the front door. She was carrying a clothes bag and a box. Her first words were, "You look worse than when I left you." Before David could say anything, she started talking, incessantly. "I bought you an outfit. I figured you were what? Five-ten and weighed what? A hundred and eighty pounds. I forgot to look at your feet so I just bought the most popular size shoe, tens huh?" She held up a shiny black dress loafer. "Alright, get up and try these on, we want a decent fit, doesn't have to be good, just has to be not bad." David stared at her. "Come on, get up and let's get busy."

David finally said, "What did you do, go out and drink nineteen cups of coffee?"

"Don't be silly, just four." She started taking a tuxedo out of the clothes bag.

He realized after seeing the tux that he probably wasn't going to a fine party but he was going to be requested to perform again. "Are we going to put on a show?" he finally asked.

"I'm not, you are. While you were in here sleeping, I was out making hay. We're booked at the Saxony. It's a bar near the Flamingo. It's ladies' night." She had already learned to talk to him without ever looking him in the eye. "There are usually a few dozen women at any given "ladies' night". We'll just test the waters, what do you say?"

She handed him the clothes and he looked around for a place to change. "Don't be shy," she said. "Just do it here." There was no way out of this so he began changing clothes right in front of her. As he put stuff on she fussed around him straightening lines and smoothing out wrinkles. All of the clothes were a little big because he was actually five foot nine, one-hundred seventy-five pounds and wore size nine and a half shoes.

After a while he said, "You know, I have performed before. I was billed as a magician and my name was Mister Orgasm."

She started to laugh, "Oh, that's precious. We'll keep that."

He started telling her about how he'd walk out, make a speech with his back turned and end with saying "The one, the only, the amazing Mister Orgasm". He said he'd spin around catching everyone's eye, throwing the audience into a frenzy. He didn't tell her all the gloomy personal details like never getting laid, but instead made it seem like it was truly a magical experience.

Once he was dressed, she turned him around a few times and said that it would do. She asked him if he had a place to stay and he said he did. She told him to go home, wherever that was and meet her back here at her place at precisely 10:00 pm. He was to go on stage at 11:00 pm. She told him to get some rest because he truly looked like hammered hell.

As he was walking out the door carrying his street clothes, she asked, "Hey, Mister Orgasm." He turned, shielding his eyes from the sun. "What's your name?"

"David Gideon." She shut the door, almost in his face.

Chapter 17

The Saxony

At precisely 10:00 pm, he knocked on her door. She stepped out wearing a low-cut red, ankle length, evening dress, slit up the side to the thigh. She had on red high heels and carried a small, silver sequined clutch purse. She had on fresh makeup and really looked nice. He couldn't imagine where she found such appropriate, clean clothes in that apartment. "You ready?" she asked as she straightened out some of his tux parts. They went around the back of the apartment complex and got into the most beat up brown Buick that he had ever seen. "You have to hold it," she said. David didn't have a clue what she was talking about. "The door. It will fly open on the turns if you don't hold it."

This, he thought, *may be the most stupid and dangerous thing I have ever done.* He had just gotten into a car, if you could call it that, with an older woman who had been around the block a few times, who he had met about fourteen hours earlier, going somewhere in a city with which he was not familiar and he had $42,000 in his duffle bag back in the hotel room. He did not like pain as proven during his high school football days and all anyone would need to do to get his money is stick a bamboo shoot near his fingernail and he'd give it up. He'd show them where the money was stashed, then take them to the bank and cash hot checks for them all day long. No, he didn't like pain. *Maybe this will be okay.*

The drive to the Saxony was pretty much straight down the Strip and entailed only a couple of left turns, during which, David hung on for dear life trying to keep from flying out of the vehicle. The pile of junk on wheels, did not have a passenger side seat belt to help hold him in. It was just gone. She pulled into a parking space behind a rather seedy looking building and started getting out of the car. David got out and tried to close the door the best he could. Finally, he put a hip into it and the door mostly shut. "Don't do that!" she said. "The paint will come off on your pants and it's a rented tux. I have to have it back in a few days."

They went in the service door, down a narrow hall and through a kitchen that led to the back of the stage. There was a man on stage, naked to the waist, being auctioned off to a group of frenzied female bidders. "What do they get to do with him if they win the bid?" David asked.

Janice replied, "Whatever they agree upon but don't worry about that." She was straightening his tux again, "Just go out there and do your little act."

"The Mister Orgasm act from college? The whole act only lasts thirty seconds and then a few minutes for the ladies to finish up."

"That's plenty of time. We're here on a mission tonight to prove your abilities and make an impression. Okay, two more guys to auction and then you're up. Will you be alright back here by yourself? I'm going to go out and stir up the crowd." She patted him on the chest, never looking up at his eyes. She left him standing there trying to figure out what he was going to say and try to get his head wrapped around what the hell was going on. It was coming at him pretty quickly. He was starting to think reenlisting for another hitch might have been the best move. *Three days out of the army and look what I've gotten myself into.*

Halfway through the second guy's auction, David began to sweat profusely in his tux. He was trying to remember what he used to say back in college for the Women's Book Club. Suddenly he realized the auction was over because he heard Janice's voice boom over the public-address system. "Ladies, J-Gold here to bring you a special treat. If you do not like sex, specifically - having an orgasm!" The women screamed hysterically. "Then by all means leave the room because this next performance is so raw that it will cost extra. This man is so sexy, that he can get you down on the floor, writhing around and grinding those hips in a mind blowing self-sex explosion. You will gladly fork over twenty bucks and beg him to do it again. Any woman that does not cum until her panties are soaking wet will not have to pay. Did you hear that girls? If he does not satisfy you, it's free of charge!" The women were screaming again. "Without any further introduction, because I know you little hussies are about to cream your panties... live, on stage, for your personal carnal pleasure, the one, the only, the amazing Mister Orgasm!"

All David could think was, *I was supposed to say the Mister Orgasm speech. Now what am I going to do?* He slowly stepped out on stage, the women were clapping and screaming in anticipation. He's thinking, what *could they possible be expecting? Do they really think I'm going to make them fall on the floor and start cumming?* It was about to happen, but it was ridiculous to be thinking that. He faced away from the crowd.

He pulled on his cuffs a little and the crowd responded. He thought, *damn, what would they do if I had any real talent.* He slowly started taking off his coat. *Now I'm a stripper,* he thought. The screams and applause got even louder. He slung the coat over his shoulder and shifted his weight from one foot to the other making his hips sway a little but that was enough for the women to rev up again. He took the coat off his shoulder, spun it in circles by his side, then over his head and threw it across the stage. The women continued to scream and clap at everything he did.

He held up his hand, elbow at a ninety-degree angle. The crowd quieted. Still with his back to the audience, he shouted, "Are you prepared to unleash the beast?" A unanimous scream rang out. "Are you really ready?" The screaming intensified. "Without further ado, I give you the one, the only, the amazing Mister Orgasm!" and he whirled around catching every woman he could with his eyes as quickly as possible.

The room was immediately thrown into pandemonium. Three of the tiny circular tables on the front row got kicked over, six women hit the floor, two waitresses dropped huge platters full of drinks and as a knee-jerk reaction, Janice slung the microphone across the bar crashing it into a stack of glasses. Then the microphone began emitting an ear-piercing squeal. David was looking around the room to determine if any women were left unscathed but he couldn't find any. He took a bow, which was completely missed by everyone. He grabbed his coat and left the stage. More moaning than he had ever heard in his life was happening right out there in front of him. He was tempted to peek around the corner to see what was going on but overcame the temptation. He put his coat on and waited for Janice to come back stage.

The ruckus died down but he could still hear some soft crying. After five minutes or so, he couldn't resist and looked around the corner. Janice, fully recovered, was standing at the front door collecting $20 or more with tip, from every woman in the house including the waitresses. Some male janitorial staff started moving through the bar setting up tables, picking up glasses and mopping the floor.

In about thirty minutes, Janice came to the back of the stage. She raised her hand up to his face and shook a wad of money at him. "Look what we did with no advertising and in a small venue. I'm so proud of you!" As if he actually did something special. It took thirty seconds to perform, required no talent, skills or practice and was done with virtually no planning.

"How much is it?" he asked.

"Over $800," was the reply. They split it down the middle.

Chapter 18

The Saxony, Round Two

Not bad for thirty seconds' work if one could call what he did work. She told him to go home, wherever that was and meet her back at her place on Thursday. He moved out of the Plaza and into a rent by the week apartment that was close to downtown. He took $2,900 to the bank and opened an account thinking that depositing a fairly small sum every week would not raise too much suspicion. He was still trying to unload his Alaskan poker money along with his new-found source of income. If asked, he would say he's a contractor getting paid in cash each week. He bought stuff to fill the apartment and spent a lot of time at the casinos staring at a quarter slot machine, playing one quarter at a time.

On Thursday, David went to Janice's place as directed. Her apartment was surprisingly clean compared to the first time he was there. She was wearing some slacks, a tee shirt and barefooted. "Baby, I have been working my ass off for us. We're set for next Saturday back at the Saxony. If we have any success at all, it will be the last time at that dump, I promise." David just nodded his head.

"Basically, we're going to do the same thing but I have been advertising and calling in favors and doing favors all over this town. If we don't double our money, I'd be surprised." David nodded his head again. "Try to stretch out your show a minute or so without giving away the surprise ending. We want to make sure they get their money's worth." She never once looked at him while she was talking. She was sharp, apparently hard working and he wondered what had gone wrong in her life. Then he realized that they didn't know each other very well at all.

"What kind of favors did you have to do?" asked David.

"Oh, you're concerned about me, that's so sweet. Don't worry about what I do, it's just business."

"What favors?" David stated firmly.

"Do you really want the truth?" David nodded again. "I had to give the bartender a blow job. He owns the Saxony and he said the payment for the damages last week was a blow job or $600. He made me promise to give him another one on Saturday before the show to cover anything that might get broken again."

"Janice, I don't like that one bit."

She touched him on the arm, "It's not as bad as you think, we used to date several years ago. It's not like I haven't done it before. It's just business in Vegas, okay?" David nodded. His nodding was becoming a bad habit.

"Meet me here at 10:00 pm on Saturday. Work on your show. I need a minute and a half. Can do, right?" She reached up, grabbed his neck, shut her eyes and kissed him on the cheek. "Now get out of here and I'll see you on Saturday." She slapped him on the butt as he walked out.

He went back to his new apartment and tried to write a minute and a half of soliloquy. It was much harder than he ever imagined. After twenty minutes of failed scribbling he decided maybe he should dance around for a minute and a half. He pushed the coffee table out of the way and tried to choreograph a few moves. What he ended up with was something that looked a lot like military marching and drill and ceremony. *Scratch that, what about singing?* In thirty seconds of practice he reconfirmed something he had known all his life, he couldn't sing a note. Can't write, can't dance and can't sing. The only two things he seemed to be good at were organizing poker games and making women have orgasms. He went downtown to play slots knowing he would think of something.

At 10:00 pm on Saturday night, he was dressed in his tux knocking on Janice's door. She answered wearing something similar to what she wore before but a different color. As they were driving to the club and David was holding on for dear life, he said, "The first thing you need to buy when you get a little money is a new car. Better yet, how about we stop on the way and pick one up now." He saw her smile a little but she dared not look at him especially driving down the Strip in the brown Buick death trap.

The Saxony looked the same except the act appearing before him was not an auction, it was men lifting weights in very exaggerated motions wearing what could only be described as string bikini bottoms. It looked very unnatural but the women seemed to love it. Every so often a man's penis would spring out the side of his "costume" and the roar from the crowd would be deafening. Peeking around the corner, David could see that the club was filled to the rafters with women. Many more, he thought, than the fire codes would allow.

Janice disappeared with the bartender, supposedly to pay the future debt, covering anything that might get broken. David wasn't sure if she was going to do the introduction like she did last time and the other act was already finishing up. He was getting nervous. Amidst thunderous applause, all the weight lifters lined up on stage gave a bow, pulled off their g-strings, fully exposing themselves and ran off the stage in his direction. The crowd went crazy.

The sight of six big, naked, sweaty men running toward him made him queasy. When they got off stage they gathered near him shaking hands and slapping each other on the back without even bothering to re-holster their junk. They were all naked and he was wearing a tux, in David's mind, something seemed terribly wrong with the image.

He then heard Janice's voice over the sound system. He shook his head trying to snap himself out of it. "Good evening ladies! I hope you have been sufficiently warmed up because we have a finale that will leave you breathless!" Screams came from the women for what David could tell was no apparent reason. "Exhausted!" More screams. "Wet!" Even more screams. "Satiated!" Continuous screaming. "And feeling guilty for having such a good time. Ladies! Ladies! Ladies! Settle down now, we have got to cover some ground rules." Light groans came from the crowd. "Everyone push away from your tables." Screeching could be heard as the women pushed the little drink tables a few inches away. "Go ahead everybody, push your tables as far away from you as possible. Now, everyone, especially the lovely and very efficient waitresses, put down all trays and drinks. Do it now, no trays or drinks in your hands. This show is a steal at forty bucks, girls. I know it sounds like a lot but you will be talking about this for the rest of your lives. And the good thing is, if you are not satisfied, then it's free!" Huge screams rang out from the crowd. "If you are really satisfied, a tip would be greatly appreciated. Everybody calm? Everybody cool? Everybody ready? Then it is time to present the best kept secret in Las Vegas. The person who made it necessary to coin the phrase "What happens in Vegas, stays in Vegas". The man your mothers warned you about. The one, the only, the amazing Mister Orgasm!"

David was instructed to prepare a minute and a half of warm up material but he just couldn't come up with anything so he had to wing it. Now, at this moment, he wished he had made a better decision. Slowly strolling out on stage, he turned his back to the audience. He raised his hand like before to quiet the ladies. Then he began to speak. "I tried to write a speech, but I failed." The audience in unison said, "aww". "I tried to sing "I Can't Get No Satisfaction", but I failed." The sympathy "aww" grew louder this time. "I tried to dance," he lifted his coat tails and wiggled his ass a little, the women screamed. "But I failed." Immediately they went back to "aww". "But I know someone who can do one thing very well. And fortunately for you he is here tonight. Are you ready to meet him?" He could hear the ladies going nuts. "If you are loud enough he will manifest himself right before your eyes." The crowd was about as boisterous as he thought they could possible get. "Because you have earned it, I would like to introduce you to my alter ego... he is dashing, debonair and sinfully deadly, The one, the only, the amazing Mister Orgasm!" He turned around and gave them the works. There were so many of them that he kept scanning the room trying to find those not yet affected. It took nearly a minute to get everybody but during the course of the scan and re-scan, he actually hit several of the women twice or maybe even three times. He did notice and his feelings were hurt just a little, that Janice had turned her head and didn't look at him directly like she did last time.

The physical wreckage was held to a minimum, a few broken glasses was all. David was glad because he didn't like the idea of Janice having to give the owner head to pay for reparations. However, the human toll was exponentially more apparent. He didn't know if it was because there were so many more women or if the double and triple whammy on some of them caused an exaggerated outcome, but there seemed to be many more bodies on the floor. The moaning lasted longer, there were some puddles on the tile that he didn't think were spilled drinks and when the moaning stopped, there was dead silence.

He was back stage peeking around the corner watching the women gather themselves together and pay Janice as they left through the front door. He could hear Janice telling them to spread the word about the act and to be watching for his appearances around the city at different venues. She was passing out what looked like business cards to every customer. He waited patiently back stage until the last woman left and the clean up crew came on for the night.

Shortly, Janice rounded the corner waving two handfuls of bills. She threw them down on a back-stage table and reached in her cleavage and pulled out three checks, each one made out for $100. "How much did we get?" he asked staring at the pile of money.

"Forty-eight hundred big ones," she said showing noticeable excitement. She closed her eyes and they hugged.

Chapter 19

The Strip Club

At her apartment, they divided the money down the middle and she told him he was going to perform again next Saturday. The place was called the Cock's Tail down town by Sassy Sally's, Glitter Gulch and the Golden Goose. He said he would meet her there since it was in walking distance of his apartment.

On Monday, he made another trip to the bank but it would take him a year to deposit all the cash at the rate he was earning. So, he opened two more bank accounts at different banks and put $2,900 in each one of those. Now it was a matter of a few weeks before he would have all of the cash out of his apartment.

With so much spare time, he taught himself how to count cards and play blackjack. Counting cards was an extremely new concept but the casinos were starting to deal out of shoes to negate the advantage of card counters. Playing single deck games only, he began low and slow but realized that over time, he could win. The trick was to manage his money and bet in patterns so the house couldn't tell that he was counting cards but still being able to take advantage of a plus deck when it came around. By Friday he was $300 ahead. More cash he would need to launder.

On Saturday, he was dressed in his newly pressed second hand tux and walking to the Cock's Tail. While he was walking and avoiding eye contact, he started thinking about his arrangement. Janice and he were splitting the proceeds down the middle which he didn't mind but somehow, he felt there should be some kind of contract. They didn't even have a verbal agreement, handshake or discussion about it. Janice just took over and ran with it. He decided he would talk with her about it after the show.

Janice was waiting for him outside the main door of the Cock's Tail. She grabbed his arm and walked him to the back where they came into the building behind the stage. She said, "Look, this place is a lot bigger than you are used to. It holds over a hundred and fifty people. It looks full and we still have an hour before you go on. There is one more act in front of you called Rough Lumber. They're guys dressed like lumberjacks and do a strip routine. When they're done, you'll go on. This place is big, can you do your thing with a crowd this big?" David said he didn't know, he may have to walk through the crowd to get closer.

The announcer made an introduction and cranked up the music. A team of six big burly guys came out wearing boots, some kind of canvas pants with suspenders and red plaid long-sleeve shirts. They kind of looked Paul Bunyan-ish. They each carried an ax. David recognized two of them from the group of weight lifters who performed last week.

They walked around in circles carrying their axes in different positions, then they would stop and take off a piece of clothing. The whole show was hokey but the women seemed to love it. At the finish, they were only wearing boots and something that looked like jock straps. They were huge guys, the smallest being six foot two and well over two hundred pounds. Some were hairy dudes too. Four of the six had beards and body hair like gorillas. The two weight lifters from the other show were clean shaven and had no body hair whatsoever. During the finale, the crew lined up and ripped off their jocks to expose their colossal genitals. They swung them in a spinning motion and ran off the stage toward David. It was like a recurring nightmare seeing six big, strapping naked, well hung men stampeding right at him.

As before, they stood in a group surrounding him with it all hanging out congratulating each other. Finally, one of the weight lifters told David that the group wanted to meet him. David shook hands with all of them trying not to look down. Some of the guys were so tall that their packages were nearly chest high on David which made him instinctively look cockeyed up and to the left. One of the weight lifters was explaining to the group that he caught the Mister Orgasm show last week and it was phenomenal. They were going to hang around and watch the show tonight. David hoped they would get dressed before they watched.

It seemed like it was taking forever, because Janice was collecting money in advance, but finally she came over the loud speaker with her introduction. David got himself set to go and the guys stood behind him, still naked. He didn't hear a word she said because he kept looking over his shoulder at the naked giants. And then he heard, "the one, the only, the amazing Mister Orgasm!"

He went out and did his routine. He spun around, jumped off the stage and went quickly through the large crowd trying to make eye contact with every lady in the house. He circled through once and started to go back for a second round to "entertain" the stragglers. On his way back through, he saw the Rough Lumber crew jump off the stage and run into the crowd. They started grabbing women in the throes of orgasm and rubbing themselves all over them, while manifesting erections larger than he ever wanted to see.

Janice ran into the crowd and started beating on the naked men trying to get them to leave their act alone and go back stage. She slapped around on two of them with no apparent result and then she ran to the third. The big guy saw her charging at him and batted her out of the way, knocking her over a table to the floor. This pissed David off immensely and he flung himself at the giant. The big guy easily batted him over the same table to the floor right beside Janice.

Sexual mayhem! That was about the only way to describe it. Two guys were getting hand jobs, two were getting head and one was screwing a woman from behind. The last guy was taking a slug out of a whiskey bottle while displaying his hard on. David pulled Janice up and they went to the front door where some of the women were exiting as fast as they were recovering. However, some women were jumping back in the pile. Janice was holding her side as they walked arm in arm through the wriggling bodies.

The club owner ran over to Janice and yelled, "What the fuck is going on here?"

"Exactly," was all she responded.

The pair of them stood by the door surveying the damage. Drinks, bottles and tables were upended all over the floor, mirrors were broken and curtains and wallpaper were pulled off the walls. All six guys were still engaging in some form of sex with a woman and at least twenty more women stood in line for their turn. Shear pandemonium. David finally said, "I hate to think how many blow jobs you'll have to give to make this right." She slapped him on the shoulder and they both started to laugh.

Chapter 20

A Better Plan

David and Janice met the next day in her apartment. When he walked in, there were three piles of money on the table. "What's this?" he asked. She pointed over in the corner and one of the giants from Rough Lumber was sitting in the easy chair. "What do you want?" David asked.

"Well, let's see. I want you to join Rough Lumber. We'll be famous, rich and well laid." He reclined in the easy chair with his hands behind his head. David started to say something but then the giant spoke up again, "And I want her to go into the bedroom with me right now and seal the deal."

David wasn't a hero but he stepped forward and said, "That's not likely to happen."

"Do you mean, that bitch going into the bedroom with me or you joining Rough Lumber?"

"All of it, not going to happen." The big boy stood up. He was six foot four if he was an inch and weighed a ton. All David could think was *this is not going to turn out well.*

"Get out of my apartment!" Janice screamed.

"Oh, I will, but all six of us will be back next time. But first, I'm going to take the Rough Lumber share of the money. After all, we were the best part of the show." He grabbed his crotch and gave it a squeeze while moving toward the table. When he reached out his hand to take a pile of money, Janice slammed a butcher knife down into the table top inches away from his right thumb. It scared the bejesus out of David and made the big man blanch white.

Janice was staring him straight in his eyes with the knife still in her hand, "If you touch that money, you'll be jacking off left handed for the rest of your life. I swear, I'll cut off your fingers." The big boy brushed his hand against his chest lightly and stepped out the door without another word.

David turned to Janice who was shaking violently. He held her in his arms until her nerves quieted down. Then she said, "Look me in my eyes." He did and she faded into his arms. He couldn't hold her up so they slowly slipped to the floor. He rolled on top of her and she wrapped her legs around him until she finished. She reached down between his legs and felt his hard on. "Let's move to the bedroom," she whispered.

Once in the bedroom she said, "I've been wanting to do this for a while but I didn't want to be one of a thousand other girls, but I think I'm over that now." They began kissing while standing by the bed.

"Well, I really hate to bring this up at this particular moment, but I might be a disappointment to you. As many girls as I've made have orgasms, I've never been to bed with a single one."

"Not a single one?" she repeated.

"Not one," he replied.

"You're a virgin?"

"Now you know. I'm a twenty-seven-year-old virgin. Every time I tried to have sex with a girl, she'd look at me and start cumming. After that, the girls didn't seem to want to do it anymore." David was fidgeting with his fingers.

"Well, Honey, this is your lucky day." The windows were covered with foil making it as dark as night, a trick of the nocturnal, so she lit a candle. She pulled back the bed covers, opened a closet and got a flimsy scarf off a hook on the inside of the door. "Now, take off all your clothes."

David did as instructed, standing beside the bed, nude with a hard on. She took great care not to look at his face as she surveyed his body. She then turned her back, removed all of her clothes and tied the scarf around her eyes making a blindfold. She fumbled her way over to the bed and laid down with her legs spread.

David never thought that any one feature on Janice was beautiful. She was nearly twelve years older than him, her hair was nice enough, her face was okay, her body was good enough for her age, her tits were average, her ass was alright, her legs were a little skinny but somehow, lying naked on the bed, blindfolded in the candlelight... damn!

They did all of things he had been dreaming of, everything he had ever heard about and then some more that only she knew. He had three of what he could describe as "catastrophic" orgasms. He came in her between her legs (a definite first), he christened her face and she did a combination of things to him which resulted in him squirting on her, himself, the bed, the pillow and the floor. His last orgasm was like a loose fire hose that had a mind of its own.

When she knew he was done, she laid back and took her blindfold off staring at the ceiling. David was laying beside her doing the same. After a long minute, he said, "I've got to know, did you cum for real? This was really good and I'd hate to think that it was a show. Because believe me, I know about putting on shows."

"I usually don't count but let me see." She started mentally replaying the escapade and moving her fingers ever so slightly. "If you must know, I came six times. And if you are worried about it, I didn't once look into your eyes."

David smiled. Then he said, "I don't want this to come out wrong, it's supposed to be a compliment, but I can see how you could pay for a $600 bar bill with a single blow job. I think I'm ruined for the next girl."

She smiled at his awkward compliment but, deep down, she knew what he said was true. What they just did came along once or twice in a lifetime, it was that good, plus it was his first. He might very well be ruined for the next girl or even the next ten.

"Where do we go from here?" he asked.

"I hate to say it, but we better get back to business. We have a show on Thursday at the Sands. It won't be a gigantic venue like the last one. I'm a little afraid of those now. This will be a semi-private showing with a few ladies willing to pay a premium. Get dressed and get out of here and let me take a nap. Some big stud just wore me out." A permanent smile was on his face. "Be sure and take your half of the money. It's on the table you know."

"Yeah, I know. Right next to the butcher knife." She smiled as she turned over in the bed to get some sleep.

Fully dressed, David grabbed half the bills and started walking back to his apartment. When there, he counted the money, $4,500. He couldn't help think it was an obscene amount of cash for what little he had to do.

Chapter 21

At the Sands

David met Janice at the appointed time at her apartment. They drove in her death trap car to the Sands. She was explaining how it was going to work this time... a hotel suite with a section of the room set up with reclining chairs in a semi-circle. David was to walk to the center of the chairs and put on his show but afterwards he needed to conduct a second show for all of those still harboring a desire. He agreed, sounded simple and no chance of Rough Lumber showing up.

When they got there, he found out that the only way it could work would be if he stood in the hotel hall until it was time for him to perform. Janice said she would do the build up and then come to the door to let him in. He had no choice but to agree.

David stood in the hall for what he thought was twenty minutes before he could hear Janice starting the program. In a moment, Janice opened the door and he stepped into the semi-circle trying to scan the audience with his peripheral vision. There were twelve or thirteen women in the room, ten were seated in reclining chairs but a couple were standing and he thought one was way in the back of the room.

He couldn't catch the exact number out of the corner of his eye and he didn't want to look and spoil the surprise. He could tell that this crowd was older. One lady looked a little like Aunt Bea from the *Andy Griffin Show*. All he could think was, *Oh God, I'm going to kill Aunt Bea with an orgasm.*

Facing away from them, he started telling a made-up story. It involved movie stars and European royalty, but at the appropriate time he turned around and gave them the magic. The ladies in the reclining chairs faired well and just squirmed around on their perches but the three women standing up hit the floor like sacks of potatoes. The usual moaning and groaning permeated the suite. Aunt Bea was getting after it just like the twenty-something on the floor in the back.

"Go back outside, hide in the stairwell," instructed Janice. David obeyed not knowing what was going on. He could hear her talking soothingly trying to restore order. David was in the fire escape stairwell down the hall looking out through the door he was holding open. He was afraid if he shut it, he may not be able to get back in.

Within a few minutes the suite door opened and some of the ladies began leaving. As Janice was seeing them out they were handing her cash. He counted six women who left, leaving seven women inside. In about thirty minutes, Janice came into the hall and called for him. They went back into the suite and he assumed his position in the semi-circle. This time he could see that seven of the recliners were filled with completely nude women. Aunt Bea was the one in the middle.

He had no idea what to say this time so he just started thanking them for the opportunity to give them pleasure because what he gave, he received back. He turned and caught their eyes. The hands of six of the seven women went straight between their legs but the seventh grabbed her tits and started pinching her nipples. All the woman finished in a reasonable time except Aunt Bea, she just kept going and going. The other ladies started egging her on. Janice told David to go hide in the stairwell again. He listened outside the door for a few minutes while Aunt Bea and her cheering section carried on. When Aunt Bea completed, the other girls let out a loud cheer and applause. David felt a strange sense of accomplishment.

As before, he was hiding in the fire escape stairwell peeking through the cracked door. After at least a quarter of an hour, he saw five more women leave, each handing Janice a handful of cash and praising her show. When the five of them entered the elevator and the hall was clear, Janice motioned for him to come back in.

Only two women lounged on the recliners, Aunt Bea and the twenty-something. They were sitting next to each other. David stood in front of them with his back turned and gushed such appreciation for them hanging around to catch the final act. He asked if they were ready and he turned to give them round three. He walked between the two of them and put a hand on each of their shoulders. Aunt Bea shot one hand to her mound and grabbed David's arm with the other, the twenty-something was mashing her nipples with one hand and going for David's package with the other. He didn't know how he felt about that but Aunt Bea had him in a death grip so he couldn't get away even if he wanted to.

The young one finished in what David considered to be a normal amount of time but Aunt Bea was working on being crowned the queen of orgasms. After a really long period of time, as far as orgasms go, David said, "Maybe we should throw a bucket of water on her." The corner of Aunt Bea's lips curled up in the faintest of smiles all the while continuing to cum. Finally, she let go of David and assumed a full resting position. She was so peaceful he thought he might need to check her pulse. Janice told him to go to the stairwell again. He complied.

After thirty minutes, Aunt Bea appeared in the door, handed Janice a stack of cash, thanked her profusely for such a magical night and went to the elevator. Another twenty minutes after that, the young one left thanking Janice over and over again. When the young one stepped on the elevator David came out of the stairwell and went into the suite with Janice. As soon as they got into the suite, she closed her eyes and hugged him around the neck. "You did great," she said. "Do you know how much we made tonight?" David shook his head "no". "Hang on to your hat... a hair over $20,000!"

"Shut the fuck up" was about as snappy a comeback as he could muster.

"They each paid $1,000, each time you put on a show, except for the waitress, she got hers for free. A $1,000 a piece all three damn times, thank you very much." Janice was all smiles.

"The young one was the waitress and got $3,000 worth of free services? What kind of business woman are you?" he asked playfully.

"The kind that can make twenty fucking thousand dollars in two hours!" She threw her arms around his neck again but forgot to close her eyes and received the full force of his gift. This time because of her grip around his neck, he managed to hold her up while she shuddered. When she regained composure and stood on her own, David said, "Oh great, another free one." She slapped him on the arm and said, "You go ahead and be an ass, I'm going to count the money."

She spread all of the cash and checks out on a table and got a final tally...$20,480. Since the suite was paid for, they decided to stay the rest of the night, order room service and enjoy their success.

What was he going to do with all of that freaking money?

Chapter 22

The Private Party

They both woke up early in the morning, victims of having the inability to really relax. They had awkward sex the night before because she didn't wear the blindfold and made eye contact several times. Obviously, she had many orgasms but they just weren't the kind that should have been between a man and a woman.

When they finished the room service breakfast, she told him there was a party on Saturday at which he would perform. She told him to meet her at her apartment and they would go together. She brought some appropriate clothes to change in to for an early morning but David had to wear his tux which he had thrown in the floor, anticipating sex instead of thinking about what he was going to wear the next day.

She asked him to take a cab home because she had to go the other way. She handed him an obscene stack of money, "I think you can afford it." She didn't look at him but he could tell she was still smiling.

David took the tux to the cleaners, went to his three banks and spent the rest of the day playing blackjack. By nightfall he had won $400 at the tables. Every time he thought about how lucky he was, he was afraid that he would jinx it somehow. He was living clean, eating right and had enough cash that he could buy a house if he wanted. It was all so new that he never once thought about the future. Whatever Janice told him to do next was about as far ahead as he thought.

At a suitable time, David was at Janice's apartment. "You ready?" she said not really asking a question.

"Always," was the reply although he never really was ready for these things. When they went to the parking lot, she stood in front of a brand-new Cadillac and said, "What do you think?"

David was speechless. The Cadillac wasn't really "new" but it was ten years newer than her old brown beat-up Buick and looked to be in great shape. "How many miles on it?" he asked.

"Only fourteen thousand. Remember the older lady from the other night, the one who stayed the longest?"

"Aunt Bea," David said.

"Well, it was hers. She didn't like the color and since we did her a favor, she gave us the car! "

"What favor did we do her? She paid us $3,000 for the show, right?"

"You probably won't understand this but she told me she hadn't had an orgasm in over thirty years and we opened the flood gates. Imagine that, us, sexual therapists. We earned this car together but I'm not going to lie to you. I want it so badly I can taste it. I'll pay you $2,000 for your half." She was waiting in anticipation with her hands in something that looked like a praying position.

"I wouldn't take a dime over fifteen hundred." She closed her eyes and threw her arms around his neck.

She opened her purse and counted out fifteen one hundred dollar bills and they got in the car. He could tell she was ecstatic. David was just glad that the door shut, locked properly and the car had seat belts. "Where are we going?" he asked after a few minutes.

"To Aunt Bea's," was the reply.

Somewhere, way out of town, they pulled off the highway on to a mile-long drive that led up to a significantly sized mansion. There were half a dozen cars parked out front, Janice's Cadillac being the low rent car of the bunch. A man servant of some sort took them to a back entrance and they waited in a fairly luxurious room even though it was not meant for real company. After nearly an hour, the servant took them to what appeared to be a grand ballroom. Instead of a long dining table or dance floor, there were seven leather lounge chairs in a semi-circle, occupied by seven nude women. Aunt Bea was in the middle as before. Two of the women were already fingering themselves.

Janice started straightening his tie, shirt and cummerbund. When she finished, she ran her hands over his shoulders and down his arms smoothing out his jacket, plus she just wanted to touch him a little before he got soiled in the lion's den. "What's the show going to be, are you the MC?" David asked.

"No," she said. "You are on your own with this one. She just wants you to walk out and do the deal. No fanfare, no stories. They're taking care of the foreplay themselves."

"This feels weird," he said. "Is there something wrong with us?"

"No Sweetie, everything's fine. It's just me and you." She closed her eyes and hugged him.

In the middle of their "moment", Aunt Bea rang a tiny bell. They both assumed that this was his cue. "A fucking bell, are you kidding me?" he said rhetorically.

"I don't care if she rings the Liberty Bell, they're paying us $35,000 for this so you need to do a good job. Okay?"

She straightened his jacket one more time and he walked around the corner with his head down. When in the middle of the group he stretched out his arms and slowly raised his head saying, "The one, the only, the amazing Mister Orgasm." He looked at each woman, starting from left to right.

Each one reacted differently. The first turned on her side in the fetal position and arms wrapped around her knees. Number two's legs shot out stiff as boards and her fingers found her clit. Number three had one leg on each side of the footrest with both hands grasping the top of the chair above her head. Aunt Bea went straight for her mound, working her fingers frantically, groaning louder than the others. Number four lowered her footrest and slid off the chair on to the floor, arching her back with both hands between her legs. Number five put her hand to her pussy and slightly spread her legs in what David thought was a more natural masturbation position. Number six went for her tits and number seven held her hips and kicked her legs, spurring the footrest with her heels.

David turned to look at Janice. She had her head turned but she was waving him over to her. When he got close she said, "Let's let it calm down a little," and they both stepped around the corner. They could hear moaning and cursing. If David didn't know any better he would have thought there was a torture session going on in the next room. A woman writhing in pain doesn't sound much different than a woman writhing in ecstasy.

After a few minutes of silence, Aunt Bea rang the bell again.

David entered the room and repeated the exact thirty second performance. The lady who had slid off the chair was not in the room anymore. The other women did their things and David just watched, amused at the variation in styles. After a minute, he heard Janice going "Pssst!" from the door. He walked over to her again. "Let them get back to themselves before you hit them again. It can be overwhelming and some of these ladies aren't in very good shape. I don't want them having a heart attack on us."

"Are we going to require a doctor's note before participation next time?" he mused.

She giggled a little and responded by saying, "No, I think we'll just post a sign that says if you have a heart condition, you're prone to seizures, have back pain or get headaches, then you can't participate. Or better yet, if you have those conditions, then you have to pay double!"

"That's my J-Gold," and they both laughed.

They could hear the ladies laughing and then footsteps out the rear door as a few of the guest left. When all was quiet, Aunt Bea rang the bell. "Ding-a-fuck-a-ling," David said in humorous disgust. Janice straightened him out one more time, spun him around and swatted him on the butt as she sent him out for the third time.

This time only three women occupied the seats, the lady who had wrapped her legs around the foot rest, Aunt Bea and the one who masturbated herself in the most conventional looking way. Die-hards he thought. He walked out and brought it to them, pointing at each one individually when he did it. He didn't know if his method made it better or if the third time was a charm because they were losing their minds. He turned back to Janice and shrugged his shoulders. She was looking past him at the shaking, shrieking bodies. The decibels were so loud that it hurt his ears.

He walked back to Janice and they stood around the corner while the aftermath of the show played out. "What did you do?" she asked. He shrugged his shoulders again. Ten minutes went by before things settled down this time. They could hear the ladies talking and laughing and repeatedly banging the foot rest up and down on the chairs. Janice and David looked at each other with their heads cocked so they didn't really see each other. Finally, Janice said, "I'm going to go find out what the hell they're doing, you stay here."

David peeked around the corner and the four women, Janice, two older naked ladies and Aunt Bea, who was bent over with her saggy butt facing directly at him, were trying to lower the foot rest of a chair. It was the chair the lady wrapped her legs around.

The women were giggling like kids. Aunt Bea told Janice, "Kathy wrapped her bird legs around my chair and broke it. Damn thing won't close up any more." David pulled his head back around the corner and sat on the hall floor with his back against the wall. He could hear Janice laughing with the ladies and taking care of business.

Chapter 23

Bad Luck

On the way back to Janice's apartment, she explained the business deal of the century. They received $35,000 for the show. Since it was so good, Aunt Bea gave them a $5,000 tip. Janice opened her purse and showed him, it was stuffed with cash. She told him that Aunt Bea wanted to do this every month, but she couldn't pay that kind of money. However, she was willing to pay a $1,000 per woman with a guarantee of $5,000 each show. "Think about it," she said. "That's $30,000 a year, each, for two hours worth of work a month. I know I can set up more shows. Maybe not as spectacular as this deal but we can triple that I'm sure. We're gonna be rich!"

David was in a state of disbelief. He had so much cash. The minimum wage was $2.90 per hour or $6,000 per year. Forty thousand dollars, nearly seven years of minimum wage salary, was stuffed in Janice's purse sitting on the front seat. They didn't speak while they contemplated their good fortune. Breaking the silence, David said, "We can't launder this much cash. We have got to go legit. We need signed contracts, incorporate or do something so we can put this money into bank accounts and write checks and, I hate to say it… pay taxes."

"I'm not giving any of this to the government." She sounded nearly angry. "I'll keep *all* of my money right here in my purse." She moved it from the console to her lap.

"You can't keep hundreds of thousands of dollars in your purse, the apartment or your new car. We're going to make a dangerous amount of money. So, we lose twenty, thirty or even forty percent to Uncle Sam, we'll still have more money than we'll know what to do with. And we can walk around out of the shadows. We need to do it. C'mon Janice, I don't even want to keep $20,000 in my ratty-ass apartment overnight. How are we going to hide that kind of money?"

"Okay, I know a lawyer. We'll incorporate. I'll call him tomorrow."

They arrived at her apartment complex well after midnight. They were standing in her rather dark parking lot behind her new Cadillac deciding if they were going to shake hands on the deal, hug, kiss or just go in and have unbridled sex. Janice had become an expert at conducting conversations with David without looking him in the eye and David was always a little anxious when he was around her, so he mostly stared at his feet. At the moment, neither one of them had any situational awareness.

Out of nowhere two men materialized from the blackness behind David and grabbed him by the arms. A third man punched him in the stomach with tremendous force. David crumbled to the pavement. Without hesitation or forethought, Janice launched herself at the man who threw the punch and started trying to scratch his eyes out. The attacker backhanded her to the ground. Both David and Janice remained conscious but were pretty much out of the fight. Three more men appeared from the shadows. David recognized them as the crew from Rough Lumber.

The tallest guy had a baseball bat in his hands, he said, "Okay Mr. Marvelous, how does it feel to be flat on your face in the gutter?" David knew no answer was necessary. "Here's what's going to happen, Mr.

Dick. You're going to ditch this bitch and you're going to join Rough Lumber. We're going to do our show, then you do yours and we'll mingle with the crowd satisfying the ladies just like last time except we split the money seven ways. What do you say there, Mr. Cool Cock?"

David, from flat on his belly said, "First of all, they call me Mister Orgasm. Secondly, I don't believe I want to work with Rough Lumber." The guy swung the bat and bashed the right rear taillight out of the Cadillac. Janice, still on the ground with two guys standing over her, groaned and said, "I just got that car today you fucking bastards."

One of the guys kicked her in the ribs, "Shut up bitch. You don't have any say in this negotiation."

"Well, Mr. Cumwad, want to join us or not?"

David sat up on the asphalt, "I don't fit the Rough Lumber mold. You guys are all giants. You're Rough Lumber, I'd be like...Fuzzy Stick."

"You think you're a funny man? How funny is this?" He started knocking out every window and piece of glass on the car. Janice's face sank. After about fifteen or twenty hits, he walked back to David, breathing heavily and said, "How about now?"

"No dice giant leader. I think I'll stick with the bitch," was David's reply. The big guy who was doing all the talking, walked over to where Janice was on the ground. He swung the bat and hit her in the shin. David heard a horrible crack and Janice let out a blood curdling scream, grabbed her leg and whimpered uncontrollably. Without any hesitation, David hollered out, "I'll do it!"

The giant leader just said, "It's too late Mr. Fuck Face," and he hit her hard on the other shin breaking it worse than the first one. Janice let out a short cry and then fell into a semi-conscious state. David tried to get up but the giants were holding him down. Then the leader said, "Now, watch this." He spread her broken legs, reached up under her skirt and pulled her black lace panties off. She just grunted when he yanked the panties over her broken legs. Her legs flopped helter-skelter on the tarmac. "Are you watching this Mr. Dickhead?" said the giant.

The giant leader pulled down his pants, fondled himself until he was erect and then mounted her, shoving her broken legs out of the way. The sadistic rapist kept saying things but David never understood a word he said. David tried to get up but one of the giants punched him behind his ear and nearly knocked him out. He couldn't focus his eyes but he knew Janice was still getting raped because she was waking up and trying to defend herself. The pain, fear and helplessness must have been unbearable. David kept wondering why none of the assholes in the apartment complex would call the police. Surely, they heard the commotion.

The giant leader finished fucking her with exaggerated violent thrusts, shoving Janice's body about a foot across the asphalt. In seconds, giant number two was on top of her pounding away with Janice's broken legs flopping with every vicious stroke. David gathered his strength and tried to rally to her aid but they kicked him in the face and he was knocked completely out this time.

When he woke up, it was still dark. He didn't know how long he had been unconscious but some really bad stuff had happened while he was knocked out. His pants were down around his knees and he was sure something had been stuck up his rectum because he was bleeding from his anus and his nuts were extremely sore. He looked over at Janice and she was a mess. She was on her back; her legs were in an awfully unnatural position with one bone protruding and she was bleeding from her face and crotch. Her purse was laying beside her, turned inside out with all of her personal stuff scattered across the ground. The money, all the money she ever had, was gone.

He stood up gingerly. Somewhere behind his balls in a place that he wasn't sure had a name, he was hurting like never before. He pulled up his pants and walked as fast as he could to Janice's side and knelt down feeling like he was going to split in two between his legs. He placed his hand on her arm and called her name. She groaned. She was alive! He saw her apartment keys on the ground, grabbed them and hobbled to her apartment and called an ambulance.

Chapter 24

The Decision

David awoke in a hospital bed. He tried to take inventory of his parts before he attempted to move. He could feel stitches inside his mouth, his head ached with a vengeance and the worst of it was his little butt hole was throbbing all the way up to his belly button. *Janice,* he thought. He got out of bed as fast as he could, which was in slow motion and started shuffling down the hall pushing an IV pole all the way to the nurse's station. He couldn't speak very clearly and was getting frustrated with the nurses for not being able to understand him. Eventually the light bulb came on and they told him that Janice was in ICU but could not have visitors except for immediate family.

At the earliest opportunity, he shuffled in stealth mode over to ICU. No one confronted him because he was beat up so badly that he looked like he belonged in the area. His gown was wide open in the back and anyone unfortunate enough could see his backside with a brilliant white bandage looking like a Kotex taped to his butt hole. The image was degrading but it was perfect for making people divert their eyes.

David entered Janice's room. His heart sank. She had both legs in traction and her head was completely wrapped in gauze. Because her legs were raised, he could see more bandages and a catheter up under her gown.

When the staff learned that he and Janice had been assaulted together they let him visit her all he wanted. He stayed in her room more than his. She eventually came around and learned the extent of her injuries. David told her that he had nine stitches in his mouth and eleven stitches around his sphincter because he believed he was raped by one or more of the Rough Lumber queers. Janice had two severely broken tibias, one a compound fracture, multiple contusions and lacerations in her genital area which required eighteen stitches, two broken ribs and thirty-four stitches on her face in various places. They would recover but Janice would not be the robust person she had been before the assault.

The police came by several times trying to get to the bottom of the incident but neither David nor Janice told them anything. They just said they were attacked by multiple persons in the dark and were overwhelmed and knocked unconscious almost immediately. The police had no choice but to let it go. With six giants stalking them, not knowing their names and only being able to recognize half of them, David and Janice thought not pressing charges was the best course to pursue. The possibility of a Rough Lumber retaliation was too great.

Then they had to discuss the elephant in the room which was what to do next. When David asked her what she wanted to do, Janice said, "Well, I guess I'll get a new car." David smiled, then grimaced because of the pain and said, "I think you need one. And after that?" Following a painful discourse, painful because of the emotional implications and painful because both of them had stitches in their mouths and lips, they decided it would be best if they left Vegas, separately, each going their different directions.

David was discharged from the hospital first because he had less severe injuries. As he was checking out, the staff brought him a bag with his filthy tux and shoes. How stupid did he look wearing his tux while walking out of the hospital but when he reached in his pockets, he found the $1,500 that Janice paid him for his half of the car. He went to his apartment, retrieved a little over $25,000 from his hiding place and took it over to Janice's apartment. He wrapped it up nicely in newspaper and put it in her refrigerator freezer behind some things that had been in there for months, maybe years. *She should be set for a while.* As he was leaving her apartment, he thought he saw one of the giants lurking around the corner, reinforcing the correctness of the decision to get out of town.

Chapter 25

The Escape

Janice was discharged from the hospital after two weeks but needed help so David moved in with her. He cooked, cleaned, helped her with physical therapy and took her to medical appointments. About every third day, David noticed one of the giants hanging out by the corner. David told Janice that he thought the giants were checking to see if Mister Orgasm was back in business. David said, "If we ever do go back into business, they'll just beat us up, rape us and take our money again. I think going separate directions and getting out of town really is our best play." Janice reluctantly reaffirmed the decision.

David passed his time by playing blackjack and taking care of Janice. The incident had caused their relationship to suffer irreparably. They were cordial but the spark was gone. Janice realized that she needed him until she got back on her feet but wasn't about to become involved.

Twelve weeks later, Janice had all of the pins removed, stitches were out and she could walk again, although very slowly and most of the time with help from crutches. She was so feeble and looked so much,

much older than her years. His association with her did not produce a positive outcome. That made him feel terrible. This relationship was a complete failure just like all of the others.

On a bright Las Vegas Tuesday morning in May, they said their goodbyes and David walked out of the apartment carrying his duffle bag. He looked back and saw her standing in the doorway wearing shorts and halter top, leaning on her crutches. He could see the horrendous scars on her shins and face and was sick to his stomach.

When David rounded the corner out of sight, she went back into the apartment and threw herself on the bed for a twenty-minute cry. *What am I going to do now? I have no car, no job, no money, no prospects, a mountain of hospital bills and no friends.* She rolled over for a second round of deserved self-pity and crying when she saw something robin egg blue under her pillow. It was an envelope.

David had left her a note with many words of encouragement and expressed his undying affection for her. Reading it, she regretted deciding to part ways. At the end of the message was a post script instructing her to look in the freezer. She rushed to the refrigerator as fast as she could and opened the freezer section. As an answer to her prayers, she found a small package containing $25,000. That amount of money would allow her to live, although very modestly, for three years without working. She would never meet another man like David "Mister Orgasm" Gideon. She kissed the package and made plans to move to Oregon.

Chapter 26

The Run From the Past

Many months had passed since he left Las Vegas. He had just been drifting, thinking about his future because the past was still too painful to remember. The Amtrak he was riding was almost empty. It was after midnight and it was going nowhere, anywhere, he didn't really remember. He had been riding the rails nearly every day avoiding as much contact with people as possible. On a crisp November morning, he stepped off the platform in Malvern, Arkansas. Since Malvern is known as the Brick Capital of the World, it didn't take him long to ditch that burg and catch a ride over to Hot Springs where he checked into a suite at the Arlington Hotel for a month.

His priority was to have a soak in one of the few remaining bath houses. Finding a functioning one not far from the hotel, he ordered up the works and proceeded to indulge himself in steam heat heaven. A big black man gave him a washing in a tub and another one rubbed him down. David had been sans woman for so long that he caught himself worrying about turning queer. That fleeting thought disappeared as he fell asleep on the massage table.

Refreshed to the point of needing another nap, he headed back to the hotel to get one. As he entered the lobby of the Arlington the lady behind the desk asked, "Are you David Gideon?" He walked over near her trying to avoid eye contact. He'd made it for months without triggering an incident by sidestepping women altogether but now he was standing three feet in front of a good looking one in the midst of a conversation.

"Mr. Gideon, since you will be staying with us for an extended period of time, we have a VIP package for you." She pulled this huge Easter basket looking thing out from behind the counter. She could barely lift it on to the counter top. It was at least two feet in diameter and a foot and a half deep, filled with bottles of booze, candy, sausages, crackers, nuts and other crap he really didn't want like soap, lotions and cologne.

"Well, thanks, I guess," he said in a somewhat less than enthusiastic manner.

Trying to convince him he'd gotten something special, she began the soft sell, "It's really a nice gift Mr. Gideon. You have Champaign, whiskey, wine and some..."

He interrupted her, "It really is extraordinary. It's just so big. Please tell the management that I am very satisfied with the gesture. Really, I am impressed but it is too much for me. Why don't you take some of it?"

"It's yours Mr. Gideon, compliments of the hotel." David slid the basket off the counter and carried it to the elevator using the handle. He swayed uncomfortably with its weight.

Once in his suite, he laid all of the contents of the basket on the desk top. It was certainly an impressive array of goodies. He stripped off his clothes except his boxer shorts and got in bed for that much desired nap.

A sound woke him up but he was too groggy to tell what it was. He sat on the edge of the bed listening, hoping to hear it again. In a few seconds, he heard it once more, distinctly, a light tapping at the door.

"Just a second," he hollered and put on a pair of jeans. He went to the peephole and looked out. It was the girl who had been working the front desk. She was wearing her hotel navy blue blazer, knee length navy skirt, dark stockings and black high heels. Her white blouse was unbuttoned almost all the way down to her waist. Her long black hair was pulled forward to cover up her open blouse.

After seeing that image out the peephole, he wasn't really sure he wanted to open the door. "What do you want?" speaking through the door.

"I am checking to see if you are pleased with your accommodations and VIP package. "

"Everything is fine," David said through the door again.

She leaned against the frame, "I was hoping we could share the package, you know, have a drink, eat some cheese on a cracker. Come on, let me in, we can have some fun."

"You don't know what you are getting in to. If I open this door, your life will never be the same."

"Cocky little bastard, aren't you?" she said softly into the peephole.

Responding to what sounded like a challenge, he swung the door wide open.

Chapter 27

A Life Changed

He left the door open, walked back to the bed, and started putting the covers back on. "Help yourself to anything on the desk," he said over his shoulder. She walked over to the desk picking up and studying the savory items. "You know my name, but I'm afraid I don't know yours," he said as a question.

"I'm Vicki."

David stood up from making military corners on the bed, still facing away and said, "Something is going to happen to you in a few minutes that you will not be able to explain. You will enjoy it if you let yourself but you won't be able to understand it. Are you really ready for some magic?"

"My, my, don't you sound mysterious." She turned around holding a can of almonds.

"I warn you, you'd better lie down on the bed or at least sit in a chair because there is a very good chance that you will fall down."

'What could possibly make me fall down?"

"An earth-shattering orgasm given to you by Mister Orgasm himself."

"I think you're a silly shit."

"Indulge me," David implored. "Please sit on the bed at least." She didn't move. "Please," he said again.

"Alright." She put down the can of almonds and slowly moved to the bed. She sat on the edge and said, "Okay, now what?"

"I hope you're ready for the one, the only, the amazing Mister Orgasm." He turned around a stared into her eyes.

She fell across the bed, one of her shoes fell off before the orgasm overtook her completely. She was really reserved, hardly making any noise with very little body movement. In maybe a minute and a half she was somewhat recovered and David said, "If you don't leave now, this will happen again and again."

"How'd you do that?" she asked, gasping for breath.

"By looking at you. I used to have an act in Vegas called Mister Orgasm."

"No wonder you were sounding a little like a crazy person a minute ago. Can you really do that to me as many times as you want?"

"All you want," he said. He was looking at the floor.

"At the front desk, I can usually get a man to at least look at me but not you. Now I know why."

"Ladies choice," he said. "You need to make up your mind if you want to stay or go."

She stood up hesitantly as if her back were stiff. David thought she was going to leave but to his surprise she began to undress in a modest but still seductive striptease. Methodically stripping off her clothes she slowly revealed an incredible body. Alabaster skin, cute feet, long legs, tight ass, flat tummy, faultless tits, jet black hair, beautiful face... everything was perfect. The bush between her legs was full, black and shiny, almost a midnight blue. She laid down on the bed. "I'm ready." David really wasn't sure that *he* was. He was in love with her body and hoped she had some substance to her personality.

"Let's get started then." He looked at her and she blasted into an orgasm, arching her back, grabbing her breasts and spreading her legs. He shucked his pants and boxers as quickly as he could and climbed on top of her. She easily transitioned from a solo act to him participating. She wrapped her arms and legs around him so tightly that he couldn't move and he so desperately wanted to move.

In a minute, she released her death grip on him, put her hand to her forehead and took a few deep relaxing breaths. He, on the other hand, was just getting warmed up, driving deeply into her for all he was worth. He was lying on her with their heads side by side so he wouldn't make eye contact. He was pumping, grinding and hunching, giving her what he thought was the best fuck of her life. However, she felt nearly lifeless under his weight and seemed completely disinterested. He chalked it up to her having two orgasms already *or* maybe he really was a lousy lay.

He hadn't been with a woman since Janice and he didn't think he was going to last very long. He was right. This girl was so gorgeous just the sight of her nearly set him off. When he was about to finish, she said, "Don't cum in me." He pulled out and exploded all over her belly. He was on his knees helping himself along when she looked up and saw his face. She smiled because his face was all contorted in a "fuck face" deluxe. Then their eyes met and *her* face began to contort.

She pulled her legs up, nearly putting her feet behind her head with her elbows inside her knees. Her beautiful, fur lined, juicy, wet pussy was right below his face and it was pulsating in the throes of an orgasm. The situation commanded it, he had to muff dive. Down he went into a sweetness where he had only been in his dreams.

She seemed to be enjoying his skills but since she was in the middle of and eye-contact orgasm he didn't really know. In thirty seconds, she pushed his head away. He rationalized that post third orgasm, she was just too sensitive for him to continue. He rolled off the bed and went to the bathroom to get her a warm wet rag to clean her up.

When he returned, she was sitting on the side of the bed with her hand out. He put the rag in her hand. Without looking up she said, "Well that was interesting." Not exactly the glowing praise for which he was hoping. She finished cleaning herself up and handed him back the rag. "You'll still be here this weekend, right?" David thought that was a rhetorical question because she knew good and well that he was checked in for the month, thus the gift basket and in turn the sex. "I have a girlfriend I want you to meet. We'll be here Saturday at eight." Never making eye contact, she finished dressing and left. He was standing there naked holding a cum rag. Although not the common phrase that it is now, he said, "What the fuck?" under his breath. In his eyes, her great beauty had already faded as did his hopes for a life changing experience. Something was definitely wrong.

Chapter 28

Double Team

On Saturday at 7:30 pm, David was waiting in his room dressed in his best clothes. He was perspiring even though he was sitting on the bed doing nothing. He heard the knock and instinctively looked out the peep hole. Of course, it was the girls.

He let them in and they walked, shoulder to shoulder, to the bed and sat down, both were looking at the floor the whole time. Vicki coached her friend well to avoid eye contact. "Okay," Vicki said matter-of-factly. "This is how it's going to work. We're going to lie on the bed and you're going to watch. You are not to touch us nor talk to us. You are not allowed to take off your clothes. Got it?"

"Then what do I get out of it?" As always, David was somewhere between disappointed and confused.

"You get the rare opportunity to witness two gorgeous chicks getting it on." They both giggled sitting arm in arm. "Now go to the chair, stay there and be quiet." He sat down not liking this at all. The girls started to strip as quickly as they could and within a minute, they were completely naked on the bed. Vicki was white-skinned and dark-haired while this other girl was dark-skinned and blonde. They were polar opposites in coloring. Both were about the same height and weight and had the exact same body types. They could have been picture perfect negatives of each other. The only difference was Vicki had beautiful natural boobs and the new girl had bigger store bought ones.

The darker girl was on top of Vicki, they were kissing. Vicki grabbed the other girl's head and pushed her away a few inches and said, "Carmen, when I tell you, I want you to look at that asshole over there in the chair." Carmen nodded an acknowledgment.

"Do it now baby, do it now!" Carmen twisted around and looked behind her at David. Their eyes connected and Carmen fell on top of Vicki grinding and grasping for flesh. Vicki was doing what she could to enhance the orgasm by putting her hands and mouth in all the right places. Finished, Carmen collapsed face down, diagonally across the top of Vicki. Vicki was holding Carmen's head in one hand and rubbing Carmen's ass with the other. Vicki was making a shushing sound.

In a moment, Vicki said, "Are you ready for another one?" Carmen's head moved slightly in the affirmative. Vicki took her hand off of Carmen's ass and wet her middle finger in her mouth. Then she placed her hand back on Carmen's butt and said. "Look at that asshole again."

Carmen twisted and raised her head just enough to make eye contact with David. As soon as she did, Vicki roughly jammed her finger into Carmen's asshole. Carmen arched her back, cried out a little and stiffened herself into a push up position slamming her pelvis into Vicki's mound. "That's it, baby, give it to me." Carmen ground into Vicki for a solid minute.

Slowly running out of gas, Carmen lowered herself on to the bed. This time she was nearly horizontal to Vicki making and X on the bed with their bodies. Carmen's ass was up in the air lying across Vicki's crotch. Carmen was breathing hard and Vicki was shushing again.

David sat in the chair as instructed with a throbbing hard-on in his jeans. He decided it was time to rectify the situation and started unzipping his pants. "Don't you even think about pulling that nasty thing out. It's girl's night. I mean it, I'll cause you all kinds of trouble if I even glimpse that stinky little dick. I'll scream rape." David decided right then and there that Vicki was a mean lesbian bitch. Vicki turned back to Carmen and said, "Let me give you one more, what do you say?" They started repositioning on the bed until Carmen was on her back sideways across the bed with her butt right on the edge and her feet on the floor. Vicki was on her knees on the floor in between Carmen's legs. "Now hold your feet up." Carmen raised her legs with the soles of her feet together and held them with her hands. Vicki said, "Look at that idiot again."

Carmen glanced at the very dejected man in the chair with an obvious erection in his pants. Their eyes met. Carmen leaned her head back and fell into an orgasmic trance. Vicki stuck a finger from one hand up Carmen's ass and two fingers from the other hand up her pussy and shoved them in as deeply as possible. Then she massaged those mysterious places that seem to allude most men. When the fever pitch was perfect, Vicki plunged her face into Carmen's pussy licking and sucking her clit with a ravenous hunger. The timing must have been perfect because Carmen let out a loud, high pitched squeal, her bronze skinned face turned red, she tore at the bed sheets and then she slowly faded into a semi-consciousness.

Vicki stood up, wiped her mouth with the back of her hand and pushed Carmen around on the bed until she was in a fetal position. Carmen relaxed into a peaceful sleep. "My turn now little dick man." Vicki jumped on the bed and looked at him, once, twice and then a third time having strong orgasms each time.

When finished, she took a couple of deep breathes like someone who just finished exercising and jumped up off the bed to get dressed. When fully clothed she tapped Carmen on the hip and said, "Come on baby, time to go." Carmen stirred slowly and dressed as if it were a great burden. Both women moved toward the door. Vicki opened the door to usher Carmen out but Carmen stopped in the doorway. She turned to David, being careful not to look at him and said, "Thank you."

She barely got the words out of her mouth when Vicki said, "Don't talk to him. Now get out." She pushed Carmen out and turned to David, "Be here next Saturday at the same time, bitch." She walked out closing the door behind her.

David was left sitting in the chair with a dwindling hard-on. He kept thinking that this could have been one of the most magnanimous nights of his life. Two insanely sexy women in his hotel room searching for orgasms and somehow it just went sideways. How could the woman with the most perfect body he had ever seen turn into the meanest lesbian bitch in the world. *Just look up mean lesbian bitch in the dictionary...Vicki.*

Chapter 29

The Second Escape

Even with the way he was treated, he still had the urge to get a release. After all, he did just witness six orgasms between two very sexy looking women. He took care of himself. Finished and cleaned up, he could now think rationally and what he was thinking was *I gotta get out of here* and then he added, *definitely before next Saturday.*

He was starting to run out of cash. He'd been traveling on trains for over a year, staying at hotels and eating cafe food. He needed to land in a permanent place and go to work doing something. Where to go and what to do were the simple questions he had to answer. He could live anywhere, he had no ties, that wasn't the problem. However, all he had ever done was work in a warehouse, run a poker game and pass out orgasms like candy.

He went down to the local store that catered to tourists and bought a map of the United States. He took it back to his room and fanned it out on his bed mentally knowing that he would never be able to correctly fold it up again. He asked himself *Where would I best fit in?*

He looked at the map for all of two seconds and then he said, "New Orleans." The decision was made just that quickly.

He went down to the lobby and asked the bellboy what days Vicki worked. She was off today and tomorrow. *Quick get away* he thought. He went out and ate a large supper and returned to his room and packed for a very early morning escape. He went to bed just before midnight and never fell asleep. At four in the morning he called the front desk and canceled his wake up call. Grabbing his duffle bag, he bolted in the middle of the night like the bitch he was.

The sun was just rising as he got on the Greyhound. Since he checked out two weeks early he received a two week refund, in cash, since that's how he paid. Counting the refund, he had thirty-two hundred bucks and some change. *How long would that last in New Orleans?*

Chapter 30

New Orleans

He was in the French Quarter carrying his duffle bag and wandering around looking for a permanent place to stay. He'd been in two really seedy hotels and one extremely expensive one but the right one had yet to come along. While blindly searching for his new temporary home, he happened upon a fairly busy open-air restaurant called Cafe du Monde. They served up a fried dough gizmo that was similar to a donut. He ordered a plate full. They were powdered sugar delights as evidenced by a ring of sugar around his mouth.

He hoisted up his duffle bag and resumed his search. He hadn't gotten twenty paces when a woman on the sidewalk said, "Those beignets must have been good." She was a wholesome looking young woman, maybe a local, maybe a tourist, he couldn't tell, but she was definitely southern.

"They were magnificent," he said. "How did you know I just had some of those things?"

"You have sugar all over your mouth."

"Oh great." He started vigorously wiping at his mouth. "I think it's dried on now. How stupid do I feel?"

"There's a water fountain over on Jackson Square. You can clean up there. I'll walk you over."

"Thanks," he said, practicing his life long habit of avoiding eye contact. "You wouldn't know of a cheap hotel around here, would you? I need a place to stay for a few days. By cheap I mean no rats and no hookers."

"I can find you several hotels with no rats, but I don't think there is a hotel within three miles of here that won't have a hooker in it from time to time. Got something against hookers?"

"No, I'm not very good around women, as you can see," he pointed to his face. "It just makes my life easier to have less women around. You're not a hooker, are you?"

"Somehow I feel like I should be deeply offended by that remark but coming from you I just find it extremely amusing. You really aren't very good with women, are you?"

"I'm sorry. If you only knew the whole story then I think you would understand. Where's this water fountain?" he asked trying to change the subject as they walked along.

She pointed to the corner of the square in a hidden spot by a tree. He washed his face and got a drink. "Now, where's a good cheap hotel?"

They walked down the side streets talking and getting to know one another. Her name was Anne Marie from Jackson, Mississippi. She came to New Orleans to get away from a dysfunctional family and find work. Not having any special skills, she found a job as a clerk/cashier at a tourist gift shop. She lived in a small third floor walk-up on Dauphine Street near the Grenoble Hotel.

Two blocks off Jackson Square they stopped and she pointed to a building front that was indistinguishable from any of the others. "This is a boarding house. They don't have many of these any more. I know the lady who runs it. You get a room, a shared bathroom at the end of the hall and two meals a day, breakfast and dinner, family style with all of the other guests."

"You sound like a salesman," he said while staring at the building.

"Maisie owns it. She's a no-nonsense proprietor, you know the kind that will throw your ass out if you do anything wrong and she's a very good friend. It cost $300 a week. Is that too much?"

"That's a little more than I was hoping for but since it includes most meals, I think it's doable."

They went in and Anne Marie and Maisie hugged like the pals she said they were. David liked the set up and he liked Maisie. They met Maisie's old man who seemed to be a loafer but Maisie was the brains of the business and her old man did the heavy work when under threat of being beaten with a broom. David had to pay a week in advance and a week as a deposit.

Anne Marie left to go do whatever she was going to do and David settled in to his new abode.

Chapter 31

The Magic Shop

After two days of getting his bearings he needed to find some work. Since Anne Marie was so helpful finding his lodging, he thought maybe she could help him find a job also. He remembered her saying something about the Grenoble Hotel so he went there and waited on the street. After two hours, he gave up and decided to return between four and seven in the evening to see if she would come home after work.

At six-thirty that evening he saw her walking toward him on the other side of the street. He intercepted her just before she went through the front door of her apartment building. "Hey Anne Marie," he said.

Her face lit up and she said, "Hey Sugar Lips, what are you doing?" He could only look at her with his peripheral vision. She on the other hand could look straight at his reddening face.

"I came to see if you would help me again. This time I need work, a job that pays me enough to cover $300 a week room and board. Got any other friends?"

"You came to the right person. I just happen to know a guy who knows a guy," she said grinning from ear to ear.

"And what would I be doing?"

"Two words," she said. "Shrimp boat."

"Oh good God." David lowered his head even further and had to shake it in disbelief. Anne Marie just laughed.

David knew nothing about boats or the ocean and the only thing he knew about shrimp was how to eat them. "I know nothing about shrimping."

"Don't worry. They'll teach you. You start out as a junior helper, then you'll get promoted to helper, then crew, then some kind of mate, then captain of your own boat. It's a good job." She seemed excited. David couldn't tell if she was kidding him or not. She continued, "I tried it once but I got sea sick and the gulls crapped all over me. It was so stifling hot and it smelled a lot less than pleasant."

"As good as you were about selling me on the boarding house, you are as equally terrible at selling me this job. A "lot less than pleasant" is not exactly what I was looking for but since you know guys who know guys and it's a sure thing, I'll take the job. Where do I meet these shrimp boat boys?"

Anne Marie said she would give her guys a call but it took two days to get through to them. David interviewed over the phone and was given the job on the spot solely because of the Anne Marie connection. He had to show up in a place called Bucktown on Monday for a two-day trial. Evidently most people reacted the way Anne Marie did when she tried shrimping which was quit after a day because of sea sickness, the smell, the heat and birds crapping on you. Go figure why anyone would quit a job like that.

On Monday, he woke up well before the crack of dawn, caught a bus, made two transfers and walked a mile before he got to the docks. He was not sure he wanted to make that trip every day. He found the boat and met the guys. The guys were fun loving, good old boy brothers who owned the boat jointly. Bob was the captain and Leroy was the first mate. They needed a flunky to do all the things they didn't want to do and David was that guy. The job paid $100 a day which was a killer salary but the work was truly "a lot less than pleasant". His official job title was "crew member".

On his maiden shrimping trip, they finally called it quits after a fourteen-hour day. Since David lived so far away, they let him sleep on the boat overnight. After changing places several times, he found that sleeping on some tackle, ropes and nets was the best place. If this became a permanent arrangement he would have to figure out something better.

At the end of the second day, the guys paid him $200 and said they would see him next Monday for a three-day week. He guessed they were breaking him in gently. He hoped so because he certainly needed more than $200 a week.

After sleeping all day at the boarding house, he decided to go find Anne Marie. He went to her apartment building but she wasn't to be found. He only knew that she worked at a touristy gift shop so he thought he'd systematically walk the "quarter" looking into every shop. At 6:00 pm he walked into Marie Laveau's House of Voodoo and wouldn't you know it, Anne Marie was behind the counter. "Tell me you are not her great, great-granddaughter," he said surprising her.

"I'll never tell," she replied with a smile. "How was the shrimp boat?"

"Less than pleasant."

"No shit," she said and they both laughed. "I get off in a few minutes, do you want to grab a bite?"

"Sure," he said thinking about missing the free meal he already paid for back at the boarding house. Until he started earning more than he was spending he had to watch his pennies.

"What do you want to eat?" she asked.

"Anything but shrimp," was the reply. She smiled.

They went for hamburgers, fries and beer from Bill's overpriced family owned bar on Bourbon Street just down from the House of Voodoo. "Any truth to that voodoo stuff?" David asked nonchalantly.

"I've only worked there six months but some of the stories I hear are pretty convincing."

"Who owns the shop?"

Anne Marie said, "I don't know. I report to a lady about my age who is almost never there. She hired six of us girls to run the shop. No one is in charge most of the time.　I just look at the schedule each week and show up when I'm told. The owner has a manual you have to read that tells you about most of the stuff. They sell shrunken heads, voodoo dolls and even Ouija boards. Ask me anything in the manual and I'll know it. But if it's not in the manual I have no practical knowledge of any of it." She took a bite of hamburger and said, "Can I ask you something?" David nodded in the affirmative. "Why don't you ever look me in the eye?"

There it was. How was he going to get around this one? The truth never worked out well for him and lies were even worse. "That's a good question. It's sorta why I was asking you if you believed in the voodoo stuff, because if you did, this would be a whole lot easier to explain."

"Well, even for a House of Voodoo employee you have managed to pique my interest. I thought you would say that you were just shy but you took a left turn at the bakery." She leaned forward with her elbows on the table and her chin in her hands. "This really sounds interesting. I'm all ears."

David started off. "I have a special ability." He didn't really want to come right out and say it. "I can't keep from hypnotizing women when I look them in the eyes. I look at them," he snapped his fingers, "and they're under my spell."

"Really," she said in a skeptical manner while subconsciously leaning back in her chair.

"And the only thing I can do when they are under my spell is convince them to have sex."

"If you are trying to get me into bed, there are other more conventional ways. I'm not saying I'm easy but I'm not that hard either. This beer and burger just about did it."

"It's not a pick up line. I'm serious, I hypnotize women into having sex and they can't help it. I can do it every single time, no matter where or when."

"Do it right here then." Anne Marie put her hands flat on the table as she offered the challenge.

"Do you really want to start having orgasms right her in Bill's Burger Joint?"

"If I had the choice I'd prefer my bed. You can drop the hypnosis con." She started getting up.

"This is always so embarrassing," he said mostly to himself as he paid the check.

They walked in an awkward silence to her apartment on the third floor of the building. At her door, she spun on her toes and said, "We just took a weird turn and you're scaring me a little. I don't know what to think about the hypnosis act, it seems beneath you to make up something like that."

"We are not going to be the same with each other until we get through this and the only way to get through it is to let me come in and..."

"Hypnotize me," she said finishing his sentence.

"If you'll let me. It's the only way to show you what I'm talking about. It's not really hypnotizing, it's more like... just looking into your eyes and you'll take it from there. But be assured there will be orgasms involved whether you want them or not. If you can live with that, then I'll come in. Neither one of us even needs to undress or touch each other."

"This is such bullshit and I think you might be the biggest liar, hustler, con-artist I have ever met and I have met some real assholes too." She crossed her arms and tapped her foot for a moment and then she opened the door and walked into her living room. David followed. Her apartment was meager but comfortable. "If you're going to make me have all of this sex," she said sarcastically making the quotation sign with her hands when she said the word sex, "then I want to clean up. I'm going to take a quick shower. Make yourself at home."

David occupied himself with snooping around and flipping through the magazines she had lying around. Then he came across the Marie Laveau House of Voodoo Manual. An interesting read. After ten minutes that seemed like an hour she walked out of the bathroom wearing a ratty house robe and some pink fuzzy footy socks. David didn't know if she was purposely trying to look unsexy or if this was the way she ran around when she was home alone. She sat down on the couch arranging the robe to completely cover her legs. David sat in the chair almost opposite of her. After a moment of uncomfortable silence, she finally said, "I feel stupid, cheap and gullible. You need to say something right now that will set me at ease or you need to go."

"Very well," David said. He stood up as if he were going to leave but instead he walked over to within inches of where she was sitting. She wrapped her robe around her even tighter, conscious of him towering over her. He spread his hands out a little and said almost under his breath, "Then I give you, the one, the only, the amazing Mister Orgasm." He looked her in the eyes.

She blinked twice and for five seconds she tried valiantly to fight it off but the magic was too strong and she succumbed. She gracefully slid down the couch into a supine position with her legs spread a modest amount with one arm across her breasts and the other hand between her legs. She moaned, her body shuddered and then she was done. David was still standing by the couch with an obvious hard-on in his pants.

When recovered, Anne Marie sat up and wrapped the robe around her again. She cleared her throat and said, "Well, is that a blessing or a curse?"

"It hasn't worked out very well for me so far."

"You'll need to tell me all about it," she said. "But first, pull your dick out and let's even the score. I'm afraid I have to do it the old fashion way."

David unzipped his fly and she eagerly helped him pull it out. He did not have a big one but evidently, she thought it was well shaped because she said, "You have the most beautiful cock I've ever seen." A compliment he had never had before and would never get again. He was standing right in front of her with his pants part way down his thighs. His rod was sticking straight out in front of her face. Being almost average size (a tad on the small side), she could get the whole thing in her mouth. When she pulled it out of her mouth to stroke it a little she said, "It's so hard," and then she pushed it all the way to the back of her throat. She made one little gagging cough sound, but otherwise took the whole thing easily.

This was not going to take long. It never did because he usually hadn't had it in a while and most of the time he had just watched a girl have an orgasm right before it was his turn, if he ever got a turn. In cases of mean lesbian bitches, he never got a turn. David warned her when he was about to cum but she kept on with the deep throat thrusting and fondling his balls. He tried to warn her one more time but the warning came out of his mouth at about the same time he lost his load. She swallowed hard three times and then started licking the remnants off the head.

She wiped her mouth, let go of his cock and said, "It wouldn't kill me if you looked at me again." He looked deeply into her eyes and she rolled back on to the couch in the same position she was in before but this time her robe fell wide open and exposed pretty much all that she had. Her body was not in the same league as Vicki's, the mean lesbian bitch, but by all accounts, she was attractive and obviously into men.

Chapter 32

Before the Next Date

David decided that this relationship might have some merit. He liked Anne Marie and she seemed to have a grasp on "the gift". She hadn't run off, she hadn't tried to exploit him and their first encounter ended in mutual satisfaction. Anne Marie didn't have a phone, nor did David so communication was a series of preplanned rendezvous. Their next meeting was at a local bar on Saturday night.

He spent the next few days exploring the quirky city of New Orleans. He rode the trolley as far as it would take him, learning quickly that he should more correctly refer to it as a streetcar. At dusk on Thursday evening he found himself standing in front of Marie Laveau's tomb in St Louis Cemetery No. 1. More than once he whipped his head around thinking that he had glimpsed someone turning the corner or standing next to him. He shivered although it was quite warm outside and twice, he felt like ants were crawling all over him. As the last rays of the sun extinguished, he left the area with a concluding thought, *don't go in St. Louis Cemetery No. 1 at night.*

On Friday, he went to the discount store and purchased "camping" supplies so he would be more comfortable on the boat for the two-night stay. That evening he went to a bar off the beaten path and started playing a twenty-five-cent slot machine, an illegal game for sure, but a crime overlooked by the authorities.

As usual, he was lucky with gambling and had amassed enough quarters to fill the large plastic cup he was given when he got change. They didn't have a cashier's cage like they did in Vegas so all coins were counted on top of the bar and winners got paid from the register. David set his plastic bucket down on the bar and waited for the bartender. The lady behind the bar was a middle aged heavy set person (that was a kind way of putting it, she was slovenly fat) with dirty blonde hair. Not dirty blonde like a coloring but literally dirty hair. She smoked and had a cigarette hanging between her lips when she talked. She never took it out of her mouth, just smoked it while she was talking and working. She blinked all the time because smoke rose directly into her face and when she moved from one end of the bar to the other, smoke sifted through her hair like her head was smoldering. She was "smoking hot" but in all the wrong possible connotations. She came towards him.

"Got a bucket full do ya?" She sounded nice but it was hard to get past the cigarette flipping up and down as she spoke and the visible aura of bluish tinted nicotine and tar laden fog swirling around her head.

"Yeah, I got lucky," and he shoved the bucket of quarters over to her getting no closer than arm's length.

"Well let's see what you got here." Since there were no coin counting machines, she took out four quarters and placed them at the corner of the bar. She repeated this process, placing the stacks of four quarters each in a row down the edge of the bar. Her fingers were fat and the opposite of nimble and her hand barely fit in the cup so it was a slow process. When she placed the last stack of quarters on the bar she counted them, four times, twice incorrectly but the last two times were accurate.

"Okay Honey, that's forty-two seventy-five." An inch-long ash snapped off her cigarette and landed on the bar. Instinctively, she swiped the top of the bar with her big paw to wipe the ashes off and accidentally hit about ten stacks of quarters knocking them on to the floor behind the bar.

"Raining quarters," she said and started positioning herself to get down and pick them up. She looked like a huge piece of machinery trying to park in a small space. She backed up two paces, looked down, backed up one more, looked down again, then she took one step forward turned sideways, grasped the bar, went down on one knee, turned back straight, went down on both knees, then to all fours and then she folded forward on her belly. She was lying on her stomach, which was ample, reaching out with her arms picking up individual quarters. She looked like she was trying to swim across the floor.

David went around the bar and started helping her pick up the money. "We'll have to count it again to make sure we have them all," she said with her face six inches off the floor. The short little cigarette butt was still hanging from her lips. So much smoke was in her face that David didn't know how she could get enough oxygen into her lungs to sustain consciousness.

"Hey Hon, can you get those over there?" She pointed under a beer cooler that was about four inches off the floor.

"I'll try," he said. After struggling a little he decided that he had to lie on his back so he could reach the quarters that rolled the farthest away. He was on his back on the floor and she was on her stomach on the floor, their heads about five feet apart. What could go wrong with this?

He heard her making a commotion and he put the top of his head on the floor and rolled his eyes up as if looking overhead but he was flat on his back. He saw her on her elbows and she was trying to crawl forward to reach some more quarters. Her movements were one elbow two inches forward, the other elbow two inches forward and then a walrus kind of jiggle until she actually progressed. Then she repeated the process all the while engulfed in blue smoke. The very tiny cigarette butt had almost burned down to her lips.

David, thoroughly amused at what he was witnessing, made a scarcely audible sound. One syllable, almost imperceptible, something like "huh". That utterance was the bane of his existence. The big blue smoky lady looked up from her endeavors and they accidentally made eye contact. She let out an extremely loud sound like she was vomiting and proceeded to have what he thought was an epileptic seizure. She put her hands by her side and undulated in quick, exaggerated movements. David thought, Hand to God, she looks like Flipper on a hot tin roof.

During her orgasm, she bumped her face into the floor and pushed the tiny cigarette butt into her mouth. It must have burned her terribly because she let out a squealing pig noise and a crooked smoke ring billowed forth. She began to choke. David thought she must have swallowed the cigarette butt. She was trying to roll over on to her back but between the coughing, cumming, cacophony of other involuntary bodily convulsions and the narrow space between the bar and refrigerator she did nothing but flounder around and arouse the attention of everyone in the bar.

David jumped up and stood over the thrashing body. A guy bigger than the gyrating woman came out of the back room and all the men in the bar stared at the lady on the floor and slowly raised their eyes to David, "What did you do to her, motherfucker?" *This is not going to end well,* a thought he seemed to have way too often.

"Nothing, she just accidentally swallowed her cigarette," he said with a pleading look in his eyes.

The fat guy from the backroom hollered, "Get that cocksucker!" and they all stampeded around the bar and dragged him out on to the miniature dance floor. The backroom fat guy was helping the lady get up. David figured him to be her husband.

Surrounded seven to one in the middle of the room, it felt like Rough Lumber all over again. Even though two of the guys were in their seventies, he couldn't fight all of them and win. They began posturing quite menacingly. With the help of the fat guy, the woman got herself righted and she was leaning against the counter. One of the skinny septuagenarians in the circle lunged forward and punched David in the face knocking him down on one knee. David was trying to recover and make a plan to defend himself, when the beached dolphin lady said, "Wait a minute boys. Buy that little sum' bitch a drink!"

Everyone looked at her including David out of his non-swollen eye. "Go on now, bring that little bastard over here and let's have a drink." They grabbed him and shoved him over to the bar and plopped his ass down on a stool. Flipper set a whiskey glass in front of him and poured it full. "Go on now, drink up, on the house." The fat guy asked, "Flo, what's going on?"

"Earl, I'll tell you tonight," and she lit another cigarette.

Flipper gave David $42.75, he drank up and got the hell out of there. "Thanks for the drink," he said over his shoulder.

"My pleasure," replied Flipper.

Chapter 33

The Next Date

Saturday night, David met Anne Marie at the designated bar. This was an upscale club that catered to the growing throngs of yuppies. The place was full of men in Izod shirts or those trying to look like Sonny Crockett from *Miami Vice*. David was the only guy wearing jeans that didn't have a design on the back pockets.

She greeted him with some excitement which made him feel good but then she noticed his black eye. "Oh my God," she said. "What happened?" She reached up and touched his face as David kept his eyes focused on the floor.

"I'll tell you later," he said. The bar was too crowded for his taste and suggested they go some place else. She understood completely and recommended that they get some food to go and head back up to her apartment so he could tell her the story of the black eye.

They picked up some Chinese food in little boxes and walked back to her third-floor walk-up. While they ate, David told her the story of why he got punched in the face. "That's amazing," she said.

"What's so amazing about it?" David said as he ate a piece of moo shu pork with his chop sticks. "I do have the power, you know."

"Oh, not that, any guy can make a girl cum, it's just a physical reaction to stimulation. The fact that you won forty dollars on a bar slot machine! Nobody ever wins on those things," she said with a smile.

"Bitch," he called her playfully.

Finished with supper, they settled in on the couch to watch some television on her thirteen-inch black and white portable TV. They manually changed channels about four times before they settled on a new program, *Murder, She Wrote.*

He was lying against the back corner of the couch and she was lying on the couch with her back against him. He had one arm wrapped around her shoulder, his hand just at her breasts. His lips were next to her ear. Being in such close proximity to someone he liked and found attractive, it only took until the first commercial before he was nibbling on her ear lobe and pushing his hard-on into the side of her leg. His hand easily slipped into her blouse and found her nipple. He tried to slide his other hand into her pants but they were unnecessarily tight and the positioning was awkward. After a couple of teenage attempts at getting into her pants, she stood up and said, "Let me slip into something more comfortable." She went to the bedroom.

She returned wearing nothing! "That's better," she said and assumed her previous position.

After about two seconds of her naked body on him, David said, "I think I need to slip into the same outfit." He stood up, disrobed throwing his clothes in a pile and then he too, assumed the same position. There they were, naked and fully aroused with Angela Lansbury on the small screen solving the *Murder of Sherlock Holmes.*

He twisted her around and put her on her hands and knees on the couch and he got on his knees behind her. He slipped into her from behind but after just a minute of doggy-style she climaxed hard and fell forward on the couch. He hadn't had an orgasm, yet, but he was extremely satisfied with himself. Giving a woman a non-eye contact orgasm was rare... and good.

Anne Marie began to stir a little. She was still lying on her stomach and she raised her butt up in the air a few inches and said "Have at it." David got down low and started positioning himself behind her again. "I'm a Brunswick, you know," she said as she wiggled her butt.

"No, I don't know," said David clueless.

"A Brunswick. A bowling ball." She waited for him to "catch" it, but he didn't. "A bowling ball has three holes." She waited for another second. "Here's a hint, you've already had two of my three holes. Why don't you take the last one." David didn't make a move, he was hysterically paralyzed. Finally she came out and just said it, "David, be a dear and fuck me up the ass."

The *ass fuck*, a very illusive maneuver, one which he had never attempted. He was still paralyzed, mind reeling on how to proceed. She could sense his hesitancy due to his inexperience. Breaking his trance she spoke, "Just spit on your dick, stick it in my ass and fuck it like a pussy." He was still frozen with indecision when she tried to give him some encouragement, but what she said had the exact opposite effect, "Go ahead and stick it up my ass and fuck me. It won't hurt, I do it all the time."

He was all of a sudden not comfortable with the whole situation. He still didn't move. "Do it now," she said in a gentle but persuasive way. He spit on his hand, wiped it on the head of his dick and stuck it halfway up her ass. She didn't make a sound. He was waiting for some sort of response when she said, "More." He stuck it in to the hilt. He was afraid that she would command him to give her "more", which he didn't have. Not the least bit surprising, she said, "Give me more."

Smashing it in as hard as he could, pressing with all of his body weight, he managed to give her another half inch "more". Getting the feeling that the extra half inch and the effort he had to go through to give it to her was not really worth it, he just started pounding away as fast and hard as he could. A jack hammer ass fuck, even with a small dick, seemed counter-intuitive to the way this should have been handled but the hard pounding and her diddling her clit while he did it seemed to put her over the top.

After the last gasp of orgasm left her body, she settled into the couch with his dick still up her ass. "Go ahead and use me to make yourself cum. Just shoot it up my ass, you won't make me pregnant," she said with a giggle. Almost as soon as she said it, he filled her up. He was lying on top of her halfway holding himself up with his arms, his dick still up her ass. She said, "Leave it in me until you go soft and I'll shit you out."

Relatively young and still being up her hole, he wasn't sure if he would go soft anytime soon. He tried to think of other things while he was waiting for her to "shit him out". Eventually, mainly due to his arms getting very tired from holding himself up, his dick started to soften. As it did, she began working her muscles and literally, "shit him out."

"Now go clean up and bring me a wash rag. Hurry!" she instructed.

Chapter 34

After the Date

They were both sitting on the couch, naked, watching the credits scroll across the screen from the *Murder, She Wrote* show. Anne Marie grabbed a box of left over Chinese food and picked out a piece of orange chicken and ate it. The image was almost more than David could take.

"You look out of sorts," she said.

"I guess I am. I have never been down that road before and don't know what I am supposed to be feeling."

"We were just fucking, no big deal. Didn't you like it?" she asked.

"Of course, I did. What's not to like… a Brunswick. Who wouldn't want that?" he said somewhat facetiously. She reached over with a bare foot and kicked him on the shin.

"What do you want to do now?" she asked.

"I don't know. Do you have any more holes some where I can fuck? Maybe a cat or something?"

She kicked him a little harder this time.

"How about a movie? Always good to kill a few hours," he suggested.

"Sure, the paper is on the table. It should have the show times in it. We can walk to the Bijou Theater from here so check that one."

They opted for a Michael Douglas film called *Romancing the Stone*. In the theater, she held a Coke cup up in her hand and made a motion with it as if she were toasting and said, "Everything goes better with Coke."

David returned the toast and said, "Everything goes better with that well laid feeling."

Once back at her apartment, they settled on the couch again with the little TV offering them some diversion, a late night low budget monster movie. As David would seem to always do, instead of taking advantage of the situation, he needed to understand it and asked, "Do we need to talk?"

"About what?" she asked in return. Before David could say anything, she said, "The sex? It's just sex. We grew up in the seventies. You know, *Deep Throat*, *Behind the Green Door*, *The Devil in Miss Jones*."

David's affect was blank.

"The *Opening of Misty Beethoven*." David still looked bewildered.

"*Debbie Does Dallas*?" Anne Marie finally hit a title David recognized.

"Oh yeah, porno movies," he responded sounding like a guy who lived like a hermit, which basically he was.

"I would have thought a man with your abilities would have been around a little more. What have you been doing for the last fifteen years?"

"Hiding mostly," he said. Then he told her his life story as depressing as it was. She listened and during the particularly sad parts she would reach over and squeeze his leg. When finished with his story, she pushed him down on the couch and started kissing him with some veracity. She remained on top the whole time and undressed the minimal amount needed for him to penetrate her. He was still fully clothed with his penis sticking out of his unzipped pants. She had just moved her panties to the side and pushed his dick in her. He was not well endowed and the layers of clothing shortened it even more. The grinding motion she was making was pinching the crap out of his cock on the zipper, jeans and underwear.

She had a quick orgasm, which was fortunate. She was clearly done but he grabbed her hips and thrust a few more times so he could finish. Announcing that he was close, she jumped off of him and stood by the couch. Since his cock was pinched up in the zipper and underwear he didn't squirt like he wanted. The orgasm just got right up to the peak and then dissipated into a mild body shudder with no ejaculation.

Anne Marie stood looking at his little dick all purple from being pinched off. David tried to get it stuffed back in his jeans but when he freed it up the largest wad of ejaculate he had ever experienced flooded out and soaked his pants. Anne Marie snorted a laugh and said, "There it is. You are the biggest mess I have ever seen." She chuckled again. "No, I mean that in every way. You are a mess." She went and got a rag and tried to clean him up as best she could.

After another hour of good conversation and bad TV, David left for the night to go back to the boarding house. He asked her if he could see her again next Saturday and she agreed but asked him if he could meet her at the House of Voodoo because she had to work late that night. It was a date.

Chapter 35

Another Date (Sort Of)

After a long hot stinky week on the shrimp boat, David was really looking forward to being with Anne Marie. He had a few questions he wanted to ask her but was afraid he would mess up their fledging relationship. However, she didn't seem like the kind of girl that got her feelings hurt easily, but he really wanted to know just how many guys had been knocking on her *back door*.

With the shrimp smell scrubbed away and dressed in his finest jeans, tennis shoes and Polo shirt, he set off to meet her at the House of Voodoo. It was dark inside but he could see several women moving around in the shop. He was hesitant to go in because it was rather close quarters and there may be inadvertent eye contact. Something he didn't want to risk.

Eventually she saw him loitering on the sidewalk. Sticking her head out of the door, she told him to come on in. He shook his head and told her that he didn't think it was a good idea. She finally convinced him by telling him that all she wanted to do was introduce him to the girls. "Just keep your head down like you always do." He reluctantly agreed.

Three other employees were in the shop... Megan, who was petite, dark-haired, wore glasses and looked to be about nineteen years old... Jody, who seemed fairly well put together, like an athlete, also in her late teens... and then there was Amber, a tall blonde buxom girl about twenty-two years old who thought she was God's gift to men and was obviously the leader of the House of Voodoo girl gang.

Most of the customers who came to the store were middle-aged women looking for love potions or voodoo dolls of their husbands' secretaries so they could stick pins in them. Amber, the big boobed self-appointed House of Voodoo queen, always left those customers to the other girls. Amber's specialty was young good looking men. Very few young guys actually came into the shop so she really didn't do that much work. David was just young and good looking enough to flip Amber's switch.

Anne Marie made the introductions and David stared at his feet. Amber homed in on him and started asking one question after another about what he did for a living, where he lived, and how they met. David answered every question while he roamed around the store inspecting various individual items and avoiding eye contact. Amber lost interest in David after she found out he worked on a shrimp boat as day labor.

Two customers were in the store, both women. One was the typical customer, a middle-aged white woman looking for something to ward off evil spirits. She was certain her dead husband's ghost was still down in his basement man-cave because the television would turn on by itself or the pool balls could be heard clacking together. Megan sold her a candle to light when she thought her husband was in the basement. "It will burn away the spirit veil and allow his soul to enter the other side," she said. It was just an ordinary candle but they sold it for $22.00! The lady left all excited about the prospect of ridding herself of the final remnants of her twenty-five years of married misery. Misery, except for the money, the four-bedroom house and the three cars in the garage.

It was 9:00 pm, closing time but the last customer didn't seem to be in a hurry to leave. She was a paper thin, ancient, dark skinned mulatto woman with long straight gray hair. David was just about convinced she was a witch. She certainly looked the part. Long finished with interrogating David after she found out he had no money, Amber looked over and saw the old woman still perusing the merchandise. Amber walked over to her and said, "You have got to leave. It's closing time."

Anne Marie said, "It's okay, let her look around."

Amber shot back, "Are you going to stay late because I'm not. I don't get paid overtime." She walked back to David and said, "Your girlfriend is too nice for her own good. Someone is going to take advantage of her someday. She's not smart like me and she doesn't have all this." She dropped her eyes to her own boobs. "I'm out of here." She snatched her purse off the counter and was gone just that quickly.

Megan said, "Well, Amber doesn't seem to have a problem with confidence, does she?" They all agreed that Amber's shortcomings were not the kind that were visible. "What are you guys going to do tonight?" Megan asked as both she and Jody raised their eyebrows.

David said. "Oh, I don't know. Maybe go bowling."

"Bowling?" the others girls said in surprise.

"Yeah, you know a big hard ball with three holes in it," David light-heartedly replied. Anne Marie was mortified.

"Okay, enjoy your bowling and Anne Marie, we'll see you on Monday, right?" said Megan.

"Right," Anne Marie said raising her index finger and pointing at Megan. Goodbyes said, the girls left Anne Marie, David and the old lady customer in the store.

David had his head down and was holding a hairy root tuber of some sort that he had been inspecting in an attempt to avoid eye contact with everyone in the store. He turned around to put it back in the bin and the old lady was right in front of his face. He was startled because he didn't hear or see her come up behind him. "Oh gosh, you scared me," he said. "You must be part ninja."

"That's a taro root you holding there boy." She was staring at his face but he wouldn't look at her.

"What's it good for? Fame, riches, a better sex life?" David asked with lighthearted inquisitiveness.

"It's good for supper. You eat it, fool. Buy it here, it be three dollars a root. Buy it at the grocery, it be three dollars for ten pounds. Best buy it at the grocery boy."

"Well you know your roots."

"I know more than that boy. I know what you sees when you sees it."

"What are you talking about?" he asked.

"Don't play dumb with me boy. I knows what you do to dem girls."

"What do I do to them?" he asked still trying to figure out if she knew about his condition or if she was just a crazy old woman who wasn't making any sense.

"Ever since your pecker started standing up on its own you done been given the gift. Look at me boy, I want to see how strong it is."

David held his head down even lower and said, "I don't think that would be a good idea."

"What you afraid of boy? You afraid Madam Defazende can't resist?"

She reached out, took his chin in her hand and slowly lifted his head until their eyes were fixed on each other.

"Oh yeah," she said. "You done got it bad." She gently shoved his face to the side, "Even Madam Defazende feel the wet down there with you boy and Madam Defazende ain't been wet for a hundred years come next Christmas."

"Why didn't you react?" David was getting excited about the possibility of discovering something new about his affliction. Maybe even a cure.

"Madam Defazende done got tired boy. I needs to go home."

"I want to talk to you some more. Where can I get in touch with you?" David went to the counter and got a piece of paper and a pencil.

"What's your phone number."

"Ain't got no phone boy."

"What's your address, I'll come by tomorrow."

"Best just let me be. You got no call to bother Madam Defazende."

"I won't be a bother, I just want some information."

"You already a bother boy," and she walked out of the store.

Anne Marie asked, "What do you make of that?"

"I don't know. But I really want to find out. I think I ought to follow her. "

"What about our "bowling" night?"

"Oh yeah," David's interest just changed gears. After all, he was a guy. He walked over to her and kissed her like there was no tomorrow. After a thirty second "shut the front door" kiss, that's exactly what they did. They shut the front door and went back to the store room where he immediately looked her in the eyes and stripped her naked while she was cumming. Her clothes came off in wadded up rolls as she writhed around on top of some large boxes.

When she settled down, he bent her over the boxes and had her from behind. The height of the boxes was lower than was comfortable so he had to flex his thighs during the whole affair which wasn't very long due to her incredible animal lustiness. She was like a living orgasm machine.

She came with a shudder and two or three good strokes later, he pulled out and shot his load to the side, soaking a box of T-shirts that had, "If Mama ain't happy... Ain't nobody happy" written on the front.

Anne Marie turned around in time to see him unload. She smiled and said, "Well, I guess Mama's happy now."

"She may not be happy but she is surely surprised." They both laughed a little as he hitched up his britches.

She stretched a little and looked up at him. She grabbed his arm, and said, "What about the Brunswick?"

"Could we maybe move this operation to your apartment? I don't think Mama will be that happy the second time."

"The only thing I have to eat in the apartment are hot dogs. If we want something to cook we need to buy it on the way or we could get some take out like we did before." She was struggling to unroll her pants and get them back on.

"I feel like eating fried chicken. Know some place where we can get that?"

She finally got her pants back on, "One block over and two blocks down. It's a bar, but it's got great chicken and fish."

At her apartment and finished with a bucket of chicken, they reclined on the couch to let it settle in. She was snuggled up close to him with her head on his chest. They were fighting off the urge for an after-dinner nap by having some meaningless conversation. David finally asked her if she had ever seen Madam Defazende in her store before. Anne Marie had not seen her before and said the old lady seemed nice enough but gave her the creeps. Anne Marie also said that her observation skills didn't really mean that much because she had never noticed the Mama T-shirts in the back room either.

"When I first found out about my gift, I used to have to look girls in the eye and think a dirty thought. It didn't have to be much of a thought either, just something like "she sure looks good" and that was all it took. In a matter of months all I had to do was make eye contact with a woman and she would go off. If I looked with a dirty thought, the orgasm was more pronounced. The raunchier the thought the stronger the orgasm."

Anne Marie added, "But the real question is, why was Madam Defazende immune?"

"Did Madam Defazende look like an angel to you?"

"Not at all, but maybe Madam Defazende will cave in eventually." Then she added, "If you are into that sort of thing."

"That old woman knows something and I'd really like to find out what it is. I hope she can resist because Geri-sex is not my thing, but talk to me when I'm seventy and I'll be telling a different story."

"What are you going to do, hang out at the store every day for God knows how long? This was the first time I saw that lady in the six months I worked there."

David thought for a minute and said, "Maybe she's new to the area and will be a regular from now on. Out of curiosity, what did she buy at the store?"

"Nothing. She was in the shop for an hour and left after your conversation."

"Well that's no help." David took a deep breath out of frustration.

"Sounds like you need to relax and besides, you owe me two more holes."

She unzipped his pants, pulled out his cock and sucked it up with a large amount of enthusiasm, getting it soaking wet with saliva. When rock hard, she pulled his pants off while he was sitting on the couch and then she shed her jeans. She faced away from him and literally sat on his cock. It was up her ass! She couldn't seem to get it all the way in so she was bearing down with her full weight. It was excruciatingly painful for both of them but a full penetration Brunswick was the order of the day and by golly it was going to happen. With a couple more bounces and twists, his dick was seated as deeply as possible. She rocked back and forth playing with her clit the whole time, sometimes reaching down between her legs and rubbing his balls. It didn't take long before the inevitable, he shot up her ass. She could feel every pulse of his dick and it was just enough to set her off. Then she clamped down on him even tighter while she was cumming. Pressing down with her full body weight, her ass-grip felt like a vice.

When done, she said, "Don't pull out. I think it is going to be messy."

"I don't think I could pull it out if I wanted to. We may be stuck. What do we do now?"

"Can you stand up with your dick still in me?"

"I think I can but we better hurry. I may not stay hard very long. This is my second time in a few hours you know."

They rotated around a little until they got upright. Then they moved in this human centipede fashion, butt to crotch, until they got through the bathroom door. She reached up and grabbed a hand towel off a hanger and held it around the base of his cock. "Slowly pull out."

In one fluid motion, she wiped him clean as he pulled out of her and stuffed the towel between her cheeks. "Now get out. As a matter of fact, go on home and I'll see you next Saturday, same time, same place. Go on now. Go."

"What about the Brunswick, I'm owed another hole."

"Out!" and she pointed with her finger, smiling.

He walked to the boarding house thinking about how tight Anne Marie's ass was and then he killed the after glow by letting Madam Defazende's face materialize. "Crap!"

Chapter 36

The Relationship

David started working five days a week on the boat. That was $500 per week with only $300 in expenses. Two-hundred a week free and clear was plenty for now. He felt comfortable with the situation and hoped it would last.

Saturday rolled around and David met all the girls at the shop just like the week before. Out of curiosity he asked the girls if they had ever been to Marie Laveau's grave, after all she was the namesake of the shop. None of the girls had ever seen her grave. He asked if they wanted to go see it after work. Amber, the blonde, buxom one had a date but she said her date could wait on her so she would go. Everyone else also agreed. The plan was to go to Pat O'Brien's for a couple of hurricanes and then to the cemetery.

While drinking hurricanes, David asked the girls if any of them had seen the old mulatto lady, Madam Defazende, during the week but no one had seen her. Pat O'Brien's was crowded with tourists and David needed to get out of there quickly. He had years of practice not looking into women's eyes but the more targets around the better chance of an accident and Pat O'Brien's was a target rich environment.

David paid the bill for seven drinks, Amber had three, and they left to walk to the cemetery. "If we linger a bit, we can be in the cemetery at midnight." "No thank you," was the consensus from the girls. They walked in relative silence until they approached the Basin Street entrance. A tourist information kiosk was still open and David fell prey to the vendor because not only did he buy a map of the cemetery plots, he also bought a complete list of some 2,600 names of all those buried there.

He handed the list of names to Anne Marie and asked her to look up Marie Laveau. The group stood underneath a street lamp as Anne Marie flipped through several pages. She found the plot number and David looked it up on the map. When he got his bearings, they entered the cemetery and moved as a group until they were standing in front of the Voodoo Queen's final resting place. Amber said, "Is that all there is to it?"

David responded. "They say if you knock three times on her grave and make a wish, it just might come true."

"I want a million dollars," said Amber who was feeling the effects of three large Pat O'Brien hurricanes.

"Knock on the grave," the group encouraged. Then David said, "I think you have to spin around three times too or something awful will happen to you."

Megan responded with, "Don't spin. It's not a necessary part of the ritual plus you'll probably just get dizzy. But you have to put three X's on the grave when your wish comes true."

"Well I want a fucking million dollars so I'm gonna do it." Amber stumbled up to the sepulcher and lightly rapped three times on the side stone wall saying, "I'm gonna spin. Why take chances?" She started a death spiral and plummeted face first to the ground just before the third rotation. The hurricanes were victorious. Megan and Jody were trying to get her upright. Anne Marie was laughing and David watched in amused disbelief. Megan and Jody grabbed Amber by the arms but couldn't stand her up. They just dragged her around a little on the filthy ground. Besides soiling her clothes, she now had gum in her hair. Back down on all fours, Amber said, "I'm gonna throw up."

As she spoke the words, she looked up at everybody. David was so enthralled with the action that he let his guard down. He and Amber made eye contact! *Poor girl* is all he thought. She started throwing up and having an orgasm at the same time. Only Amber and David knew for sure what was happening. The other girls thought she was having an exceptionally hard time evacuating the hurricanes. Suspecting more than just a drunken purge, Anne Marie stood beside David and asked in a very low whisper, "Did you look at her?"

"I didn't mean to."

"Look at that bitch go," Anne Maria said laughing even harder now. Amber finished with both activities and curled up on the ground. She was dirty from being on the ground and not only did she have gum in her hair, but now she had vomit as well... plus she peed her pants.

Jody said, "Damn, that Marie Laveau curse worked really fast. Amber must not have done it right."

"No, I guess not," David said stifling his desire to belly laugh. "Well, let's get her home and cleaned up." He got her on her feet with Megan and Jody propping her up on either side. "Anybody know where she lives?" No one knew so they decided to take her back to the shop and let her sleep on the boxes in the back, maybe using the Mama T-shirts as pillows.

Anne Marie was laughing again, "Oh Mama ain't going to be happy about this."

After stumbling through the French Quarter, looking like every other bunch of drunks that night, they reached the shop. Stacking boxes and spreading out "If Mama ain't happy" T-shirts, they made a fairly comfortable bed on which Amber could sleep. They lit several "good luck" and "better sex" candles and lounged in the corners of the store room. They sat in an awkward silence for a moment until Megan said, "These candles make me think I'm going to get lucky and get laid tonight."

"You wish," responded Jody. After a chuckle, they settled into some decent conversation. David always wondered when someone would ask, and finally Jody did.

"David, why don't you ever look at us? Is it a cultural thing or are you just shy?"

Anne Marie squirmed on the box upon which she was sitting. "I think we need to get Amber home," she said. She started to get up but the other girls decided that it would be best for Amber to stay right where she was until she woke up on her own.

Jody didn't let it go, "So why do you never look at anybody."

"Just shy, I guess," said David, forced to still look away.

Jody dared him, "Look at me."

Anne Marie literally jumped up off her box and said, "I'm sorry, we have to go," and grabbed David by the hand to drag him out. Jody, built like an athlete, grabbed Anne Marie by her arm, spun her around, and asked, "What's going on here?"

Anne Marie pulled away holding her hands up in a defensive position. "Girls, just let this go."

Megan stood up and entered the fray, "You're scaring me. Anne Marie, what's going on?"

Jody added, "You're not getting out of here until you spill the beans." Amber groaned and rolled over on the box and t-shirt bed. She was coming around. All eyes turned to her. "What's going on. Where are we?" Amber asked.

Meagan told her that they were in the storeroom at the shop. "What are we doing here?" Amber asked.

Megan explained, "You passed out on us and we didn't know where you lived so we drug your filthy ass back here to sleep it off."

Amber didn't seem to be paying any attention because she had discovered the gum stuck in her hair. Jody helped her understand, "Yeah, that's gum. If you smell your hair you should be able to smell your own vomit. And, I'm pretty sure you pissed yourself too."

proprietor, was standing on the front steps. David didn't even get the words "Good Morning" out of his mouth before Maisie told him he would have to move out within the week.

"Let me guess," said David. "Anne Marie."

"You bet your sweet ass." Maisie turned and went into her part of the boarding house.

Chapter 38

On the Road Again

David was sitting in Cafe du Monde eating sugar coated beignets and reading the paper looking for another job. He didn't have much money and was being evicted from the boarding house on Friday. He needed income and had no prospects. He tried to make up with Anne Marie but he was greeted with a middle finger on one occasion and a door slammed in his face on the other. He was on his own.

He didn't really want to leave town because he was still interested in talking to Madam Defazende. How to find her was the question. To continue the search for the Madam, he would have to quickly find a new place to stay and get a job.

After reading the classified ads and finding only truck driving and waiter jobs, he started reading the rest of the paper. The headlines, the sports, the financials, the comics, and finally the fluff. He set a whole section aside that had pages and pages of names on it. So many names were on the pages that it looked like a list of Civil War dead.

Finishing the last beignet and having nothing else to read he decided to glance at the section of the paper with all the names. The names were in alphabetical order and without thinking about it he looked where his name should be on the list. David O. Gideon was on the list! "What the hell?"

He was looking at a national list of names of people who had dormant bank accounts with over $10,000 in the account. He couldn't believe there were thousands of names on the list and he really couldn't believe that he left Vegas without cleaning out his accounts.

He rushed to a local bank, opened an account with fifty bucks, got a large pocket full of quarters and started making calls on a pay phone. When it was all said and done, he found that he still had three bank accounts In Vegas with money in them. One account had just over $10,000. Thank goodness or it wouldn't have shown up in the paper. The other two accounts were around $8,000 each.

He'd done it again, rags to riches. He got one of the Las Vegas banks to transfer $2,000 to his New Orleans account and he told all the banks to close the accounts and invest the money in a get rich quick stock. Since he just got through reading the financial section of the New Orleans Times-Picayune he felt like an expert and decided the stock should be Microsoft, a company that was currently having an initial public offering. Transaction confirmed, he had nearly $23,000 invested in Microsoft. Fortune or folly, he didn't know.

With his new windfall, he purchased two nights in a moderately priced hotel. He moved all his things, one duffle bag full, into the hotel. Good riddance to the boarding house. He was afraid that Maisie might try to poison him if he continued to stay there the rest of the week. He emptied his pockets on the dresser. Among his things were a wallet, a room key, twenty-three quarters left over from the phone calls, a map of the cemetery and a list of the dead buried in the cemetery. He grabbed the map and the list, kicked off his shoes, and laid on the bed. He studied the map a few minutes until he located Marie Laveau's plot. He then started looking through the list of names with the dates of birth and death. He didn't know what he was looking for but the last list he looked at, the dormant bank accounts, was extremely good to him so he thought he'd just give it a once over.

He flipped through several pages of the list until his eye caught a line that didn't have a date in the birth column nor one in the death column. He thought how sad. No one knew when this human was born or died. Then he looked at the name. Holy shit! The name was Defazende! Lot number 20.

David put his shoes on, grabbed his crap off the dresser, and headed out the door. First stop was a pay phone to call information. No Defazendes were listed or unlisted according to the telephone company. Next stop was the court house for a search of records. He searched census, property, births, deaths, marriages, divorces, and taxes. No records were found. Defazende was not a name associated with anything in modern New Orleans.

Next, he went to the library. He related the story to the librarian leaving out the details concerning his affliction. She helped him look through some historical books and records but they didn't find anything. After scratching their heads, the librarian reluctantly suggested reviewing the books in the Haunted New Orleans section. She showed him where they were and returned to her duties at the front desk.

David examined the haunted books but they were not user friendly when trying to find a single name. Defazende was not listed in any of the indices, glossaries or chapter headings. He came to the last book which was more of a stapled together Xerox copied pamphlet. He flipped through it quickly seeing that it had many more old pictures than the other books. He started turning through the pamphlet page by page and reading the captions of every picture. He stopped in amazement at the twelfth daguerreotype picture in the book. The caption was simply "Marie Laveau Gathering: June 23, 1874". Marie Laveau was maybe a tiny, blurry, moving figure in a group of tiny, blurry, moving figures in the back ground. However, perfectly still and perfectly focused was a haunting figure in the foreground. It was Madam Defazende's spitting image! The mulatto, gray haired old lady was standing less than ten feet from the camera, just as she looked in Marie Laveau's House of Voodoo two days ago.

He decided that he had to show Anne Marie. After making copies of the daguerreotype picture, he set off to find Anne Marie. Since it was a weekday, she was probably at the shop. He really didn't want to see her there because he had no desire to see Amber, Megan or especially Jody. Standing outside the shop and across the street, he was hoping beyond hope to catch Anne Marie as she came out the door for a break. After an hour, he went to the shop window and looked in. He saw Megan behind the counter. She saw him and came outside, "You're not welcome here, pervert."

"I need to see Anne Marie," he said, disregarding the pervert name calling.

"Well you're shit out of luck because she called in sick this morning,"

"Where's Jody and Amber?"

"Jody's in the back. You want me to get her?"

"No, she'll probably try to kick my ass. And Amber?"

"She went to the doctor. Her date the other night got pissed because she didn't show up and slapped her around a little. He's a worse asshole than you."

"I didn't do anything to you," David said.

"Yeah you did. You mind fucked me. I feel so... used."

"I didn't mean to do it. Actually, I can't help it. I hypnotize women into having orgasms. That's why I never look women in the eye."

"Well you did, didn't you?"

David ended the argument with saying, "Keep in mind that a hypnotized person won't do anything that they don't really want to do."

"If you're saying that I wanted you to mind fuck me then you're crazy."

"Listen to yourself, Megan. You're the one that sounds crazy."

She didn't know how to respond. "That's it. I'm going to get Jody and she will beat your ass bloody."

David just said, "You win," and he ran off down the street to Anne Marie's apartment.

Standing outside the door he rehearsed what he was going to say. None of it sounded sincere so he just knocked on the door. He was excited about showing her the picture and the remote possibility that they could get back together. Then his hopes were dashed.

Captain Bob answered the door. Fucking, stinky, shrimp boat Captain Bob was inside bowling with Anne Marie.

David was stunned but he managed to say, "Not working today?"

Captain Bob said, "I wouldn't call what I'm doing work but I am putting an effort into it." He smiled with a fucking, stinky, shrimp boat smile. David hated everything about New Orleans at that very moment. Then Captain Bob said, "Looks like you're not working at all."

"Tell Anne Marie I just came by to share some information I found on Madam Defazende."

From back in the apartment, "Tell him to fuck himself." Anne Marie was obviously still angry with him.

As David turned away, he could hear them both laughing. He decided that he was leaving New Orleans and never looking back. He returned to the hotel, packed his duffle bag, and went to the train station. "A ticket on the first train out, please." He bought a $500 package that was good for three months and eight stops. He was back to mindlessly riding the rails.

Chapter 39

The Trip to Graceland

He was riding a train called the City of New Orleans, a train made famous by the song, but it was one more reminder of what he was trying to leave behind. He traveled, head down, in the observation car periodically looking at the view out the window. In Memphis, he got off the train using the first of eight stops.

He decided Graceland was worth a visit. After all, Elvis had never done anything to him before. However, in the back of his mind, he was worried about funds. He was short and it needed to last as long as possible, but it *was* Graceland.

There had been numerous Elvis sightings across the country, mostly concentrated in Vegas and Graceland. With his recent experience with Madam Defazende, meeting Elvis seemed like a real possibility. The self-guided tour of the home was enjoyable. He especially liked the Jungle Room. However, when he came upon the grave in the backyard, he was a little startled. He never knew that Elvis was buried on the grounds.

Standing next to the grave, feeling like an intruder, he decided to go back through the house to exit. Aware that some of the home was still occupied by family members he crept around cautiously trying not to enter the private section. Two wrong turns later and he was thoroughly lost. Throwing his hands up, he turned to retrace his steps. A young woman was standing behind him in a doorway and asked, "Are you lost?"

"For most of my life," replied David.

She pointed, "Two rights and a left and you'll be back in the front lobby, but most people go out the backyard."

"I didn't know. I saw the grave and felt out of place, so I came in here trying to retrace my steps. I failed miserably as you can see."

She said, "Don't worry. Daddy's grave has that effect on a lot of people."

Shit, he thought. *I'm talking to Lisa Marie Presley.*

"Thanks for the directions," he said trying to remain calm and not appear star struck. She was only 17 or 18 years old but she had him flustered.

"Enjoy your day," she said as she turned and disappeared from where she came.

He floated out of Graceland feeling more like he had seen a ghost than what he would have felt if he had *really* seen one. He went to Beale Street to listen to some blues and eat some Bar-B-Que. What a great day this turned out to be. Hell with Anne Marie and three cheers for Lisa Marie.

But he made a mental note to himself: *In the future, avoid women with "Marie" in their name, it's flirting with disaster.*

Chapter 40

The Chicago Arrangement

David liked the feel of Memphis and decided to stay for a while. He found a job at a movie theater, cleaning up the nasty floors after the movies. It was a good job for him because he did most of his work alone, plus he got to see the movies for free.

He was staying in a sleaze bag hotel that only cost six bucks a night. His pay for an evening at the movie theater was $15.00, a positive cash flow especially since he sometimes ate the free popcorn and hot dog for supper at the movie theater. It was a good set up for a month but then it was time to leave. With a few hundred extra dollars in his pocket he boarded the train for Chicago. No plans for the future was his new way of life. Whatever came his way, he'd handle it, making sure to avoid women named Marie.

At the train station in Chicago, he decided that the first order of business would be to purchase a deep-dish pizza while at Wrigley Field watching the Cubs play the White Sox. *Okay, get real, just the deep-dish pizza.*

He told the taxi driver to take him to the best pizza in town. The driver said, "You got it." In a few minutes, they pulled up in front of a place called, Marie's Pizza and Spirits. David just said, "No fucking way. Not the name Marie." How could a place of business have both the name Marie and the word Spirits in it?

The driver shrugged his shoulders. "Your nickel," he said. A couple of turns later he asked, "You don't have anything against women named Constance, do you?"

"Nothing at all." They stopped in front of a place called Connie's Pizza. He paid an exorbitant cab fare and went in for what the driver described as "the best pizza of your life". Not to his surprise, it was in fact, the best pizza he had ever eaten. While he ate the three-meat pizza, he thought of nothing but Lisa Marie Presley. Somehow, he felt that he had missed a golden opportunity. What would have happened if he had given her just one glance? Then he thought better of it, he probably would have gone to jail.

Next order of business was finding a place to stay and getting a job. Without too much trouble, he found another flee-bag hotel that he could afford for a month. The job was a little harder to find but he was now the head dish washer at the Grand Buffet, a Chinese restaurant. The hardest part of the job was going to be avoiding the dozen or so young female Chinese waitresses.

On the fifth day, after his shift was over, the Boss Lady, a slightly stocky woman, older than him by ten years, called him into the back office. She was not unattractive and had a name he couldn't pronounce and certainly couldn't spell. She screamed at him, "What you work for here!"

He didn't understand what she was asking. "Money," he said rather meekly. She evidently didn't like the answer because she yelled again. "What for money when got girls!" He was really at a loss now. Then he just decided to go for it and screamed back at her.

"Need money. Don't want girls!"

"You queer!" she screamed. They were getting so loud that several waitresses came into the office to see what was going on. David was losing the argument but he wasn't sure what point he needed to make. Within five minutes, the Boss Lady had every waitress in her office all screaming at the top of their lungs, calling him queer. The only reason he could figure they were ganging up on him was that he always moved among them with his head down and didn't pay the normal amount of attention to a bunch of young women. Add the fact that a terrible AIDS scare was running rampant through out the country. The Chinese put two and two together and got five, an AIDS epidemic plus him not showing interest in the girls equals him being queer. The girls started pushing him and yelling for him to get out. They didn't want an AIDS infected dish washer. They backed him into the far corner of the office and started trying to kick him in the groin. He decided enough was enough.

He looked at all of them in quick succession. They screamed in their own personal orgasm way and simultaneously, hit the floor of the office. Thirteen Chinese women piled in a quivering mass on the floor, squirming around him like eels. As they recovered, he looked at them again and again until they all collapsed in a semi-conscious state on the floor. "Who's a queer now?" he demanded. Then he said, "Hell, who's your Daddy?"

The Boss Lady stood up from behind the desk having been "untouched" by his attack. She must have been quick, ducked for cover, and stayed there. He hit some of the girls three and even four times depending on how fast they recovered and looked at him again. The Boss Lady said, "You no queer boy. You magic man."

"That's right, Boss Lady. I'm Mister Orgasm and there is a new sheriff in town."

"I don't know new 'sherf' but you honey boy. I make you good deal."

The girls started getting up and straightening out their clothes. They were chattering among themselves. It appeared that they were recounting the episode and bragging about who came the best. The Boss Lady ran all the girls out of the office. "Let's make deal."

The Boss Lady gave him two options. Either he takes up residence in the room on the second floor above the Grand Buffet and each night, one of the girls would come up and be serviced. "Happy wait-ress no look for husband and leave me." The deal involved a different girl every night for thirteen nights and then David would get a night off. He still had to work as a dish washer but he would get free rent and all the Chinese food he could eat. Or, the Boss Lady would call the police and all of the girls would testify that he tried to rape them. At least all of the girls with legal papers would testify.

He was caught in another fucking trap. "What the hell," and took the first option.

That night he moved into the room above the Grand Buffet which was furnished nicely and was one of the better places in which he had lived. He was watching MTV and finishing his last bite of egg foo young when he heard a light tapping at the door. When he opened the door, two girls ran in giggling and closed the door behind them. The tallest girl said, "Don't tell Boss Lady, but we get picked for number one night and number two night." She pointed to herself first and then her companion. "We talk and decide to share. Share okay with Mister Orgi?"

"Mister Orgasm," he corrected.

"Okay Mister Orgi, we get ready." They started unceremoniously taking off their shoes, socks, black work slacks, and white blouses. Beige panties and white bras still on, they went to the full-size bed. They helped each other get their bras off then they shucked their panties on the floor. Both women were thin and less buxom than most. They had fair skin and dark black hair.

They got in the bed and held on to each other. It didn't look to David like they were lesbians but more like the were about to take a wild carnival ride and were trying settle each other's nerves. Then he thought, a carnival ride is more like what this was going to be. He said, "Are you ready?" The ladies held on to each other tighter and shook their heads affirmative. "Let's get started then."

He said very loudly to make sure he got their full attention, "For your sexual pleasure, I present to you, the one, the only, the amazing

Mister Orgasm!" He looked at them both and they squealed with delight, writhing around in a snake dance twisting motion still intertwined. *It is truly a carnival act*, he thought as he watched the girls start to slow down. He made a mental note to consider a carnival act sometime in the future.

When finished, the girls both sat up in bed and hugged again at a job well done. David liked what he saw in his bed and asked, "Mind if I join you?"

He started to undo his belt but both girls shrieked, "No can do! Boss Lady say you have AIDS and no can touch us."

"No can touch!" David repeated.

"Touch self. No touch us. We want another go. Boss Lady say you give us all we want."

"Get ready then," he said as they both laid back on the bed. "Once again, the one, the only, the amazing Mister Orgasm!" They started going instantly. The tall one played with herself between her legs trying to enhance and prolong the experience. The shorter girl just held her thighs. David thought, *touch self*, and unzipped his pants. He masturbated in front of them, finishing up in a handful of tissues that he threw in the trash. He was reasonably sure that the girls never even noticed him doing it.

The girls were shiny with sweat and their hair was matted against their necks. The taller girl wanted another go but the shorter one was done. The short one just rolled over facing away from David while he continued to satisfy the taller one for a third and then a fourth time. When she was finally done, they both began to get dressed.

David started to speak to them but the taller one raised her hand like a cop stopping traffic. It worked because David ceased to speak in mid sentence. Neither one of them said another word. They just finished dressing and left. David heard them go down the stairs and when outside of the stairwell, they began to laugh. He could tell there were more than two of them so some of the other girls must have been waiting outside to get the story.

The good thing was that it was over fairly quickly and he did get off so it wasn't that bad. The things people do for free rent and food, he thought. He also thought about how quickly people figured out ways to capitalize on his ability. They always saw what was in it for them and never once considered how their schemes might affect him or others.

Chapter 41

Chinese Take-Out

The next night the same two girls came to his upstairs apartment. This time the taller one gave him the cop stopping traffic sign and said, "No speaky." They shucked their clothes in record time and were wrapped in each other's arms naked on the bed ready for the show. David unzipped his fly and pulled out his dick. When the girls looked at what he was doing he quickly said, "The one, the only, the amazing Mister Orgasm!" before they had a chance to protest.

The girls started hugging each other more tightly and competing in some kind of leg squeezing contest. Each one was trying to get a better grip around the other's thigh. When they started to slow down David walked over to the bed and made eye contact again.

The short girl turned toward the wall and made herself into a tiny ball on the bed. The taller girl rolled onto her back and spread her legs as wide as she could, holding her feet about a foot off the bed. She stroked herself with some verve. So did David. He was losing the race to finish first so he caught her attention and she went off a third time. He finished, shooting into a wash rag. She was about to run out of steam when he looked at her again. This time she cried out as if it were painful. David secretly hoped it was. Once done, the girls dressed quickly and left without a word of conversation involving David.

This is going to be a long two-week rotation, David thought as he drank an ice cold canned diet Coke straight down. It burned the dog shit out of the back of his throat. The next work day was over before he knew it and he was in his room waiting for girl number three. Within ten minutes, he could barely distinguish a light tapping on his door. He never heard anyone walk up the stairs.

When he opened the door, the smallest woman he had ever seen was standing there. She must have been four foot, six inches tall at the most and she didn't weigh more than a kennel size sack of dog food. He was afraid that she was not yet grown up. The first thing out of his mouth was, "How old are you?" She said she was eighteen. It was cutting it close but it was legal.

She asked him how it worked and what she was supposed to do. David laughed and told her he didn't have much experience with this arrangement but he said the other girls took off their clothes and laid down on the bed. She said she would do that and hesitantly started removing her blouse. She was facing away from him sitting on the edge of the bed. After each piece of clothing was removed, she looked over her shoulder to see what he was doing. He wasn't doing anything, just sitting in the chair.

When she was finally disrobed completely, she scooted into the middle of the bed on her back. She crossed her arms over her breasts, pulled her legs up, and pinched them together at the knees. From what he could tell, she really didn't have any breasts at all. As a matter of fact, she was completely flat chested and had the smallest nipples of any woman he had ever seen. He was really beginning to suspect that this girl was more like twelve years old instead of eighteen. He glanced between her legs and didn't see any hair. David started to panic. "Wait here," he said as he ran out the door down to the restaurant and found the Boss Lady. She was always in the office.

"What do you mean by sending me babies," he said sternly.

"Mei is eighteen years. You no worry 'bout being baby!" she screamed. "Go back up and give her magic. But no touch her, you got AIDS."

David said, "I don't think I want to do this anymore."

"You go back up queer boy before I call cops and tell them you got baby girl in bed."

"She's not a minor," he said.

"I know she not. She all grown up but she not legal with no papers and she will say she thirteen years. She will swear you rape baby girl."

David could not figure out how things deteriorated so quickly. Once again, he knew he was trapped and it was only the third day of the arrangement. When he went back to his room, the girl was sitting in the middle of the bed with the covers wrapped around her. Well, let's just get right down to it. "Here's the one, the only, the amazing Mister Orgasm." He looked at her and she fell back on the bed with the covers nearly obscuring her completely. All he could see was the covers moving around and he heard something like a little puppy crying. He almost laughed.

When the covers stopped moving and the whimpering could no longer be heard, he walked over to the bed and jerked the covers off the little naked woman. She startled and tried to cover herself but David was too fast. He caught her with a sideways glance. She flipped up on her knees, then went face down, flat on the bed and began a horizontal dirty dance with the sheets. She started the puppy whimpering once more.

While she was going for it on the bed, he started thinking about how most women have the same type of orgasm over and over again. Besides the position, the orgasm is exactly the same. Then he wondered why the need for orgasms drove people to do stupid things if they knew the orgasm was always going to be the same. It was like eating a hamburger. They're good but why would you want one every meal. When he realized he was making no sense, even to himself, he snapped out of his thoughts. When the girl started trying to sit up, he said, "Hey!" She looked at him and went down again. She was undulating just like before and the crying puppy arrived back in the room. "See," he said to himself. "It's the same." When she finished this time, he let her get dressed and go.

Chapter 42

Girl Number Four

He just finished his busboy/dish washer work and had gotten back up to his apartment when he heard the knock on the door. This rap was not timid. He opened the door to the most mature waitress of the bunch. "May I come in?" she asked.

"Sure," he said.

She came in, sat on the bed and crossed her legs. David sat in the chair and said, "What's happened the last three nights is the girls take their clothes off and lie down."

She responded with, "Can I ask you a question?" David nodded. "Are you really a homosexual?"

"No."

"Do you really have AIDS?"

"No."

She took her shoes off. "Do you like this arrangement?"

"Probably no more than you do," said David

"I have to be here if I want to keep my job," she said. Her voice was flat and her eyes stared into the distance.

"Why don't you just leave and be a waitress some place else?" he asked.

"I'm not legal. I've been in America for over ten years now and have worked at the Grand Buffet for the Boss Lady the entire time."

"Your English is very good."

"I learned in China and had a tutor here for five years. Then the Boss Lady told me I had learned enough and if I had time to study, then I had time to do extra work. I didn't get to study anymore after that." She took off her blouse.

"Do you think you are better off here or back in China?"

"Here for sure. I would be working in a rice paddy if I were back in China." She took off her pants.

David found himself speechless waiting for the bra to be removed.

She continued, "I would probably be married to a local farmer with a water buffalo, or two, if I married well." She laughed a little. The bra fell off exposing relatively full breasts with large brown nipples. Exquisite, David thought. She continued to talk.

She told him that she was raped three times on the way over from China to the United States. "Once by the man who took my money and made the arrangements, once by the boat captain." David immediately thought, *I hate fucking boat captains.* "And once again by the guide in Burma." She said several other close calls occurred and twice she traded sex for food and shelter. She said she also had to give a hand job to a Chicago cab driver when she came up short on fare. When she finished her story, she pulled her white panties off, laid back on the bed and said she was ready.

As beautiful as she was, David just didn't want to do this, especially to someone who had been through what she had. He felt like he was about to rape her again. She had her eyes shut and legs spread.

"I'm ready," she said again placing her hands on her thighs.

"You have to look at me so I can hypnotize you."

She raised her head and looked. Cumming quickly, she stayed flat on her back, knees bent, legs spread and soles of her feet on the bed.

She was also one who played with herself to increase her pleasure. This was a sight to behold. David took his clothes off and stood beside the bed with his cock sticking up at a sixty-degree angle.

When she finished herself, she reached over and grabbed his shaft. It surprised him because she was not even supposed to talk to him let alone touch him. Two seconds later she went carnivore, sat up, and shoved his dick into her mouth. Another pleasant surprise! He went up on his toes leaning into the mattress. She pulled him closer and sucked his dick, expertly. Obviously not all of her sexual encounters were against her will.

David had to concentrate on other things so he could get control of himself. Regrettably, he was not going to last long. He pushed her head away because he wanted to get between her legs. He crawled on top of her with his eyes shut, and slid himself into her. It was like fucking hot melted butter. He lasted long enough to allow her to cum again but he was not so naive to think that he was giving her an orgasm, it was more like being used to have an orgasm.

She had wrapped her legs around him and it was feeling good. She dug her nails into his back and said something in Chinese in his ear. He had no idea what she said but it sounded dirty. He announced to her that he was about to cum. She said, "Put it in my mouth."

They made some quick moves on the bed, she getting on her knees and David standing up. He stroked himself a few more frantic times and she waited with her mouth open like a baby bird. A second before he was at the high point, she guided him into her mouth. She did it by grabbing his balls, firmly...wvery firmly and pulling him deep down her throat. He nearly cried out from the nut squeeze and did cry out when he shot his substantial load into her mouth. She swallowed it in rapid succession.

His knees gave out and he had to lie down on the bed. He was on his back and she put her head on his chest, throwing a leg over his. He instantly liked this girl, felt comfortable with her and always appreciated real sex. Unfortunately, he had to service twelve more girls before he got around to her again.

They had a short conversation about their current predicament and how their lives had gone wrong, then she stroked him up hard a second time and mounted him from the top, facing away. He grabbed her hips and pulled her down, penetrating her as deeply as possible. When he had no more inches to give her, she would raise up on her knees until the head of his cock almost slipped out. This action, repeated continuously, created long and powerful strokes. The alternating motion of their selfish desires blended to perfectly satisfy them both. She had two more orgasms while riding him and when he announced he was about to cum, she spun around and threw her mouth on his cock. She looked at him as she spun around and was cumming again while she had him in her mouth. He unloaded for the second time which felt great but his balls hurt like they were collapsing in on themselves.

She didn't swallow his load like she did before, she was too busy having her own orgasm. Instead, she let his juice run out of her mouth back down the shaft of his cock into his hair. Recovered, she crawled up the bed to lay her head on David's chest. "That was fantastic," she said.

"That was messy," said David, looking down at his crotch. His whole pubic area was a mass of hair, saliva, and cum. She gave him a playful slap.

"It nearly hurt to cum a second time that quickly," he said not really expecting any kind of response.

"Poor baby," she said. "Let me make it better." She started massaging his balls.

He said, "That feels good," but what he was thinking was, *please don't get me hard again.*

After a few minutes of a great nut massage, she said, "I guess I better go." David got up and went into the bathroom to clean up and she got dressed.

Both dressed and standing at the door, he said, "I suppose I'll see you in a couple of weeks."

"I'm already not liking the fact that you'll be with all the other girls before I see you again."

"I'm not sure what to do about it. It's our arrangement. No telling what the Boss Lady will do if we don't honor it."

"You're right. We must honor our arrangement. I will see you in two weeks." She stuck out her hand and David shook it. Then she closed the door behind her.

Chapter 43

Two Weeks to Repeat

The girls came in night after night. Most were very respectful and just disrobed, had their orgasms on the bed, got dressed and left. No girl had less than two orgasms and one lady had seven from the best he could tell. Hers were nearly continuous and it was hard to discern the end of one and the start of another. The heaviest waitress came three times. He knew this for a fact because she farted each time she came.

He took care of himself on most nights with the girls still present but sometimes he waited until they left to satisfy himself. All was progressing as planned. He had finished girl number thirteen and was looking forward to his night off.

It was Sunday. He didn't have a busboy/dishwashing shift that day and no services to perform that night, so he went out. He bought a book by Louis Lamour, *Last of the Breed*, shopped for some clothes, and bought a few groceries that had nothing to do with Chinese food. Back at the room he decided to read his new book. Within minutes he was asleep on the bed with the book on his chest open to page six.

He awoke thinking he heard a knock on the door. He sat up in bed and listened intently. Yes, it was a knock. He thought maybe it was girl number four, returning for a special visit knowing he was off that night.

He flung the door open hoping to see girl number four but instead, the Boss Lady stood in front of him. "Oh my God," he said.

"My turn," she said. "I wait two weeks for this." She stepped inside without an invitation just like she owned the place. Of course, she did own the place. "You no look, you no talk," and she gave him the cop stopping traffic sign like most of the girls did. She evidently taught them what to do. "Face away," she instructed with some authority. David turned around as told.

He could sense that she was disrobing. Then he heard the bed squeaking. "Turn around now." He turned to see her naked on her hands and knees with her feet and ass at the very edge of the bed. Her legs were squeezed tightly together so the only hole he could possibly get to was her ass. "Take off clothes," she said. Again, this was not a request. David stripped and stood naked with a half hard on.

"Now, get harder, stand behind me and fuck my ass."

David didn't want to do this so he stood there. "I don't want to go bowling," he said under his breath.

"Now!" she screamed.

"But I have AIDS. You said so yourself."

"I make bullshit. Fuck ass, now!"

David's half hard went to quarter hard. "I really don't want to do this."

"Don't care what you want. Stand behind and fuck ass or I call police."

David walked over to the edge of the bed and stood behind the Boss Lady. He thought, *If I can just get her to look at me, I think I can end it.* He stood right behind her and placed a hand on either side of her hips. He was limp as a dish rag and he knew dish rags. He thought if he stood idle long enough, she would turn around and yell at him again.

She wiggled her hips and pushed back trying to make contact with his dick but he kept himself just inches away. It would have been the cruelest of teases if that had been what he was trying to do but all he wanted was for her to look at him.

It worked. For someone who always got her way, this must have been extremely frustrating for her. She looked back over her shoulder, looked him straight in the eye, "Fuck ass now or I call police!"

Their eyes locked for a good three seconds before she turned back around. Nothing happened! Not a fucking thing. No heavy breathing, no spasms, no cries of emotion, no orgasm, no nothing! David was stunned. Could she possibly be a Chinese Madam DeFazende? "Do you feel anything?" he asked.

"Of course not, limp dick cocksucker."

For a guy who had the world's greatest gift for women, he had the knack for stepping into every conceivable emasculating situation. He stood back a couple of steps and asked, "What's wrong with you?"

"What's wrong me, what wrong you!" she screamed as she jumped up off the bed and pointed at him.

And the answer became apparent. She was standing in front of the bed naked, with a large, erect, uncircumcised dick poking out in front of her.

"Oh my God, you have a dick," David said reiterating the obvious. "What are you?"

"I Boss Lady and you do what I say."

David all of a sudden felt like he had the upper hand. He walked over to the chair and put on his jeans. He was not going to have an argument with a naked something who had a hard on while his own dick was hanging out. David turned around and faced the Boss Thing and said, "Why don't I just beat your ass unconscious and you can call the cops when you wake up?"

The Boss Thing had no immediate response. David directed, "Put your clothes on, get the hell out of my apartment and don't ever step foot in here again." The Boss Thing stood there dejected, the dick on it shrinking like a punctured inner tube.

"Go on now. Get your clothes on and go before I feel the need to kick your nuts up to into your mouth. I swear you'll look like a squirrel getting ready for winter." The Boss Thing slowly got dressed and left the apartment without saying a word. David won that round but he was sure a retaliation would be inevitable.

All the girls lived in a dormitory style building at the end of the block. The Boss Thing had done well for him/herself and owned the restaurant and the two apartments above it, Boss Thing's apartment and David's apartment. She owned the dormitory made up of eighteen living cubicles and she owned a warehouse at the other end of the block. It was at least a couple of million dollars worth of property. With that kind of capital, she could easily hire someone to do harm to him. It had happened before with Rough Lumber. Assholes. He decided right then that he had to get away. He couldn't trust the Boss Thing long enough to let the sun rise.

He finished dressing, packed his duffle bag, and went down to the dormitory to see if he could find girl number four. He didn't even know her name but he found her after talking and gesturing with several of the other girls. He decided to tell her the story before he asked her to run away with him. He told her that the Boss Lady came up to his apartment and wanted some entertainment but when she took off her clothes, she was really a he.

Her response was, "We all know that. It's part of the arrangement. Before you got here, she made us all suck her dick and fuck her. We had a two-week rotation. She is very insatiable and she's been rotating through all the girls for ten years. Now she gets us one night and you get us the next."

David was incensed. "And you didn't tell me!"

"No need to tell. I thought you'd find out soon enough."

"Just how many times have you sucked that thing's dick?" he asked not really wanting an answer.

"In ten years, hundreds. I swallowed it almost every time." Way too much information.

He just turned and walked away. Back up in his apartment, he grabbed his duffle bag and bolted. It was deep into the night before he made it to the train station, one of the only places he felt comfortable. He used his eight-stop ticket, headed to nowhere in particular, and left Chicago with no regrets and regretful all at the same time.

Chapter 44

In Search of a Home

"Next stop, Albany!" he heard the man say. Albany, New York and the question was always in his mind, *do I get off or do I stay in the relative safety of the train?* David got off, found the usual dump of a hotel and bought some food and a newspaper. Starting all over again was becoming his specialty.

In his room, he had just eaten a sandwich and was reading the classified ads by the light of a bare sixty-watt bulb. Clerks, tellers, laborers and some professionals, there was not much to choose from. He threw the paper on the floor and went to bed.

In the morning light, the hotel room looked worse than it did the night before. He thought maybe he should try to find a better one but his funds were running really low. A job was imperative. He cleaned up, ate a Honey Bun, got dressed, and went out on the streets of Albany looking for work. He was walking in a blue-collar neighborhood looking for any help wanted signs in the windows of the shops and businesses. After four or five blocks, he started to take notice of some posters on the telephone poles: The Arabian Nights Circus.

From the posters, he could tell that the circus had passed through Albany eleven days ago. *A carnival act*, he thought. If he could hide anywhere, a circus should do it. The circus always had an assortment of misfits and freaks and it never stayed in any given town for more than a day or two. He just made up his mind; he was going to "run off" and join the circus.

Tracking down a circus with an eleven-day head start was going to be a tall task. He started by going to city hall to ask about permits. The clerk in the office said that he didn't know where they were going next but they circus loaded on a train heading west. *Crap*, he thought, *not back to Chicago.* After doing a little more research, mainly talking to people at the train station, he decided that his best bet was the Empire Service train. It went through Syracuse, Rochelle, Buffalo, and Niagara Falls. He called the city offices of each of those towns and discovered that the circus had already been through and was currently set up outside of Buffalo.

He jumped on the train and by the next day, he was standing in line for a ticket to the Arabian Nights Circus. The "circus" was a one big tent outfit with a midway of food booths and unbeatable games leading from the front gate to the big tent. More smaller tents were off to one side of the midway with freaks, palm readers, and fun houses. Off to the other side were the rides.

David got himself to believing this might be a place to land, never staying in town more than a couple of nights and there was no shortage of characters. At precisely eleven in the morning, the gates opened to a rush of teenagers and children. The adults were slower to respond. The only things open that early were the rides and the midway. They were always ready to take one's money at the carnival games and sell you a foot-long hotdog that was really only eight inches long for three times the price of any other hotdog known to man.

David heard one kid ask a worker why they didn't open up the other stuff until night and the carnie's response was, "It's the Arabian Nights Circus kid, not the Arabian Days Circus." David decided to ask a different worker his questions. "Hey man, who do I see about a job around here?" The guy pointed to a purple and gold tent.

Standing outside the main flap of the tent, David realized that he didn't know how to knock. He finally just yelled, "Hello." A man's voice said, "Come in." David entered and was met by a man and a woman. Both were in their mid to late forties and both looked sun tanned from work and not from a day at the beach. The male said, "You want a job, don't you?" David took his duffle bag off his shoulder and set it on the ground, "Yes, I do."

He looked scornfully at David and asked, "What can you do?"

"I can work hard."

"Shit," the guy said. "You ain't never worked hard a day in your life." He looked at the woman sitting behind the desk, "Another free loader. You know what I think, but you're the boss," and he walked out of the tent brushing David's shoulder as he passed.

The lady said, "Don't mind Jimmy. He's got a lot on his mind. My name is Carol. Jimmy's got a small percent but I own the show. Do you have any carnie experience?"

"No, I don't."

"What can you do? And make it quick, I've got a meeting with some potential investors in five minutes in the Big Top."

"You're not going to make it."

"What are you talking about?" she asked.

"You're not going to be on time for your meeting because I'm going to show you my entire act and it will take longer than five minutes."

"What are you going to do, sing the Star-Spangled Banner?"

"No, but you might stand up and sing it when I get through with you."

"Alright, I've had about enough of this nonsense. Tell me what you're talking about or I'll call Jimmy back in here and he'll help you out the front gate. "

"There is only one thing I can do. It's make women have orgasms." She started to get up from behind her desk and she had an ax handle in her hand. "Wait now. Here me out. I do it by hypnotizing them and they have no power against it. Do you believe me?"

"Not a single word out of your mouth."

"Can I show you?"

"You're going to make me have an orgasm by hypnotizing me?"

"Yes, right here in the next two seconds and there is not a damn thing you can do about it."

He looked at her and she did not pass "GO" and did not collect $200. She hit the ground behind her desk experiencing a powerful orgasm accompanied by moans, shudders and rolling around. When she was almost done, David looked at her again. She got up on her knees and was squeezing her crotch through her blue jeans. He noticed her rub it a little every few seconds. She tried to get in her chair but David hit her again. She slid back down to the floor with her head on the seat of the chair. She had a hand on one arm of the chair and the other hand was still between her legs. "Please," she said but he hit her again. She went to the ground once more. "Please," she said. "Enough."

He let her recover. Eventually she stood up, dusted herself off and sat in her chair behind the desk. She laughed and shook her head. "You're hired. I don't know what the fuck we're going to do with you but you're hired."

"What's the pay?"

"It's $100 a week and twenty percent of the gate."

David countered with, "I want $100 a week and forty percent of the gate."

They shook hands. "I'm not even going to argue with you," she said. "Now go find Jimmy and he'll show you where you'll be staying. Come back to this tent tomorrow morning at nine. Got it?" David went to find Jimmy who was incredulous about him being hired on the spot. David's place to stay was in a semi-truck trailer converted into an apartment with four bunk beds. His was a top bunk. He threw his duffle bag on his bunk and went to explore his new home, the Arabian Nights Circus.

Chapter 45

Circus 101

David met with the co-owners in the morning. Carol was the lady he "hit" four times yesterday and Jimmy was the tough roustabout guy who showed him to the semi-truck sleeping quarters. Carol bought the circus from her Dad nine years ago and Jimmy contributed just enough to become a ten percent partner, plus Carol and Jimmy were an on again, off again item. They've been scraping by ever since.

Carol explained to Jimmy what happened the day before but he wasn't believing any of it. She assured him it was real and they could make a fortune, but they needed the right venue, the right advertisement and the right clientele. "You just go and muck out the camel pen and let me plan." Carol sent Jimmy off to do busy work.

David stood waiting for something to happen. Carol got frustrated with him so she sent him off to find Jimmy and help him. David didn't like Jimmy that much so he went to the Big Top to look at the acts practicing. There were clowns riding tiny bicycles, dancing dogs dressed in tutu's, a pig wearing a top hat and three camels that were acting just like…camels.

David moved on to the midway. He introduced himself along the promenade meeting a few stereotypical carnie types, toothless and greasy. They seemed pleasant enough, they were just down on their luck, loners, one step ahead of the law or just needed work and this was available. These guys showed him how the games worked or more accurately how they didn't work. He never knew there was an art to stacking metal milk bottles in a way that a major-league pitcher couldn't knock them all down. The ring toss wasn't really rigged either but the rings were so tiny compared to the bottle tops that it would be a one in a million chance of actually getting a ringer.

There was a coin toss game played by throwing quarters on top of a horizontal board with a target drawn in the center. If one were to throw a quarter and have it stop in the bullseye, the customer would get a giant stuffed panda bear. If the quarter stopped in the ring next to the bullseye, they would get their quarter returned. The carnie showed David how the board was slightly slanted making it harder to stick the quarter where it was aimed. The board was slanted a different direction every few minutes by using a peddle beneath the board. This made it very difficult for return customers or for those who played for a long time to make the correct adjustments. On top of that, the bullseye was ever so slightly crowned and highly polished which made quarters slide off even easier. In his three years working the game, the carnie had only given away four major prizes.

David visited the food booths and watched them prepare for the day. They cleaned off grills, washed out pots, chopped onions and thawed out meat. All in all, it was more hygienic than he ever thought it would be, but still something far less than restaurant quality hygiene.

He learned that each carnie got a small salary and a cut of the game or the food booth, just like he was going to do. He wondered just how much money these guys made. Then for some reason, he thought, how much does it cost to feed a camel? And then he quit thinking about it. He needed to concentrate on $100 a week and forty percent of the gate.

He then went to the cafeteria, neatly set up in an old army tent. There was always coffee and something to eat. Meals were served at the regular times but all circus people had different hours so stuff for a sandwich or a bowl of soup was always available.

He sat down on a bench at a long table, ate an egg salad sandwich, and drank a cup of really strong coffee. The tent flaps on either end of the tent were open and he could see out toward the animal pens one way and the sleeping quarters the other direction. A woman stepped out of a small travel trailer and stretched. She was wearing some short cut-off blue jeans and a spaghetti strap halter top, with obviously no bra. She started walking in the direction of the cafeteria tent. David thought this might be a problem because it was going to be hard not to look at her.

She came in to the tent and said good morning to the cook in a familiar way, like family. She got a cup of coffee and sat down across from David. "Hi, I'm Zelda or Blanche or Salome depending on what part I happen to be playing but my real name is Betsy." She stuck out her hand. He shook it, raising up a little off the bench seat and just said, "David."

"Obviously, I've never seen you before so you must be new. What's Carol got you doing?"

"She's working out an act for me. I've kinda got this hypnosis thing going. I'm just waiting for the details."

"Good. I'm the actress and dancer of the troupe. I generally play half-naked dancing ladies, or whatever they need at the time. I was in Hollywood for a few years and landed one beer commercial. I was the woman in the background in a bar. All I did was raise my glass." She demonstrated with her coffee mug.

"Well, you do it better than anyone I have ever seen."

She gave a little chuckle and said she needed to get going. Besides being the half-naked dancing lady, she had some other carnie duties she had to perform. She said she would see him later somewhere around the grounds and they could talk some more. David said goodbye never looking any higher than her chest. Being the half-naked dancing lady, she must have been used to men staring at her chest because she didn't seem to be the least bit uncomfortable.

David finally left and found Jimmy who made him push wheelbarrows full of animal dung up a hill to the pile of manure to be sold to local farmers for fertilizer. Carol made a penny off everything. All the carnies he met seemed to be content with their work so Carol must have been treating her people well. However, like any small business, she had to make a buck where she could, including conning local farmers into thinking that camel shit had better plant nutrients than anything one could buy at the local farmer's supply houses.

About the time he finished with the last wheelbarrow, a pick-up truck stopped next to the pile and David shoveled all the dung into the bed of the truck. He and the driver secured a tarp over the load and the driver told him he already paid for the merchandise. Out of curiosity David asked him how much he paid for the "premium fertilizer" and the driver told him an even hundred bucks. He thought, *That's my weekly salary. My talent is worth the same as a pile of camel shit.*

Chapter 46

The First Show

Three days later, just outside of Cleveland, David was going to have his first show. Carol's team had been posting flyers stating there would be a special treat for the ladies in the Ali Baba Tent at exactly 10:00 pm on Saturday. The show was only for "single women and free female spirits."

On Saturday, thirty minutes before the show, he was feeling uneasy about going down this road again. These things never, ever seemed to work out right. He was pacing in the back of the Ali Baba Tent peeking out between the curtains every two minutes. Sixty old wooden folding chairs were set up in front of the stage and none of them were occupied. He kept pacing back and forth thinking that he was going to be a monumental failure.

Carol came in the back of the tent to see if he was doing okay. She had a yellow flower that she picked from somewhere and stuck it in the button hole of his purple long tail jacket. His tux was an old ringmaster's outfit from the 1940's. He felt ridiculous. Carol straightened his collar and said, "Break a leg." She exited the way she came in.

He peeked out the curtains again and saw several groups of women chatting and looking around as if they may be in the wrong place. He hoped they wouldn't bolt into the night after reconsidering. He paced some more while practicing his lines. "This is not going to be good," he said out loud. He peeked through the curtains again. Twenty women milled around in the tent now. "Maybe it'll be alright."

Carol went in the front door of the tent and started playing a mixed cassette of instrumental music. It was supposed to be Arabian music but it sounded like Greek. David looked out the curtain again and the tent was more than half full. After ten minutes of the music playing, Carol turned the volume down really low and started talking. "Ladies, we have a special treat for you tonight. After searching the world over, we found an ex-patriot living in Baghdad who studied the ancient art of the Kama Sutra." She put her hand up to her mouth like she was whispering, "Ladies, that's the art of satisfying a woman. You know what I mean girls." She rubbed her crotch a little, said "ooh-la-la" and fanned herself. The audience applauded and laughed. She continued. "If anybody has a jealous husband or an insecure boyfriend, you better leave now, because this is going to be a special treat. If you love to, you know, enjoy the finer things in life," she rubbed her crotch a little more, "then this night is for you. I'd like to introduce you to the host of the evening, here he is.... Saladin!" She bowed and backed off the stage.

David stepped out in his ridiculous purple tux. "Hello Ladies." They applauded politely. He noticed that the tent was filled to standing room only. "As Carol said, they found me in a bazaar in Baghdad on the Tigris River. I had been servicing the harem of Prince Sahara-kan when the Sheik of Arabi caught me. I was banished and have been hiding out ever since. Carol rescued me on the condition that I would now service the nice people who visit the Arabian Nights Circus. So ladies, without any further ado, I give you the man who steals your most prized and intimate possessions, the Thief of Baghdad, Saladin... known in America as, the one, the only, the amazing Mister Orgasm!" He looked at all of the women, working his way through the crowd to ensure one-hundred percent saturation. Carol was poking her head in through the back curtain.

Every woman started to have an orgasm. The flimsy wooden folding chairs were no match for the more matronly bodies and at least half of the ladies went to ground. David continued to walk through the crowd, dishing out the full measure. Guaranteed satisfaction. When David had made his rounds for a third time, he heard Carol say, "That's enough. We don't want to kill anybody the first night." David exited stage left and Carol stepped out to restore order. David stood behind the curtain trying get himself together. These things always took their toll. He looked out and about half the women had left and the others were struggling to regain their strength and recover their senses enough to walk out. Carol was running around giving encouragement trying to gage if this was a success or if the sheriff was going to raid them later and serve arrest warrants or throw them out of the county.

David went to his trailer bunk and changed clothes. Then he went to the cafeteria tent to grab a sandwich or something. He was too nervous to eat all day so he was really hungry. The cooks made a big chicken casserole and cut him a fair-sized wedge. He hogged it down in a matter of minutes. He got a cup of coffee which had been made since seven in the evening and decided to wait for Carol right there. She would find him sooner or later.

A little before one in the morning, Carol walked into the cafeteria tent. She got a cup of coffee out of the big urn which had to taste like black paint by then and sat down across from him. "Well, I'm not sure," she said. "We had seventy-three paid. Which was more than I expected, but I don't know if we can do it again tomorrow. So many things can happen... no one can show up, some irate husband can come after us with a shotgun, the police can shut us down, hell I don't know."

"So, we'll try it tomorrow, right?"

"Damn right! By the way, " She said. "Your cut of the gate is $292. Thank you very much. I'm doubling the entrance fee tomorrow. What have we got to lose?'

"\$292," he replied.

"Yeah." She took another sip of the coffee and asked, "What are you doing right now?" David shrugged his shoulders. "Can you take care of me the way you took care of them?"

"You mean right now?"

"Go to my office tent. We should be alone there." She set her coffee down and said, "Give me a few minutes before you leave."

David waited five excruciatingly long minutes and then headed over that direction. When he arrived, Carol was sitting behind her desk. "Can you do it from there?"

He was standing three feet in front of her desk. "Sure, you ready?" She shook her head, yes. He looked at her and she started to cum. He noticed that her pants were in the floor and she was furiously masturbating. David stood with a growing hard on waiting for her to finish. When she appeared to be complete she looked up and said, "Again, please." David looked at her and she was lost to the orgasm once more.

When she finished this time, she said, "This is so strange. I'm sorry, I can't help you right now. I'm just not ready."

"That's okay," he said. He left the tent to find somewhere he could be alone and do himself.

Chapter 47

The Second Show

It seems that circus people stay up very late but still rise early in the morning. It was about 8:00 am and David found himself in the cafeteria tent drinking coffee, lots of it. Most of the other workers had already been through and gotten breakfast. David was just draining his cup when Betsy, the half-naked dancing lady came into the tent. She went straight for the coffee urn and then joined him at his table. "I hear you were a big success last night."

"I don't know about how successful I was but the house was full and we made a little money. I'll know more tonight. Carol is worried that it was a flash in the pan and I might already be washed up."

"It might be better if you were a has been. This life is hard. Always moving from town to town, never making any normal friends, just other carnies." She sighed and took a drink.

"That's what I'm looking for right now. I don't want roots. I just want to be lost."

She finished her cup, "I've got to go practice my belly dancing. I will play Scheherazade, the Story Teller until they find a real belly dancer. The last one, Jennifer, ran off last night with a banker from Dayton."

"She must have been a good dancer," David said.

Betsy laughed and got up to leave. "We'll catch up with each other in a couple of days. You know they break down tonight after closing. You'll be busy."

"Where are we going next?"

Betsy shouted back through the tent door as she was exiting, "Kentucky."

Carol and Jimmy never liked to stay in one state for very long. Their circus was not known for employing the most up standing citizens and two days in one place was enough. They couldn't afford to hang around because they cut corners on health regulations, they certainly had dubious midway games, they performed exotic shows, and they had the usual pick-pockets, con-men, plain old thieves, and burglars. Every county's crime rate went up when the Arabian Nights Circus came through.

David was about to go try to make himself useful when Jimmy came into the cafeteria tent. "Where do you think you are going?" he said more like a statement than a question.

"I was going to see if anyone needed help."

"I got your help. You're coming with me. I heard you put on a good show last night but don't let that go to your head. You'll shovel camel shit if I tell you to, I don't care who you hypnotize."

"So, I'm going to shovel camel shit today?"

"Don't be a wise ass. You're going to wash the vehicles today and you'll break down tents on a four-man crew tonight. You'll start with the first tent on the midway and won't quit until you have all of them squared away. If you start at midnight, you might be done by sunrise. Meanwhile I'll be laying up with Carol in my trailer. You think about that tonight while you're out humping canvas."

David wasn't sure why Jimmy didn't like him. Maybe Jimmy just didn't like anybody or maybe he felt threatened. In any case, David sure wasn't going to tell him that he "had" Carol again last night. He was positive that would be detrimental to his health and well-being.

Two hours before the next show, Carol found David in his semi-truck living quarters and gave him a new tux that looked more like a regular tux instead of someone's misguided idea of a pimp suit. She also gave him a large turban with a feather in it. "You have to wear this. It's part of our theme." David didn't argue and just took it. "You'll be in the Big Top tonight. I've put you in between some of the more traditional circus acts. I'll charge for the early circus act show, clear the tent, charge for your act, clear the tent and then charge for the finale. This is going to be great for business, provided anyone shows up."

Carol was a nervous talker and she was nervous about tonight. "I'll do my best, " David reassured.

"I know you will." She reached out and touched his arm before turning and going off to organize and worry.

At T-minus thirty minutes, David was in the back of the Big Top wearing a rather ill fitting tux and an outlandish turban. He peeked through the curtains as he did the night before and saw only a smattering of women in the bleachers. The Big Top had bench bleacher seats and accommodated a thousand people, so a crowd like last night would look paltry. He didn't know if he could make eye contact if the women were very spread out. He refrained from peeking out anymore and just paced.

Before he was ready he heard the Greek-sounding music start to play. Ten minutes after that, he heard Carol's voice giving the spiel. Then he heard the cue, "...Saladin!" David threw the curtains open and walked out on the stage. The venue wasn't full but there must have been a couple of hundred women on the bleachers. He approached the microphone, cleared his throat and said the exact same words he said the night before, and then "...the one, the only, the amazing Mister Orgasm!"

He ran to the bleachers going in and out of the rows trying to catch the eyes of every woman. He couldn't focus on anything, they were just a blur of faces passing before him. By the time he was finished, he was actually out of breath. He went back to the stage, stood with his arms crossed and surveyed his work. He was thinking the crowd couldn't be much bigger because he wasn't sure of his ability to "get" everybody. Plus, many of the women fell to their sides, lying on the bleachers. If they had a full house, there would be no place left for them to fall over.

As the crowd settled, he ran through again making sure the ones he may have missed the first time got a healthy dose and the ones looking at him with wanton eyes got their second drink from the cup. He was back on stage when a woman in the far corner caught his attention. She was crawling on the ground wearing a costume, a belly dancer costume. He had zapped Betsy, the half-naked dancing lady, who came to his show as a sign of support.

Carol was poking her head through the back curtains. "David, run through again." He did as instructed, running through, dodging bodies, hitting anyone still capable of having another orgasm. He'd never worked a crowd this large before. The scene was surreal, over two hundred women going at it all at once. The roar, moans and shrieks of the crowd were deafening. It sounded like a torture chamber. It reinforced his thought that, a woman's sound of pleasure was similar to her sound of pain.

After working the crowd for a third time, he saw Carol waving him back to the stage. "Leave them wanting more," she said. "You're done. Now, get changed, go find Jimmy and help him start breaking down. I'll clean up here." David hated the "go find Jimmy" part of that. He didn't mind the work but he just didn't like Jimmy.

Clothes changed and walking through the grounds, he asked everyone if they knew where Jimmy was. Some said they hadn't seen him for a while or they acted like they knew where he was but they weren't going to tell him. He resorted to searching nooks and crannies and calling out Jimmy's name.

David noticed a blue light on in Jimmy's trailer. "There he is," he said to himself. He banged on the door three times before Jimmy finally answered. He was half dressed, holding his pants up with one hand and trying to put a shirt on with the other. "What are you doing in your trailer, taking a nap?" David asked.

Jimmy seemed flustered and couldn't get the door shut behind him fast enough. It took a few seconds for David to realize it, but all the signs pointed to Jimmy banging someone in his trailer while Carol was busy running the circus. David pointed and said, "Someone's in there."

"There may be or there may not be but it's none of your fuckin' business. Why aren't you breaking down tents?"

"Carol sent me to find you, so I did."

"Shit for brains, I told you what to do earlier so you wouldn't bother me. You don't get it, do you? I'm the boss and you have to do what I say and I say that you go break down tents right now."

"Sure boss," David said and spun around to join the guys on the midway. *I wonder who's in there?* he thought, hoping that it wasn't Betsy, the half-naked dancing lady.

David worked until the sun came up breaking down the tents. It was excruciating work and not that rewarding. In the cafeteria tent, sometime after the sun was up, David was at his table drinking a cup of day old mud. Betsy came in looking fresh in jeans and a T-shirt. Being awake the last twenty-four hours and doing physical labor all night, David looked like he had been hit by a truck and he smelled like a skunk. Why now, he thought.

She came over. "We need to talk," she said.

"Now is not a good time." He was so tired that he wasn't sure he could comprehend a difficult conversation.

"Tonight then, when we get to Louisville." They both nodded their heads and she left the tent.

Carol, entering the tent, passed Betsy exchanging salutations. Carol looked animated. She stretched out her hand and gave him a giant wad of bills. "Sorry it's in small bills but your cut of the gate is $1,800. That's more than any of my headliners have ever made. You're going to be a big star and we're finally going to make enough money to operate in the black comfortably."

"What's your biggest expense?" David asked out of curiosity.

"Technically, you are. Your cut is the biggest single-person outlay. The transportation is expensive. So is feeding everybody and the live-stock. Oh my God, those fucking camels."

"Can't you get rid of them and quit calling this thing the Arabian Nights Circus? Call it Carol's (We Have No Camels) Carnival and operate at a higher margin?"

"Probably, but then it wouldn't be my Dad's circus anymore." Jimmy came in the tent at that moment looking dirtier than David. He walked over to the table after getting a cup of coffee. Carol said, "It looks like my boys have done a full night's work."

"Your boys, since when did this prick become one of your boys?"

Carol stood up and put her hand on his chest, "Jimmy you're tired. Go get some rest. I'll go with you. We could use a nap."

David was still sitting with a cup of coffee in one hand and a wad of bills that could choke one of those camels in the other. "Where did you get all that?" Jimmy asked in a not so friendly way.

"I gave it to him," said Carol quickly. "It's his cut Jimmy. Everybody gets a cut. That's how it works."

"That's not a cut. That's something else. Are you fucking her?" David still sat silently.

Carol was up in his face now trying to get him to focus. "Jimmy, he made us $3,000 last night for his act and another two grand by split-ting the main acts and charging twice. He made the money, Jimmy. It's good for the show. It's good for us." She shook him a little at the end.

David stood and stuffed the wad of bills into his pocket. He drained the last of the coffee which lost its taste when Jimmy walked in. "I think I better go and let you two talk business." Jimmy made lunge at him but Carol got between them. David walked away, not looking back but he heard them yelling and it wasn't about business.

Chapter 48

A Taste of Circus Life

At the next location, the troupe busied itself with set up, practice and maintenance. Jimmy assigned David every mundane, physically exhausting, menial task that he could think of. Shoveling camel shit was the best of the jobs.

By mid-afternoon, David found a little free time and went searching for Betsy. He found her in her performance tent practicing her belly dancing. He watched her from the curtains for a while and she was really good, very sexy.

She caught a glimpse of him while she was spinning and stopped in her tracks. She turned the music off and motioned with her hand for him to come in. As David walked up to her he said, "I guess an explanation is in order." He was referring to the orgasm he gave her during his act.

"You're right." She paused a second and just before David started to tell her everything, she blurted out, "I'm sorry you caught me with Jimmy the other night."

David was stunned. Once again, his worst fear realized. "That's none of my business. I thought you wanted me to explain why I was making two-hundred women, including you, have an orgasm."

"Of course not. That's your act."

"That doesn't bother you?"

"No. It's not even the strangest act in this circus. There's a lady, Jean, who swallows a snake. I don't mean the head, but the whole damn snake crawls in her and somehow finds its way back out. We have a guy who pierces himself with knives through his nut sack. Lola smokes cigarettes with her pussy while her husband shows off his two dicks." She held up her fingers indicating, two, and said it again in a whisper, "Two dicks."

"Well, I just hypnotize girls into having orgasms. I feel inferior."

She put her hand on his arm and playfully said, "But it was a good orgasm." They laughed a little. "Why do you make them have orgasms instead of making them think they're eating apples when they are really eating onions, or sing a Madonna song or something like that?"

"Honestly, I don't hypnotize them. All it takes is a look, a fleeting glance, an accidental peek, a momentary glimpse or if I get caught staring, they'll have an orgasm. I have found no exceptions. It's inevitable." Then he thought of Madam Defazende and shuddered.

"That's why you never look at me."

"I never look at any woman."

"Can you do it now?"

"Sure. Do you really want me to?"

"I think so."

David looked around, "Do you want to lie down or get more comfortable?"

"I guess I should." She sat down on one of the dozens of folding wooden chairs. "Okay, I'm ready."

"The way the act goes, is I say a few words, blah, blah, blah, and then here's the one, the only, the amazing Mister Orgasm," and he looked at her.

She said "Oh fuck," but maintained composure fairly well. She even giggled once while she was cumming. When she was done, she rubbed her face making a sound like "whew" and said, "That was fun. What a great act." She fanned her face with her hands.

"Unfortunately, I can't turn it off so it's not an act to me. It's real life. I'll tell you all about it someday."

Betsy stated, "I guess Carol knows."

"Of course, she needed to experience the act before she hired me. I wanted the job so I didn't stop with just one."

"How many?" asked Betsy excitedly.

"Four."

"You made her cum four times?"

"Yep."

"How did she take it?"

"Like the carnie she is. She just got up, dusted herself off and started thinking of ways to make money."

"God love her, she treats me so good" said Betsy. "How many times have you done her since the audition?"

"Are you jealous," he teased.

"Maybe," she responded.

"Just one," he said. She looked relieved but didn't say anything.

"And thanks," she said.

"For what?" he asked.

"For not asking about me and Jimmy,"

"It's none of my business. If you want me to know you'll tell me. Look, I've got to get going. I'm sure Jimmy is looking for me and it won't be long before he decides to check in with you. And he'll catch us together with you still glowing."

"It's from dancing."

"Don't kid a kidder. I'll come see your show if I can get away."

David walked out into a bright sun. He can't remember when he was ever this tired. Even in the Army he never got this bone tired and he had been with the circus less than a week. He was walking to

Carol's administrative tent to ask her about the format of his show that night when Jimmy came up from behind him. Jimmy annoyingly punched him in the back of the head. "Where've you been boy? I've been looking for you. There's work to be done."

David twisted around to look at Jimmy and rubbed the back of his head. "Well you found me."

"Get over to the Big Top and help them put together bleachers."

David just turned and walked toward the Big Top without saying a word.

"And you better keep your ass away from Betsy. She's mine."

David turned around, "What about Carol?"

"That bitch is mine too but I've about used her up. I think I might give her to Dale"

He didn't want to ask but he couldn't help it. "Who's Dale?"

"The two-dick man, Two Dick Dale." Jimmy laughed. "I may give her to Dale anyway."

"Jimmy, you got it good here. Carol is a great person, she treats all her people good. She is this circus. Without her what would you be doing, working at a convenience store?"

Jimmy approached to within a few inches, well into David's personal space. "You just stay clear of Carol and Betsy." He waited a few seconds. David couldn't tell what Jimmy was thinking but he could tell it was taking an effort. "And stay away from Jean. A snake is not the only thing she swallows if you get my drift."

He never wanted to call anyone an asshole as badly as he did Jimmy. Jimmy was six-foot two and weighed 215 pounds. His body was hardened by years of circus work. David was five-foot nine and weighed 175 pounds. Jimmy would kill him in a fight. David just walked off.

A hundred feet away, David turned and yelled, "Hey Jimmy! Is it okay to fuck the camel or are you doing that too?" Several of the men in ear shot laughed and stopped working to see what Jimmy would do. To David's surprise, Jimmy just kept walking away.

Jimmy went into the administrative tent to find Carol sitting behind her desk. "Hey Babe," she said. "Do me a favor and go find David. I need to talk to him about his act tonight."

"Find him yourself, bitch." Jimmy walked out of the tent to find Betsy or Jean the snake swallower. He found Betsy first and the outcome was not mutually satisfying.

Jimmy walked into Betsy's tent, grabbed her, spun her around and shoved his hand down her leotard. She was dripping wet from dancing and the orgasm she had just had. Jimmy stuck his finger up in her as far as he could. He held his other arm around her neck, tightly.

"Jimmy, come on, don't. I need to practice." She tried to pull his hand out but he was too strong.

"You used to like this," he said roughly biting her ear.

"Ow! Jimmy, you're hurting me." She pulled her head away, still trying to get Jimmy's finger out of her, but there was no way. From prior experience, she knew that Jimmy could go off at any time and hurt her badly. In the beginning, he showered her with affection but lately he'd been restless, moody, and violent.

She knew he was "getting some" from somebody else and she was more relieved than angry because she wanted it to end amicably and she hoped he would just drift to the other woman. His true colors did not paint an aesthetic picture and she didn't want him as an enemy.

He pulled out his hard and relatively large cock, walked her over to some bales of hay, and started pulling her leotard down. At this point she knew it was pointless to resist. He got her leotard down around her knees, bent her over the bales and penetrated her from behind.

He started pounding away like all "Jimmy's" do. He grabbed her hair and pulled it so hard that she cried out. "Damn Jimmy, not so hard!" He kept pounding away. She could tell he was about to cum and said, "Let me finish you up with my hand. I don't want you to cum in me." He kept going. "Jimmy, let me jack it now." He was getting really close. "Don't cum in me!" She was trying to get away. He now had both hands on her hips pulling him into her. She started flailing at him, trying to get him to break contact. She reached back and scratched his face.

He reacted instantaneously and punched her in the kidney as hard as he could. She straightened up in excruciating pain. She grabbed her side and held her forehead trying to keep from passing out. He bent her back over and finished filling her up with a heavy, angry load.

Betsy started to cry. She pulled a tissue out of her sports bra and tried to clean up between her legs. Jimmy just stuck his dick back in his pants and said, "You nasty, fucking bitch," and walked out of the tent to go look for Jean.

Jean was sitting in her tent on the floor with about a dozen snakes in cages all around her. She was drinking a diet soda and eating a salad. Jimmy walked into the tent with out saying a word. "Well, hello Jimmy. Ever heard of knocking?" He stomped over to her and grabbed a handful of her hair. "You're gonna suck my dick and then we're fucking."

"Okay, okay." Unfortunately, Jean knew Jimmy's dark side also. He pulled his dick out and started rubbing it in her face. "Shit Jimmy. Did you just fuck somebody else? I can smell it."

"What do you care?" he continued to stick it in her face but she wouldn't take it in her mouth. He got frustrated quickly and slapped her across the temple. "You eat that dick before I really get rough."

She had no choice but to open her mouth. He grabbed the hair on both sides of her head and stuck his flaccid cock all the way in her mouth. He ground on her face until he could feel it start to grow. As he got harder, it filled up her mouth and throat to the point where she started choking. He wouldn't let her breathe. Her nose started bleeding when he smashed her face against his pubic region. As he got hard, he got more out of control. She tried to fight back but he was suffocating her with his big cock.

She settled in her mind that the only way she was going to survive was for him to cum quickly because she couldn't break out of his hold.

He didn't cum quickly because it was his second time in only a few minutes. She was losing the battle.

Long before he came, she passed out. He held her head in both hands and continued to fuck her mouth. Somehow, fucking her seemingly lifeless skull turned him on and sped up his orgasm. Fortunately for Jean, the amount of the load was far less than it was for Betsy, otherwise she might have choked to death. He dropped her head and her body slid to the ground, unconscious but still alive. He stuffed his dick back into his pants and walked out of her tent looking for his next victim.

Chapter 49

The Small Audience

David just finished bolting together his umpteenth bleacher when Jimmy walked in to the Big Top. "Carol wants to see you now. And she doesn't like to be kept waiting."

"Okay, I'll get on over that way, " David said, thinking Jimmy was acting strangely, even for him.

Carol was sitting behind her desk buried in a pile of papers. "Damn, these bills. There're so many of them."

"I can help you with those. I do have a degree in accounting."

"Really? Can you really straighten these out, no bullshit?"

"Sure," he said. "But I can't do it putting bleachers together. "

"No bleachers, got it. But you have to continue to do your act... and I can't pay you more than the hundred a week."

"Deal," said David and they shook hands. "Now let's see what you've got here." He pulled up a folding wooden chair next to her and started looking at each piece of paper and putting it back into another stack. She intently watched his every move. "Carol, you don't have to be here for this to get done."

"Oh, you want me to leave?"

"Yes."

"Okay, I'll give you some space." She grabbed a few things and left the tent.

While sorting through the papers, he did learn one crucial tidbit of information that had been gnawing on him for days. It cost $77.39 a week to feed a camel. He laughed to himself. He worked right through lunch. About four in the afternoon, Carol came back in to find her desk in a semblance of order.

"Well, you've been working."

David stood up pointing to each stack in succession and said, "Pay these today, these by next week, don't pay these at all. As a matter of fact, throw them away." He picked up the whole stack and threw it in the trash. "Pay this stack at the end of the month. Then you will be caught up. The totals you'll need to pay are on these cards on top of each stack." He picked up one of the cards and showed her.

"I could kiss you." She actually shut her eyes, leaned in and started to kiss him on the lips but he pulled away.

"I don't want any trouble with Jimmy. He and I aren't getting along very well right now and I don't think kissing you will help."

"You're right. Let's keep it professional. But thank you, just the same."

"You're welcome. What do you have planned for me tonight?" David changed the subject.

"A whole new lineup. I'm giving you a tent of your own for private showings. Joyce, the backup lady for palm reading, will be the ticket taker and clean up girl. You just do your thing. You're going to handle small groups, one, two, four, six, but no more than six. You'll have your own sign out front." She waved her hand across her body like she was showing his name in lights, "An Evening with Saladin" She looked at him for confirmation. He smiled.

"Sounds good," he said.

"You go on at nine. Don't be late. Go get some rest and thanks for cleaning up my desk."

He went to his trailer bunk and tried to take a nap, but all he could think about was Betsy, then Carol and then Jimmy. *Damn it!* At 8:00 pm he got cleaned up and dressed for his show. He was in his tux and turban. He walked to his new tent and met Joyce who had everything under control. She was a very capable woman.

A small gathering of customers was waiting out front for the 9:00 pm show. Carol had been doing some serious advertising and they were expecting a big crowd. Joyce told David to stay behind the curtains until he was introduced and then he could step out, do his thing once or twice, and then retreat behind the curtains. She would take care of the rest. "Easy peasy," she said.

David went into the back of the tent behind the curtains. Joyce had put a chair, a pitcher of water, and a couple of *Field and Stream* magazines back there to make his waiting a little more comfortable. He kept looking at his watch and at exactly 9:00 pm, Joyce started letting women in, six at a time. At four minutes after nine, she started her introduction. At five minutes after nine, David unleashed himself on the women and a wail went up that could be heard by the line of women forming outside the tent getting them even more ready for their experience.

As the hour moved on, Joyce stayed on course, getting a set of women through every ten minutes. The hardest part for Joyce was recovering the women in the allotted time. David was busy doing the math: 6 women every 10 minutes, 36 women per hour, 108 women by midnight.

At 11:00 pm, David went out the back of the tent to take a look at the line. About 100 women still stood in line. He thought he recognized some he had already "seen" earlier in the night. He went back in and continued to work.

At midnight, closing time, Carol showed up and asked David if he could keep working. "There are still a lot of customers." Of course, he could keep working. It wasn't very hard, walking out on stage every ten minutes, looking at some women a couple of times, and then sitting down and reading magazines.

At 2:15 am, the audience size was only four women. The end of the line! When Joyce got the last woman out, she said, "That's a wrap. Good job. I'll see you tomorrow night." She walked off with the tent looking ready for the next show. David went to the trailer bunk and crashed.

Chapter 50

Cleaning Up the 10%

At ten in the morning, David entered the administrative tent where Carol was working on the finances. "Good, you're up." She was shuffling stacks of money this time. She handed him a huge wad of bills. "Here's your cut." David took it, weighing it in his hands like a big cantaloupe. "It's $7,600. What a hell of a night," she said smiling at him.

David looked at the money apprehensively and said, "This is too good to be true. When's the other shoe going to drop?"

Carol crossed her fingers and said, "Don't jinx it. Just ride with the tide and go with the flow."

He stuffed the money in his pants and asked if she needed any help with the accounting. "No, I don't need help. You're going to do it all. I'll be back in a while." She grabbed a satchel and left the tent. David matched up invoices and cash to determine the night's profit. His show was by far the biggest grosser. He even beat the Big Top.

He was riding a small high, thinking that he was contributing to the success of something when Jimmy walked in the tent. "Where's Carol?"

"I don't know." David said. "She doesn't tell me where she's going." As soon as he said that, she walked back in.

"I forgot my....oh, Hey Jimmy."

After an awkward moment, finally Carol said, "We had a good night Jimmy. David is going to be our new star attraction."

"Oh, he is? You think hypnosis is hot shit? Betsy's dancing draws them in pretty good if you ask me. I worked her show last night and her tent was packed." Jimmy made some preposterous dancing moves as he was speaking.

Carol said, "David had over 190 paid at his gate."

Jimmy countered with "Betsy had over 300."

Carol smiled, "But at what ticket price?"

"Thirty bucks a pop!" Jimmy crossed his arms, satisfied that he just got the upper hand in the conversation.

"David's act cost $100 per ticket. What do you think of that?" Carol told him this thinking that Jimmy would be happy about the success of the circus. Instead, Jimmy flew off the handle.

He reached over and grabbed Carol by the hair, his favorite move. He shoved her head down to the level of her knees and then shoved her all the way down to the ground. "I don't care how much those stupid bitches pay to get hypnotized. I'm still the big dick around here."

Carol was sitting on the ground with her legs curled up underneath her, "Sure Jimmy, you're the big man, you're an owner." David was standing behind the desk not sure what to do.

Jimmy unzipped his pants and actually pulled out his dick. "I am the big dick around here. I think I'll open my own show. I'm sure the ladies would pay twenty bucks just to catch a glimpse of this." He was displaying it for them to see.

David went to help Carol up, but Jimmy jumped in between them with his pecker still dangling out. David tried not to look down but it was difficult not to. David said, "Jimmy, I don't want to fight and I'd really like it if you'd put Big Jimmy back in his stall." Jimmy snorted and pushed it back in and zipped up his pants. He just turned and walked out of the tent.

Carol jumped up and said, "Check the receipts."

David didn't know what to think. "Are you alright?"

Carol said, "Yes. Did you hear him? He said she had over 300 customers at $30 a head. What did he turn in at the end of the night?"

"Don't you ever stop thinking about the gate?"

"Never."

David checked the receipts. Jimmy had turned in $6,000. He was short $3,000!

Carol looked furious, "I knew he was stealing from the circus. He worked Betsy's front gate last night. I wonder if Betsy's in on it?" She looked at David and he looked back. They instantly realized their mistake. She started to have an orgasm. She stayed on her feet and fought through it. David could do nothing but help hold her up and apologize, "I'm so sorry."

"Don't worry about it. That's our money maker." She barely got the words out and then she said, "Damn it, David." She was still cumming. As soon as she finished, she said, "Wow, that was a good one."

Changing the subject, "What are you going to do about Jimmy?"

She rubbed her crotch a little. "Sorry," she said trying get things correctly situated down there. "You leave Jimmy to me. Go on and get some sleep now. You're starting early tonight, 7:00 pm."

"Yes Ma'am." David went to the cafeteria tent to get a cup of coffee and something to eat. He kept looking over his shoulder for Jimmy but never saw him. While eating a bowl of chili, Betsy walked in. She saw him and gave a high sign. After loading up with cereal and toast, she plopped down at his table.

David said, "I hear you killed it last night."

"Yeah, I had some big crowds. Four shows. It was fun. I hear you had some long lines too."

"I had about 190. Not near as many as you."

She leaned in a little closer to him, "I made over $600 last night. All in about four hours. It's not like that every night but last night was a good one. I think the husbands were at my tent while the wives were at yours." She giggled. "We make a good team." David didn't tell her that his cut was $7,600.

They finished eating and parted ways until the next day. For people who had an act that only lasted four or five hours a day, finding spare time seemed impossible. All alone in the semi-truck trailer, David fell asleep in his bunk with all his clothes on. When he woke several hours later, Jimmy was standing next to him. Jimmy's head was even with David's on the top bunk. It scared the piss out of David. "Jimmy, what the hell are you doing here?"

Jimmy sat down on the bottom bunk across from David's. "Carol found out I was skimming money," he said to no one in particular.

"Why would you do that?" David slid off the top bunk on to the floor. He was trying to position himself for a fast get away.

"It was easy because Carol is a stupid cunt and she never would have found out anything if you hadn't come along." He looked up at David. "I took care of her and now, I'm going to take care of you."

"What did you do to her?"

Jimmy smiled, "She liked it. I gave her a big stick."

"What the fuck did you do to her?" David was just about ready to rabbit. He was no match for Jimmy in a fair fight.

Jimmy started to stand up and that's all it took. David bolted out of the trailer and went hauling ass down the hill towards the administration tent. He busted into the tent to find Carol naked on the ground behind her desk. Her face was bloody and she had the end of an ax handle stuffed up in her vagina. She was out cold.

"What a sick motherfucker," David said to himself. He tried to revive Carol and she made some signs of coming around so he knew she wasn't dead. He called the police and an ambulance on the rigged-up office phone and then he looked out the tent to see if he could locate Jimmy. He was racing down the hill straight for the admin tent. David was about to panic. He looked around the office space for a weapon. He wanted to run but he couldn't leave Carol at his mercy.

He looked out again and Jimmy was ten paces away. "Shit!" David had no choice but to pull the ax handle out of Carol's body. She made a terrible groaning sound when he did. Just as Jimmy stepped into the tent, David bashed him right in the face with a swing that rivaled the home run that got him a prom date in high school.

Jimmy grabbed his mouth because the blow caught him just under the nose. David didn't hesitate and swung again hitting him in the forehead with what he thought would have been at least a double. Jimmy went down for the count.

David contemplated for just a fleeting moment about whether or not he should knock a triple right between Jimmy's legs. As much as he wanted to smack Jimmy in his "big dick", he let the ax handle fall from his hands. He knelt down to attend to Carol.

The police came, the ambulance came, and David went to jail. From the circumstantial evidence, it looked like David went to town on them both with a deadly weapon. When Carol recovered enough to give a statement she explained how Jimmy was the one who brutalized her. She couldn't say what David did to Jimmy in the tent afterwards because she was unconscious but she was sure that Jimmy got exactly what he deserved.

By the time the smoke cleared, six other women from the circus came forward and pressed charges against Jimmy for sexual assault or aggravated assault. The women included Betsy and a very angry Jean. Carol threw in an embezzlement charge on top of her aggravated sexual assault charge and two women from the town chimed in with various charges, but mostly they were pissed off because they gave it up to him thinking they were special.

The circus ground to a halt for several weeks while they sorted out the mess. Carol spent three nights in the hospital and racked up a huge bill, the performers and workers had not been paid and the animals had to eat. And the biggest insult was Jimmy still owned 10%

of the show. Carol had to figure out a way to buy him out without going bankrupt.

The circus was easily worth a million dollars so Jimmy's share would be a hundred grand. Carol didn't have that kind of cash nor could she readily get it. David suggested dropping all charges for his share of the show. Carol found that suggestion to be too unpalatable and dismissed it. Two days later, she thought maybe the idea had some merit.

Carol visited with all parties concerned and they agreed. Jimmy copped to simple sexual assault, would do six months to a year in the county jail, and he would give up all rights to the circus. After nearly a month of idleness the circus was on the move again. Supplies ran low, gasoline was short, the animals were hungry but spirits soared.

David gave Carol the money he had made in the short time that he was with them, nearly $10,000. Carol shamefully accepted it, cried and hugged him for thirty minutes. Then she jumped up like nothing was ever wrong and started planning the next show. He thought that she probably cared for him as much as any one but her heart would always belong to the circus.

Chapter 51

The Benefits

Without Jimmy, the circus seemed to run more smoothly and much more profitably. Within a week, they were operating in the black and within two weeks Carol was clearing $5000 a week after she paid all of the expenses and bonuses to the staff for putting up with the huge delay and sticking with her. She was revered by her employees.

David was given the title of assistant circus manager which meant he did the books and kept things running smoothly while she was away doing errands or promoting the acts. She agreed to pay him 80% of the gate until he got all of his money back which only took a week. She was a good hearted and smart boss. Her employees would kill for her if necessary. David at least proved that he would bash someone in the face with an ax handle, which gave him huge "street cred" among the crew.

About every third day or so, David met up with Betsy in the cafeteria tent. With Jimmy gone, everyone loosened up and it was a shear pleasure being with her. David was starting to like her a little more than he wanted. She invited him back to her tent and asked him to give her the "look". She explained that since her caustic relationship with Jimmy was over, she didn't have anybody to help her through the lonely nights, and she was asking David to be the guy. "A casual relationship" as she put it.

David was okay with that but asked what was in it for him. She said she would give him "massages" if that was okay. She made a "jacking" motion with her hand. She didn't want to become too intimate. After all, it was the circus and anything could happen at any time.

She told him that she had the relationship with Jimmy because he threatened her sister when they were both dancers with the circus. Betsy made a deal so her sister could leave the show but she had to stay and do disgusting things with Jimmy or he would hurt her. So, she said, she went through the motions and Jimmy had his way. "That is until my new hero bashed his teeth out with a two by four."

"An ax handle," corrected David. "So... are we ready to start our casual relationship?"

"Just a second." She went over to a couple of bales of hay used as seats. She started unloosening her jeans and laid down on the bales. Her pants were just loose enough for her to get her hand in between her legs. "Okay, let's go."

David looked at her and she started cumming. This time it wasn't part of the act and seemed so much more intense. She didn't hold back anything and all David could think was, *Jimmy did not deserve any of that*. She was working her fingers over her clit and David couldn't help but get a hard-on. When she finished, she laid still for a moment with one hand still down her pants and the other arm draped over her eyes. Her ripped, six pack belly was exposed.

David said he was going to pull out his dick. She just shook her head a little indicating okay. David dropped his jeans to his knees and held his shirt up with one hand. Betsy looked over and said "Ooh," in a quiet voice. Then she looked at his eyes and she started working it again. This time her pants slid down a little further and he could see her fingers working her clit. About every third stroke she stuck a finger half way in.

He didn't know if the insertion was a "finger fucking" or if she was just keeping her finger moist to continue rubbing her clit. David was looking at a completely shaved, naked pussy. She shaved thoroughly so she could wear the skimpiest of costumes.

It took her twice as long to finish the second time, but when she was through, she sat up on the hay and said, "Come here." David moved closer.

He stood a foot away with his pants still around his knees. She said, "Look at that angle." She was talking about his dick sticking up. His wasn't big but got hard as a rock and did, in fact, have an impressive angle to it. He felt a little uneasy because he knew that she was mentally comparing it to Jimmy's big dick.

She reached up to his hips and turned him toward the hay bales. She said, "You ready?" Juice was dripping out of the end of his dick. "What am I talking about? Look at that wet, throbbing cock." She spit on the head of his dick and rubbed it in along with his juice. It only took about ten of her expertly delivered circular strokes before David exploded with a huge, magnificent load. The bale of hay was drenched and David was barely able to stand it rocked him so hard.

"Wow." she said. "What a shot." David stood with his hands on his hips. His jeans were all the way down to his ankles and his little dick was still bouncing up and down.

"I nearly passed out," he said. She laughed and they both started getting their pants pulled back up.

She laughed a little to herself again and said, "I'm going to see who sits on that bale of hay tonight and just smile."

"Shouldn't we turn it over or something.?" David looked at her waiting for a response. Staring at the bale, she shook her head "no" and laughed again. "Okay, it's your venue."

"I'll see you in a couple of days," she said and kissed him on his cheek. David went to his new private tent and had a blissful nap.

Chapter 52

The Best of All Worlds

The road was grueling but the circus was turning a large profit without Jimmy terrorizing everyone and skimming money. The crew was well paid and on time and there was no friction between anyone except George and Ramon. George was the Tilt-o-Whirl operator and Ramon operated the Spyder Ryde. For three years, they had been having a friendly competition to see who got the largest gate. Ramon had the edge for the last few weeks and George was taking it personally. Carol had to intervene by threatening to take away their rides.

Sometimes the circus traveled by train, offering David the only real rest he ever seemed to get. The train rides just weren't long enough. A train felt like his home. He was always more comfortable leaving a place behind than arriving at a new destination.

In a town in Pennsylvania, on a crisp fall evening, Betsy and David met in her tent several hours before her show. She was wearing her usual circus casual outfit, a pair of low cut jeans, a T-shirt tied at her waste and flip flops. She always looked... "long". Her toes were long, her feet were long, her legs were long, her torso was long, her neck was long, her arms were long, and her fingers were long. The only thing that wasn't "long" on her was her pixie cut blonde hair. She kept it short so she could wear the many wigs she needed for her costumes. David thought she looked like a ballerina.

She said, "I need you to do something for me tonight." She got really close to him. "I want you to make love to me."

David was in shock. " What? I mean, when?"

She got so close they were touching. "Now."

She closed her eyes and started kissing him like she was hungry for it. Then she took his hand and led him back stage where she had made a pallet to lie on. They slowly took each other's clothes off and went to the ground kissing again. She laid back with David on top of her. In one quick, skillful movement, she got David's hard-on deep inside her and had him wrapped tightly in her long legs and arms.

She felt wonderful beneath him. He was making every effort to give her as much pleasure as possible. He was not a good lover, or at least he didn't think he was, but he really wanted to make her feel special. She was beautiful.

In moments, she had an orgasm. He could feel it. Her body shimmied, her pussy tightened around his cock and she dug her nails into his back. She whispered something in his ear. He didn't understand it but he imagined it was the highest level of praise. He kept going, plowing her with every grinding, twisting, sliding stroke he could dream up. She loosened her grip on him and put her hands on his shoulder. David wondered what was going on.

"Didn't you hear me?"

David said, "Sorry, I heard you say something, but I was too busy to listen."

"I said, can you go down on me now?"

"Sure…sure I can do that."

He slid down the blankets until his face was between her legs. He kissed around her smooth mound a little to start because he had never tasted a bald one before. It felt good to kiss it, so soft. Then he licked between the lips hoping to hit the magic spot. He must have done it right because she started rubbing her feet on his back and holding his head in her hands. He thought she might pull out some of his hair. She had another orgasm...a hard one as he feasted on her sweet spot. It left her spent, lying limply on the blankets.

"I'm sorry, I can't go again. Just use me," she muttered. David did as instructed. He climbed back up on her and started using her to satisfy himself. Just before he came, she said, "Fill me up. I'm on the pill." He started squirting in her and making the rawest grunting noises he had ever made in his life. He heard her say, "Goodness."

They lay together naked and comfortable which was an odd combination for David. In his mind, he was wondering how long this could go on.

Chapter 53

The Beginning of the End

Thirteen years. That's how long it went on. In 1998, when Betsy was thirty-six years old, she decided that she needed to leave the circus. Her body was starting to break down a little, a strain here, a pulled muscle there. It was just enough to tell a smart person that a dancing career was coming to an end and Betsy was smart. She did not want to turn into one of the toothless, greasy carnies that held on until one day they were found in their sleeping quarters dead, curled up with a bottle of rot gut whiskey.

She announced her retirement and set a date for the last show. At midnight on November 10, 1998, Betsy performed her last show to a packed house of nothing but other carnies. When she finished her routine, the audience of co-workers detonated with a thunderous round of applause, cheers and whistles. Everybody hugged her neck and Betsy cried.

Carol stood by David, holding his arm and watched like parents might do if their daughter were leaving home to go off to college. At least Carol looked that way. David looked like he was losing his best friend and lover for over a decade, which he was. They never even discussed if David was going to leave too, it was just assumed, and rightfully so, that David would stay behind and continue to live out his days with the circus.

A dark cloud came over the circus after Betsy left. She seemed to be the ray of sunshine that always brightened the day. Carol and David were lost without her but they bonded together and somehow continued to manage the show.

A month after Betsy left, Omar, the camel wrangler, came to see Carol. Omar was really Mexican but passed for Persian when doing his show. Omar told Carol that Maximus, the middle-sized camel was really sick and Glutius the large camel was acting a little peaked too. Carol asked, "What about Sphinxter?" David fought the urge to laugh. He always thought it to be a great joke that the camels were named Glutius, Maximus, and Sphinxter.

However, the camel illness was no joke. All three died within a week. Carol, never skipped a beat and overnight, the Arabian Nights Circus became, Carol's (We Have No Camels) Carnival. The Big Top was gone and the only things left were the midway, the rides and a few shows. David's show was keeping the carnival afloat.

In the summer of 1999, in Michigan, Carol told David that she would be gone for a week or two and for him to handle the business affairs. She never said what she was going to do and David wasn't the curious kind. In ten days, she met them in South Dakota and told David that she wanted to see him that night after everything was shut down.

David was in the administrative tent at nearly 1:00 am in the morning when Carol walked in. David was at her desk with the day's receipts piled in front of him. She sat in one of the wooden folding chairs and took a deep sigh.

"This is not going to be good, is it?" David asked.

"No," and she started to cry.

David walked over and put his arm around her. She folded into him like he was the only safe place in the world. She cried a little harder.

David just waited for her to start talking and it wasn't long before she pulled back, wiped her eyes on her sleeve, and then opened up.

"I have cancer." David's stomach turned. "I knew something was wrong with me but I've been putting it off to make sure the circus ran well. I don't know why I did since you've been with me. It's just an old habit." David's sinking feeling continued all the way into physical illness.

"David, I have cancer...everywhere, pancreas, colon, stomach, lungs, my fucking tits." David just held her more tightly. "There is zero hope, David. The doctors just recommended that I "live the fullest life possible" until the pain becomes too great and then go into hospice."

David still hadn't said anything. She folded into him again. While her head was buried in his chest she said, "They say I'm going to lose weight at an incredible rate over the next few months. Then I'm dead. What is going to happen to the carnival?" she said more or less rhetorically.

David's mind reeled from the news but he had this fear that she would ask him to carry on when she was gone. Without Carol or Betsy, the carnival had no meaning to him. She finally said, "I have a niece in Sacramento. Maybe she'll want the carnival?" David still hadn't said a word. "That's what I'll do. I'll call my niece tomorrow. I haven't seen her in twenty years but she's the only family I have."

It was the beginning of the end. Carol made David swear that he wouldn't tell anyone and he promised he wouldn't. He would have promised her just about anything at that moment. For the next few days the carnival ran with the utmost efficiency. No one was the wiser.

That night while counting the gate, Carol told David that she talked to Celeste, her niece, who was more than willing to accept the carnival as part of the will. Looking at Carol, David thought she might have already lost a few pounds. She also told him that after she was gone, she wanted bonuses given to all the staff as a special thank you for their hard work and loyalty. She said they needed to start saving now for the bonuses because she wanted them to be substantial. Then she said she wanted to make an annual plan for the towns, routes, and modes of transportation for the carnival so it wouldn't be so overwhelming for Celeste.

David listened intently, took a few notes, and then she said, "And now I want you to look at me and do me until my pussy bleeds." David did a double take. "You heard me Mister Orgasm. I want a private show and I would like to have it in the next five minutes. You hear me soldier. I'll meet you in the back."

Carol slept in the back of the administrative tent. In all his years with the circus/carnival he had never had the privilege of being invited in. David finished up a few piles of receipts and money counting and then went to the back with Carol. One candle was lit in and old style lamp. Carol was on the bed, naked, with a sheet draped seductively over one leg.

She said, "This may be my last time so make it good. And could you take off your clothes, please?" David was having real mixed emotions but complied with her request. He stood naked before her while she burned a hole in him with her eyes. Without any physical contact or words between them, he started getting an erection. She watched him grow until it was throbbing up and down. She wet her lips and her hands instinctively went to her breast.

"Are you ready?" he asked. She spread her legs a little further and threw the sheet off her body. David took that to mean she was more than ready. He looked at her and she started. Her hand went to her pussy and her legs went up. She was fifty-six years old and she was going at it like a teenager. David was forty-six and felt half his age.

When she finished the first one, he stepped closer and she grabbed his cock. She started jacking it straight away. "Such a hard dick," she said. She sat up on the edge of the bed and started massaging his balls with her other hand. David put his hands on his hips, leaned back and closed his eyes. Just as he was relaxing into it, he felt her take half his cock in her mouth. He grunted in appreciation.

She was taking deep strokes with her mouth. One of the benefits of having a smaller dick was that a woman could take most, if not all of it, down her throat. What a wonderful feeling. She took a couple more licks and nibbles at the head and then released him, leaning back on the bed. David took this to mean she wanted to get fucked. He obliged.

While he was on top of her, she had a natural orgasm. David was always prouder of that accomplishment than giving a woman a visual one. She made some moves that indicated she wanted to change positions and before long he was going at her from every conceivable angle. When he was ready to cum, he was in her from behind. She was in a position that looked like a Muslim prayer. She called it "frog style". He announced that he was about ready. She said, "Go Go" instead of "Cum Cum". No matter how she said it, he "Went Went" filling her up with an obscene amount of juice.

They both fell on the bed gasping for air. She had cum eleven times. David came just once, but "Wow." She finally broke the silence and said, "This is usually the part that I hated the most."

"What's that? Sleeping in the wet spot or some how running the guy off without hurting his feelings or having him fall in love with you."

She laughed a little chuckle. "No. Nothing like that. That would be normal. This is when Jimmy would usually hit me. He had a huge dick, of course you know that. But he couldn't keep it up and he always blamed me. I don't know if he faired any better with the other girls he screwed but I always felt inadequate."

"Carol, that's silly. You're gorgeous. You made me feel like my nuts were getting torn off when I came. You just fucked me nine ways to Sunday and that sideways, cheerleader split, leg-wrap thing you did to me was a first and I wasn't sure any human woman could do it, especially one who is fifty years old."

"Well, you're not so bad yourself for a middle-aged old broke dick." She reached over and put her hand on his chest. "How much longer before you're ready again."

"Well, if I had a little help..." Without hesitation, she rolled over, put his little soiled dick in her mouth, and worked it with a reckless abandon. She seemed starved for sex even though she just had eleven orgasms. In a few minutes, it started to grow and she seemed to be getting more excited with every inch of extension.

When fully firm, she positioned herself on top of him with her ample tits hanging down near his face. He was most obliged to put the long brown nipples in his mouth. "Be rough with them if you want." He wanted to please her so he tore them up. He was sure that his sucking, biting, pulling, and twisting would hurt her but the more he punished her, the more she responded. He kept thinking, *I've known this woman for nearly fifteen years and never knew she was such an animal.* She came two more times on top of him. She was rubbing her clit into his stomach to make herself cum and only using his dick as an anchor. The third time she came, she collapsed, breathing heavily into his ear with her large boobs buried in his chest.

"Almost done," she said. She slid down so she was sitting cross legged between his knees. "Now it's your turn." She leaned over and sucked him a little bit and then started a very skillful hand/blow job. Even for his second time around, he could tell that it wasn't going to take very long. She was really good at this.

In no more than two minutes, she knew he was getting ready and worked his cock with just her hand. Right at the very instant that he was about to cum, she stuck her finger all the way up his ass and he squirted cum up over his head. He made an "Argh" sound which she thought was funnier than hell. They both laughed afterwards even though his balls hurt so badly that he didn't think he would be able to walk.

She rolled over on her back with a sigh and they both stared at the top of the tent. David broke the silence, "I never knew."

"What?' she asked.

"That you were so incredibly good in bed."

"I had a run of bad men. Believe me, Jimmy wasn't the worst but he was the last. After he left the show all those years ago, I became celibate. I just gave up. The show became my lover. It just about was anyway. I always liked you, but Betsy was around and she was such a sweet girl that I couldn't hurt her feelings so I just let it go."

"You mean I just fucked a ten-year virgin?"

"Yes, except for taking care of myself. I haven't had a man in over ten years."

"That's....sad."

"I know, and now, it's too late. I only have a little while to be here and I have so much to do. You have to promise me that you'll help me get the show ready to turn over to my niece when the time comes."

"I can do that," David said with all honesty. He didn't want any part of it after Carol was gone so he planned to help get it ready for Celeste and then he was in the wind.

Chapter 54

The End of the Line

At least twice a week for the next month, Carol and David got together for an hour or so of wild monkey sex. Each session seemed to be better than the last until she asked to beg off for a night or two which turned into a week and then she asked to stop altogether. Her body was starting to give out. She'd lost a dozen pounds and she was experiencing some pain now. She thought she might have six months left but at the rate she was deteriorating, a couple of months was all she could reasonably expect.

She wasn't bitter because she was so focused on the legal paperwork and financial preparation necessary to transfer ownership of Carol's (We Have No Camels) Carnival to Celeste. David had never met Celeste but she was coming out in a week to sign the papers.

Just before Thanksgiving in 1999, the carnival was starting its winter tour through the south. They were holed up on a rainy day in Columbus, Georgia. Carol was almost bedridden. Celeste was flying in to Birmingham, Alabama and one of the employees was going to pick her up and bring her to Columbus.

David was standing at the main gate to the carnival waiting for Celeste to arrive. He'd been going outside to stand for ten minutes and then back inside the admin tent for ten minutes for over an hour. He was anxious. Finally, he saw the purple zebra striped carnival sedan driving down the road. It was hard to miss. It pulled right up to the gate and Celeste stepped out.

Celeste was not anything like her aunt. She was rail thin and dressed in designer garb from head to toe. "Are you fucking shitting me with this clown car! Take me to Aunt Carol," she said without a "How do you do." David just pointed in the direction of the administration tent and she stalked off in that direction with her stiletto's stabbing in to the muddy earth. Before she got to the tent, her left shoe popped off, the heel stuck deeply in the red Georgia clay. "Fuck!" she exclaimed as her pedicured toes dug into the muck.

She reached down, grabbed her shoe off the ground and continued on. When she entered the tent, she looked around and said, "Is this the office?"

David said, "Yes, and it's Carol's living quarters. She sleeps in the back."

"You're fucking shitting me! Where can I sit?"

David looked around. Six wooden folding chairs, open and scattered throughout the tent were available to receive her royal ass. "Any of these chairs," he said.

"You're fucking shitting me! These things better not stain my pants." She sat down and started trying to wipe off her foot. David grabbed a hand towel from the top right desk drawer. Carol kept it there because she was always spilling her coffee. He handed it to Celeste, "Here, use this."

While she was cleaning up her muddied shoe and pedicured toes, David said, "I'll go get Carol."

"You do that." David was quickly developing a "Jimmy-like" loathing for Celeste. David slipped behind the tent divider and helped Carol out of bed. She was slow but she made it to the front and sat behind her desk. Once seated, Carol looked up and told Celeste how thankful she was to have her take over.

Celeste responded with, "Whatever. How much is it worth?"

Carol was so tired. She could hardly keep her head up. "About one point five million."

"You're fucking shitting me! This fucking thing is worth a million and a half?"

"At least that much. It has a good earnings history. David can tell you more about that. Today though, we just need you to sign some papers so things will be legal. Are you ready to do that today?"

Celeste asked if she would own the carnival after signing and Carol said she would. Carol explained some bonuses were to be paid to the staff but after that, she was in control. Celeste said she would be back with a lawyer. Then she looked at David and said, "Now get that stupid-ass car for me."

As she was exiting the tent she turned and said to Carol, "You look like shit. You need a spa day. Maybe a spa week." She walked out and the tent flap closed behind her.

Carol and Celeste never even exchanged pleasantries, but it had been over twenty years since they had seen each other so it was just a business deal to Celeste. David opened the door to the purple zebra striped carnival car, Celeste got in, cursing the mud and rode off to find a five-star hotel in Columbus, Georgia. *Good luck.*

When David returned to the admin tent, he couldn't help himself, making quotation marks with his hands, "Are you fucking shitting me? Are you really going to give the carnival to that spoiled skinny bitch?"

"She's the only family I have." The answer was "yes", the spoiled skinny bitch gets everything.

The next day Celeste came back with a "suit" and he pretty much rewrote the entire paperwork. Carol was too weak to fight it. Carol signed and the carnival belonged to Celeste just like that.

Chapter 55

The Carnival Payback

The carnival played Columbus but Celeste decided to cease business operations after the current run and sell the carnival immediately. Celeste put Carol in a hospice home. Then she purchased a two-bedroom trailer and had it moved to the carnival location so she could have a decent place to live until the carnival sold.

The new contract didn't include the staff bonuses and as each day passed, a performer, roustabout or cook just vanished from the scene. The carnival was getting smaller and smaller through attrition. Celeste didn't seem to notice and she sure didn't care.

When a potential buyer finally showed up to review the assets, there were very few assets left. Celeste showed him around and took him back to the trailer to offer him some sex for a better deal but the buyer wasn't going for it. He left without making an offer.

Celeste found David and cursed him out, blaming him for everything that was going wrong. David listened politely and responded, "Yes Ma'am." Fighting with her wasn't worth it because he was going to abandon ship the next day anyway.

Just before sunrise, David walked out of Carol's (We Have No Camels) Carnival, or what was left of it, and started hiking into town. After a few miles, he found the Georgia Pines Care Center and visited Carol for the last time. She was so weak he only had time to say a few kind words to her before she fell asleep.

Carol passed away, alone in the room three days later. Celeste never came by to see her nor did she show any interest after she passed. Celeste just gave instructions over the phone which basically amounted to telling the Georgia Pines Care Center staff that Carol had no assets so they needed to take care of all the expenses. Carol was buried by the county in a cardboard box in a grave marked by an aluminum plate.

Celeste had two more potential buyers review the carnival assets. One guy left quickly after seeing the state of the equipment and the morale of the remaining staff. Celeste offered him sex but he passed being anxious to get back to his wife in Milwaukee.

The second potential buyer was a carnie himself, looked over the assets, and realized that the biggest grossing act, Mister Orgasm or as he saw on the manifest "Saladin", was no longer active on the inventory. Celeste sensed that he may still make an offer so she took him back to her trailer and gave him a blow job hoping to seal the deal. However, after shooting his load in her hair and having it dribble down on her new Manolo shoes, he declined to make an offer. She was furious and physically assaulted him. He ran for his life out of the trailer and jumped in his Ford F-150 truck. She pursued him and threw a rather large, thick, glass ashtray at him and broke his windshield as he sped off.

To Celeste's dismay, the guy returned the next day with a deputy sheriff who served her an arrest warrant for assault. She got hooked up in cuffs and transported to the county jail. Now she was the recipient of county hospitality; the same county hospitality that buried her Aunt Carol for free just days before.

In her absence, the carnival staff pawned or stole most of the carnival property and divided up the profits. Then each loaded up the carnival and personal vehicles with everything that wasn't nailed down and departed to find greener pastures. Nothing was left of the carnival but scrap and trash. When Celeste got herself out of jail, she found that she had rung up $28,000 of civil fines and fees for cleaning up the site. She also sold her trailer for a ten-grand loss. Celeste hired a lawyer for $5000 and she settled out of court for $30,000 to get the victim to drop her assault charges. All totaled, Celeste lost $63,000 as a result of inheriting her Aunt Carol's 1.5-million-dollar carnival. Plus...she gave a greasy haired, toothless carnie a blow job. And they say there ain't no justice in the world.

Chapter 56

The Big Apple

Two days before Christmas, David stepped off the train for the last time at Penn Station in New York City. He looked up and saw the Empire State Building. For some reason, it made him feel good.

He first secured a week-by-week hotel room not too far from Times Square. Then he began scouring the classified ads for a suitable job. He didn't really know what he wanted to do but thought another warehouse job would be safe, plus he had a little experience in the warehouse field. Anything but show business.

He found something called an inventory specialist that paid a reasonable amount of money. He left on the subway two hours early because he wasn't familiar with New York's Financial District where the interview was scheduled. Even with a two-hour lead time, he could not find the right address, or maybe, he subconsciously didn't want to get the job. After three hours of walking the streets and searching, he gave up.

Back at his sparsely appointed hotel room, he sat in what passed for an easy chair and soul searched for an answer about what to do with himself. Instead of an answer, he fell asleep. When he awoke almost two hours later, he had a nearly divine revelation. Something Janice said to him during their heyday in Vegas. He should be a Sex Therapist!

He knew he couldn't really call himself a "therapist" because he wasn't licensed and he certainly wasn't going back to college to get the right degree. He didn't think "counselor" was a good description either. "Advisor" sounded ridiculous based on what he would do to the clients. He needed a good title. Chuckling to himself, he also ruled out being Mister Orgasm, not again, not ever. With an exhausting effort that took the rest of the afternoon, he finally came up with "Coach". That's it, he would be the best Climax Coach he could be.

Chapter 57

Setting Up Shop

David had been sending his circus money back to his banks in Las Vegas for them to invest so he didn't have much working capital, only about $6,000. It would have to be enough. He needed an "office" or clinic, furnishings, advertising, maybe a secretary, and most of all clients. What he really needed was a New York Janice to help him get started. *That's the ticket*, he thought. *I'll get an agent. A tough New York Jew just like Janice.*

A three day, including a lonely Christmas Day, search of the yellow pages and about ten miles of walking up and down Broadway netted him the names of three potential agents: Wilma Bronstein, Leslie Kravits, and Abigail Schwarz. He read their advertisements and looked up the location of the offices on the map. He made appointments with their secretaries to see Wilma and Abigail but Leslie was a one woman show and she wasn't in when he called. The highlight of the search was when he passed by Rockefeller Center which really looked nice at Christmas time.

At exactly 10:00 am sharp on the first Wednesday after Christmas Day, David entered the offices of Wilma Bronstein, Talent Agent. She was a sixty-year-old woman with a wig that looked filthy. She smoked and the ashtray was piled high with cigarette butts. Her office smelled like the ashtray looked.

David turned around and walked out. He took a small note pad out of his pocket and crossed her name off the list. Leslie Kravits was the next name on the list. Her office was in Brooklyn, a long subway ride away. When he arrived at the closest subway stop he searched for a half hour before he found her fourth-floor walk-up office. The letters on her office door read: "Leslie Kravits, Literary and Talent Agent".

David knocked and heard a woman yell, "Come on in." Leslie was younger than David giving him the impression that she may not be experienced or tough enough to handle the task. She pointed to an over-stuffed chair and said, "I have a few minutes before my next client arrives. What can I do for you?"

"Well", David started, looking down and shuffling his feet on the floor like he always did. "I have this singular talent that I want to showcase in a private setting."

"What's your talent?"

"I know you won't believe this, but I give women orgasms."

She snorted a kind of laugh and said, "I hate to break it to you Casanova but women can get an orgasm from just about any man. Hell, they can give themselves one. I do every Thursday."

"I know I'm not saying this right but I can give a woman an orgasm just by looking at her. And I'd like to start something like a clinic, and coach those women who have trouble achieving orgasms or for those who want an orgasm discreetly without having any real sex. I want you to help me set up a clinic and send me clients."

"Alright," she said, placing both her hands on her desk top. She pushed herself up. "I think I need you to leave now." She got up and started walking toward him. Halfway across the office, David looked at her.

"Holy Fucking Moses!" she exclaimed and went to her knees in the middle of the floor. She was wearing a dark skirt and blouse with dark panty hose. Before he entered, she had kicked her high heels off underneath her desk. In a couple of seconds she slipped over on her side to finish up her orgasm. David stood silently like he always did waiting for her to recover. When finished, she struggled to get into a standing position. She waddled back behind her desk and plopped into the chair. Her black outfit was filthy with floor dust. It was evident her custodial staff needed remedial training.

"Shanda fur die goy," she said in a marked New York accent.

"I don't know how to respond to that," David said thinking she was speaking Jewish. It wasn't a stretch for his wee little East Texas brain to extrapolate that if German people spoke German and French people spoke French, then therefore, shouldn't Jewish people speak Jewish?

"Never mind, it's just a saying in Yiddish. Now what is it you want me to do?" She fumbled with a cigarette and eventually got it lit. David was astounded by how quickly these kinds of people recognized that there was a buck to be made. There was no, "How did you do that?" or "What kind of magic is this?" just, "Okay, lets make money."

"What I just did to you, I want to do to any women who ask for it. I want to help women if I can or at the least give them some pleasure or satisfaction. I want to coach these women in a clinical type setting, I want you to help me set up the clinic, and send me the clients."

"What's in it for me?" she asked.

"I'll pay you to help me set up the clinic and I'll give you a cut of what each woman pays me for my service."

Being all business she asked, "How much of a cut?"

"Ten percent sounds fair."

"Twenty sounds fairer. It is a very difficult client pool." She blew a large cloud of smoke in his direction.

David smiled, "Sounds like we just agreed on fifteen percent. When do we get started?"

"Whoa boy. How much start up cash do you have?"

David reached in his pocket and pulled out a great wad of hundreds. "Six thousand." He pitched it on top of her desk.

"That's not much," she said but grabbed it up like a duck on a June bug. "I'll call you in a couple of days. Leave your number on my desk. If this isn't enough, I'll cover the rest and you can repay it at twenty percent vig a week." It was obvious she had loaned out some money before.

"If vig is interest, then I think ten percent is plenty," he countered.

"Sounds like we just agreed upon fifteen percent." She blew another cloud of smoke. David took out his note pad, wrote down his number and left it on her desk. She said, "Okay, Hon, I'll call you in a couple of days."

David left her office thinking, *how stupid is this?* He seemed to always be thinking that. He just gave six grand to a woman he had only met once, they didn't have a contract nor did they even shake hands. Maybe it is true, you can't fix stupid.

Chapter 58

Open for Business

Three days later, David was in the hall of his apartment complex talking to Leslie on the communal phone. She had secured a three-room office in the Financial District, furnished it like a clinic and paid the first two months' rent. David was now $2,700 in her debt with $405 interest owed a week until it was paid off.

He met Leslie at the specified address and she gave him the nickel tour. The clinic consisted of a waiting room, an exam room (the room where the act would take place) which had a small bathroom shower, and a spare room to be used as an office/storage. It was not a bad set up. Leslie told him to go get himself a suit and be ready for business on the following Monday.

David was down to his last $300. Just barely enough to buy the cheapest suit on earth, pay his rent, and keep him in bagels for the New Year's weekend and celebrate New Year's Eve at Times Square. And before he could turn around, it was January 1, 2000.

Early on Monday morning, David was waiting for Leslie outside his new office. Leslie showed up a little after nine. They went in and

Leslie trained him on how to use the cash register which was a computerized machine with credit card capability.

"First client will be here at 1:00 pm. Babe, do you know what you're doing?" Leslie did not think he exuded confidence.

"I don't have a clue," said David.

"Your first victim is one of my girlfriends so don't fuck this up." She lit a cigarette.

"No smoking in my clinic."

"Your clinic? Ain't you got a set of balls." She stepped outside. "I'm going to run along. I've got other clients besides you. You know, regular clients. They sing and dance and go to cocktail parties." Leslie handed him her card. "Call me when you're finished." She made a big kissing motion in the air and walked off.

David paced like a caged animal until about 1:15 when the door opened. Enter client number one: thirty-two-year-old Lorene from Portland, Maine, a chorus line dancer for *Cats,* the musical. "Hey Sweetie, Les says you got a special treat for me today. Do I get naked or what?" She started taking her clothes off in the lobby.

"Well, I'd prefer that you get as comfortable as you want but could you do it in this room?" David pointed to the exam room which had a stuffed chair and a full bed. "Do you know what is going to happen today?" he asked her.

She walked into the exam room and said, "No, not really. I assume you're going to give me a massage or something. Les gave me a $100 to come here. I guess I'm kinda like your hooker for the afternoon."

"She paid you to do this?" David was flabbergasted.

"Yeah. Isn't that how it works. The girl gets paid and the guy gets his rocks off or some other kinky shit. I've seen it all. I had a guy pay to pee on me once. It's tough out there." She was completely naked now. "Ok, where do you want me and what are we going to do?"

David was still shaking his head. "Just lie down on the bed I suppose." She was put together like a brick house and he could understand why men paid her to pleasure them.

"You aren't going to hurt me, are you?"

"No, I won't lay a hand on you. My goal is to give you the most and best orgasms you have ever had in your life without even touching you."

"Good luck with that. I haven't cum since I left Maine. I don't have a husband, no boyfriend. All I've been around for the last ten years is the producers and their casting couches and the gay guys in the show. So, I'll make you a deal. If you make me cum without touching me, I'll give you Leslie's hundred bucks. I have no faith that it will ever happen." She laid down on her side, head propped up on her elbow.

"You ready?" David said nervously. What if she could beat him at his own game. He'd be a failure before he even got started. "Well, let me introduce you to the one, the only, the amazing Mister Orgasm!" He thought to himself, *Crap, I swore I wasn't going to use that shtick.*

He looked at her. She looked at him. She raised her eyebrows as if to say, "So?" Then her face began to contort. In three seconds, she was experiencing a full-blown orgasm. What a show! He wasn't sure if he gave her a really good one or if it was the absence of orgasms for so many years but she arched her back like only a professional dancer could. She was straining so hard that he thought she might hurt herself.

She started to settle down a little, but she looked at him again. A second orgasm grabbed her. She rolled away from him, stuck one leg straight up in the air, and pointed her toes. Again, only a professional dancer could possibly enjoy an orgasm in that position. He could tell she was rubbing herself.

When she finished, she rolled on her back and put her forearm over her eyes. "I thought you were bullshitting me."

"No bullshit. This is what I do. But if it will give you a more familiar feeling, I'll pee on you."

She gave a short chuckle. "I'll pass."

David got out of the "coach's" chair and sat on the edge of the bed. He put his hand on her stomach. She instinctively looked at him and started up. She sat up this time and threw her arms around him. His little cock was about to burst out of his "new" second hand grey slacks. She reached down and started rubbing him through his pants. Although he was knocking on fifty years old, he couldn't help but blow his load in his pants.

He realized that he hadn't had an orgasm since he had been in New York either. He had about a four-inch wet spot on his crotch. She squeezed him one more time right on the wet spot saying the obvious, "You soaked yourself through."

She got up and started getting dressed. "For the love of God, don't look at me again." David walked out and stood behind the counter in the lobby trying to hide is wet spot. In a minute, Lorene came out shading her eyes pretending not to look. "As promised," she said and handed him a hundred-dollar bill. "And here Doll, for a job well done." She put a twenty on the counter.

As she walked out the door, she said, "You're going to be a big hit. Leslie picked a winner." David had been through all of this before and was wondering how long he could keep it up before it came crashing down around him. He was also wondering if he had to give Leslie 15% of his tips.

Chapter 59

Business is Booming

Word of mouth spread quickly. Within weeks he had three customers a day and within two months he had six a day. Lorene had set the precedent with a $100 per coaching session. He was making $600 a day plus tips which were substantial. Every customer he had except the brand-new ones had returned at least once.

Because Leslie was all business, she upped the fee to a $150 per session. David never lost a single customer and within six months, he was handling eight customers a day for a total of $1200 plus tips. David had paid Leslie everything he owed including the 15% vig and he was paying the office rent and other expenses with ease. His only surprise was the amount of linen he had to wash. He installed an industrial washer and dryer in the storeroom and did all of the laundry after closing.

He had purchased some nicer clothes and learned quickly which customers were most likely to soil his pants for him. He tried to keep his clothes clean when the grabby ones had appointments but he always kept several spare outfits in the laundry room in case things got out of control.

The most notable case of bad timing was when two women arrived in the waiting room at the same time. He tried to space it out where the appointments were an hour and a half apart so two women wouldn't be in the lobby together. These two ladies started chatting with each other and found out that they had absolutely nothing in common... except the fact that they were both there at the same time for the same reason.

They decided "wouldn't it be a kick if we went in together?" When David escorted the previous client out of the exam room, the two women asked if they could go in at the same time. Since they were the last two appointments of the day, David thought, *why not, I can finish my day two hours early.*

The ladies went in and disrobed. They were new customers but they had learned a lot from listening to their friends who recommended the "treatment". They sat on the bed, side by side. The younger woman was in her twenties with smooth skin and small, super-model type breasts. The older lady was in her forties, bigger than average breasts that sagged in the "every boy's dream cougar" look. Both of them were on the high side of average looking.

David asked a few questions to try to relax them and more importantly, to determine if they were going to grab him during the service. When he asked how they usually acted during an orgasm or while masturbating, he got an unusual response from the younger one. She said that she could mask her orgasms well and had them all of the time. She said she even masturbated in the cab on the way over. She promised that she was the epitome of self control.

The older lady said she usually came once or would almost cum when her husband was screwing her. About once a week, he'd climb on top of her, hunch until he finished, and then he'd roll over and go to sleep. Her husband told her that if she wanted to come along for the ride she could, which meant if she had an orgasm...great. If she didn't, maybe next week, but he wasn't going to do anything different for her sake.

David was sitting in his "coach's" chair listening to the stories and nodding politely. When they finished, he said, "Sounds like I'm in no danger from either of you. On rare occasion, I get attacked." They both shook their heads, "Oh, no." they said in disbelief that a woman couldn't control herself.

They talked a few more minutes until both ladies no longer cared about their nakedness. At the perfect time, he asked, "Are you ready?" They stopped in mid-conversation and looked over at him. He slowly raised his eyes from their feet, to their knees, to their breasts and finally to their eyes. Somewhere along the way, he left behind announcing Mister Orgasm and just went straight to the eye climax

As soon as the first inkling of an orgasm hit them they shot off the bed on to their knees in front of David while he was sitting in his chair. They started trying to get into his pants, all the while fighting the effects of the auto-orgasm. The younger woman, "who had much better control because she apparently had several orgasms a day and was more used to it," got David's zipper undone and had her hand in his pants.

David learned a long time ago that it was better to go with the flow rather than to try to fight them off, because, number one, he wanted a return customer and, number two, sometimes people got physically hurt, mainly him. He always made a cursory attempt to push them back and he said "No" several times but most of the time he got groped anyway. He really didn't mind most of the time, but not all of his customers were the girl next door, or the MILF down the block. Some were just ugly, dirty women who scraped up a hundred and fifty bucks and thought they were entitled to as much as they could get.

In a couple of minutes, after the second orgasm, the women got David's shoes, socks, pants, and underwear off of him. He was still wearing his sport jacket, shirt and tie. The younger woman was giving him head while she was cumming. She had one hand wrapped around his shaft and the other was circling her clit, just like she did "several times a day".

The older woman was rubbing his balls and running her hands up and down his thighs. Every time she had an orgasm, she stopped what she was doing to him and concentrated on herself. David was thinking, *not a bad finish for the day.*

When the ladies completed their next orgasms and had recovered, not that the younger one needed to recover, they decide to move the operation to the bed. No one said, "Let's move to the bed." They all just got up together and slowly started moving in that direction. The young one was holding his really hard cock in her hands and the older one still had his balls wrapped in a death grip. Both were acting like they were afraid if they let go, they wouldn't be able to get it back. They were holding on so tightly it was painful.

David stood facing the bed, with a woman sitting on each side of him, one with his little hard dick clamped in her fist, the other with a handful of balls. He was desperately trying to shed his jacket, shirt and especially his tie. "Okay," the young one said, "Let's do it again." Both women looked up at him and he caressed them with his eyes.

In his extraordinary life, he had made a million mistakes and done a thousand things that, in retrospect, should have been handled better. But, at this very moment, he had just done another one he would regret for weeks to come. When these women started their fourth orgasm, they each fell backward on the bed trying to pull David over on top of them. Usually, a natural love making movement. However, the younger woman went one way with his dick and the older woman went the other way with his balls. Both refusing to relinquish their grasps and both badly needing to feel David's body on top of them.

What David felt was a "pop" at the base of his dick when it twisted off to the left and the worst nut cracking he had ever had in his life when his balls stretched several inches at a ninety degree angle off to the right. He let out a sound that was not anything like the usual love making sounds. In fact, it sounded more like an industrial steam whistle going off at five o'clock.

The girls let go and David lurched back and fell into his chair. The younger woman sat up with her hand over her mouth and the older one said, "I'm sorry," three times in rapid succession, and then, "Are you alright?"

Nope, he wasn't alright. Nothing was permanently damaged, pride maybe, but he healed. It took three weeks before he could get a good hard-on again and the first ejaculation had traces of blood, but he recovered and the business continued with a few new rule changes: Try harder to keep your clothes on and one woman at a time in the exam room.

Chapter 60

The Big Time

Leslie and David sat in his office discussing their next move since the mishap. She thought his story was hilarious and couldn't keep from laughing at him every chance she got so he hit her with an eye climax every chance *he* got. Finally, David got the best of her and she called a truce.

She said it was, "Time to get the kids off the street. Your fee is now $500 a session and I hired you a girl to help with the laundry, appointments and cleaning." David was a little surprised and had doubts about how the new girl was going to work out.

"Does she know what I do?"

"Of course not. She thinks you are a clinician of some sort which isn't far fetched. She'll start this Monday."

When David arrived at the office that Monday, Gisele was waiting outside the door. She was everything else but what he thought a Gisele should look like. She was maybe five-foot two, at least ten pounds over weight, medium length brown hair with average facial features. Regardless of looks, she had a great personality and worked from the minute she stepped in the door until she went home. He didn't know what he was paying her, Leslie handled all the finances, but whatever it was, it probably wasn't enough.

She truly didn't know what kind of work he did, but guessed that he was a sexual therapist and helped women achieve orgasm. She could hear the moans of appreciation emanating from the exam room. David always appeared from the exam room first, fully clothed, so she assumed he wasn't a gigolo or male whore of some kind.

With the increase to $500 a session, he lost many of his customers and only serviced about four a day. Leslie knew her business though. She maximized revenue with David putting in less effort than before. And, most of the women tipped. What a sweet deal. Every Friday, he left $100 in an envelope for Gisele. She seemed exceptionally appreciative.

With his extra money, he moved into an apartment in Chelsea. It was the most comfortable place he had ever lived. Things were going really well. Happiness and success were unsettling to him because he knew how quickly they could be taken away.

That was never proven so true as on September 11, 2001. Since they had so few customers, David only had the clinic open from 10 am to 4 pm. The attacks on the World Trade Center occurred before the clinic was opened. Thank goodness Gisele didn't go in early that day. New York was a mass of confusion and his business was closed for the time being.

Leslie lost some people in the attack and was out of touch for several months. David gave Gisele $5,000 as a retainer so she could keep her household going and for her promise to return to work for him when the time was right. He broke his lease on the clinic because it was buried under two feet of soot. It cost him three months' rent to get out from underneath the lease. His new apartment was costing him an arm and a leg and was draining his savings at an alarming rate. It all can fall apart so easily.

Chapter 61

Regrouping

In January of 2002, Leslie told David that she would help him get started again but after that she was going to leave New York and go to Nashville. David had no choice but to say, "Okay." Then she showed him a client list and left him to his own devices. She also let him out of their 15% contract.

Within six weeks, David had a small office suite downtown near where the first one had been located. He now called it a spa. Gisele returned to support the operation and all that was needed was a pot load of customers. One day while sitting around the office, Gisele asked David why he never looked at her. David told her that staring into a woman's eyes was the way he hypnotized them into being sexually relaxed enough to climax. He said he sometimes accidentally hypnotized acquaintances and people on the street so he learned that it was best just to keep his head down and look shy.

She accepted that answer but David could tell that her curiosity was not completely satisfied. He knew that somewhere down the line he would have to take her into the exam room and give her a taste and he felt sure that it would somehow ruin their working relationship. He would put the inevitable off as long as possible.

While they ate some street souvlaki in the back room, the front door opened and someone said, "Hello." David wiped his mouth and went to greet the visitor. She was a striking late fifty something year old woman who looked familiar. Gisele came out and positioned herself behind the counter.

The lady asked, "Are you open for business?"

"Yes, we are. We just haven't had much exposure since the attack. Please sit here while Gisele takes care of you." David went into the exam room while Gisele started giving her the spiel.

The lady said, "I know Leslie very well. She helped me get started in the business. She told me about you guys months ago but I was in LA and couldn't get out this way." She leaned forward over the desk and whispered to Gisele, "Is it as good as they say?"

Having no clue, Gisele responded appropriately, "It's better." The woman leaned back and smiled.

Gisele ran the lady's credit card and explained that the charge would show up as "Day Dreams Spa." The lady shook her head in acknowledgment. Then Gisele saw the name on the card...Emerald Ferrari, the clothing designer and Hollywood icon who dressed all of the stars. She was nominated for an Academy Award for costume design on three different occasions. Gisele was even wearing a pair of Emerald Ferrari panties. When they finished the paperwork, Gisele said, "My name is Gisele and Mr. Gideon will see you now."

David was sitting in his "coach's" chair and directed her to sit on the bed. She strolled over ever so slowly and lightly glided onto the bed. The air of grace about her was thick. He wasn't sure that these treatments were going to be her cup of tea.

"Do you know what is about to happen here?" he asked.

"If I understand it correctly from Leslie, you are going to make me hysterical and then so contented I may fall asleep afterward."

"I've never heard it put that way before but that would be a fair description. So, you know Leslie?"

"Yes," She said. "She gave me my start in show business. I may have been her first client when she was just getting started and we have remained friends for all these years. You don't recognize me, do you?"

"I'm sorry to admit it, but I don't know who you are. You look vaguely familiar. Are you an actress?"

"I tried to be about a million years ago but I couldn't get past bit parts in B movies. I found out that I could dress the stars in the movies better than I could act. I'm a costume designer and have my own line of clothing. My name is Emma Ferrari." She stuck out her hand and he shook it looking away as he always did.

"I'm David Gideon and I don't act either."

"What are you going to do to me today, exactly?"

"Officially, what I'm going to do is hypnotize you until you have auto-orgasms. What I'm really going to do is just look into your eyes and give you an orgasm. Since you're paying $500 for this service and no other customers are waiting, you can take your time and have as many orgasms as you want."

"Should I undress?" she asked.

"Only if you want to but most women do. It tends to get quite steamy and I think wearing clothes makes it uncomfortable."

She started to disrobe. David always looked at the clients from the chest down, not wanting to accidentally start the session before the client was ready. She was totally naked, standing in front of the bed. David could see that she had some work done on her boobs. They were large, but not enormous, and they stood out like a grapefruit was tucked into each one. He couldn't see any scars so it was very high quality work. She laid down on the bed and her boobs didn't even move. They just pointed at the ceiling. She said, "I'm ready."

David stood up and walked to the edge of the bed. He lightly touched the outside of her leg at about the knee with the knuckle of his index finger. He slowly moved it up her thigh, right by the pubic hair, cut in a tight little strip. He continued to move his fingers over her flat belly with a diamond navel stud. He slid his fingers up the side of her ribs, around her perfectly sculpted breast, up her neck, and then he touched her cheek. When he did, she grabbed his hand and kissed it. Then he looked into her eyes.

She started cumming like all the women did but she held his hand. This was a first. When she was winding down, she held his hand to her chest right between her bosoms. She breathed deeply for several breaths and then said, "That...was good."

David replied with, "You ain't seen nothing yet," and he looked at her again. She went off once more experiencing an orgasm that seemed much stronger than the first one. She still held his hand but moved it briefly to her little patch of pussy hair where she hunched on the back of his hand for a few seconds. When she was finishing, she moved his hand back up to her chest. She was squeezing the daylights out of it and it would have hurt if it wasn't part of the process. Lovemaking pain always seemed so much more tolerable than regular injury pain.

Completely done, she released his hand and asked if she could have some water. David went to the tiny refrigerator in the corner and retrieved a bottle of water for her. She sat up in bed and drank half of it in one guzzle. She had her knees up and leaned over to cover all of her private parts. "What you do is incredible. I'll have to admit when Leslie told me what was going to happen, I didn't believe it. You must really help a lot of women like me."

David was curious, "What do you mean, women like you?"

"You know. Over the hill. Put together with plastic. Not married." She held her hand up pointing at a bare ring finger. "All alone. Don't date anymore. Kids only call at Christmas. Drink too much wine. Too tired to masturbate. Worried about business. Fighting an ulcer over next year's award ceremony. You know, just generally screwed up."

"I really don't know. I just do what I do and they get out of it whatever they get out of it. I suppose some may find a kind of comfort or escape. To others it's just a brief sexual encounter. But I really would like to think I'm helping people." They both sat in silence for a minute. Each contemplating their respective situations.

She sat up on the edge of the bed and asked, "Is that a wrap?"

"Why don't you lie back down. We're just getting warmed up." Emma smiled and complied.

David kneeled by the bed and stared into her eyes. She went off really hard, holding his hand with both of hers. She stuffed them between her breasts. Her legs flailed. When she quit kicking, he looked at her again. This time she became verbal and under her breath she said, "Fuck it. Fuck it." David thought she was talking to an imaginary lover.

When she finished this time, he let her rest. She rolled on her side and faced him. David sat back in his chair. He noticed that even on her side, her tits poked straight out. She looked down at his crotch and saw the unmistakable bulge. She pointed to his pants and asked, "Who helps you out, Gisele?"

David chuckled, " No, she doesn't even really know what we do in here. She truly thinks I hypnotize women and get them to achieve orgasm as part of a therapeutic process. I think it would be best if I kept it that way. My life is way too complicated as it is."

"I'll help you out if you want me to." She sat up on the edge of the bed again. "It wouldn't be fair for me to get all of this and you get nothing."

David was starting to weaken, after all, he was a guy and there was some logic to what she was saying. "I don't know," he said trying to give the appearance of being strong.

"Come on over here," she said patting the mattress beside her. "Come on," she said again in a soft pleading voice. Against his better judgment, he stood up, removed jacket and sat beside her. "That's better," she said and pushed him gently backwards. When she got him down, she started unzipping his pants. He initially objected, but then just caved in. She pulled out his cock with the expertise that only a woman who had done it a thousand times before could do. "Oh, that's a nice one," she said. "And it's so hard."

David was no dummy and knew that was a coded compliment to mask the fact that he had a small one. Nonetheless he appreciated the sentiment. "Let's just see what we can do here." She started stroking him from stem to stern. She made about five slow, deep stokes all the way up and down his little hard dick and then she started rubbing the head in a circular motion with the palm of her hand. After watching her have four consecutive orgasms, her manual manipulation was just too much for him. She could tell he was about to shoot and asked, "Are you ready?" David's scrunched up fuck face gave her the answer. She switched to jacking just the head with her long fingers held in a position that looked like the "Okay" sign.

David shot so much cum that she commented, "Wow, you're just a fountain aren't you." David had cum on his shirt, tie, belt, pants, underwear, the bed, the floor and her hand. She got up and walked to the door in the corner which she was hoping was a bathroom. It was a three-quarter bath and she washed her hands bringing a towel back for him to make some attempt at cleaning up.

He put himself back together and sat down in his chair. She sat on the bed, still naked. The women he dealt with seemed to quickly become comfortable being naked in front of him. He assumed that if a woman exposed herself to him so totally through orgasm there wasn't much else to hide.

Sitting on the edge of the bed, leaning forward over her knees like before, she appeared to be in deep thought. "Is the session over? Or is it still going?" she finally asked.

David said his sessions were like all you can eat buffets. "When you have had enough, then it's over."

"Oh goody," she said playfully. She laid back on the bed, took a deep breath and shut her eyes. David stood up over the bed. Just like before but using the pads of his fingers instead of his knuckles, he touched the inside of her thigh. He ran his hand lightly up the inside her leg until he touched her right between the legs. As he moved over her slit, he sliced his middle finger through her wetness. She moaned and pushed her herself forward wanting more. David continued to slide his fingers over her belly and up to her heaving chest. He hesitated at the base of her breast, caressed it, then pinched and rolled her nipple. Her back arched at an unbelievable angle. Then he told her to open her eyes and he looked at her. She grabbed his hand and held it tightly while she came.

He sat on the edge of the bed, holding her hand and looking at her again and again. He was telling the truth when he said it wasn't over until she said it was. She must have cum a dozen times but she never said quit. The way the session ended was when she just physically could not open her eyes again. He left her on the bed sleeping and went to the storage room to get a change of clothes. When he went through the office, Gisele ask him what was going on and he just said that it was a particularly difficult case, which wasn't a lie.

David and Gisele sat at the little table out in the lobby talking while Emma slept in the exam room. No other customers came in and the phone never rang once. After several hours, Emma came out with a smile and messed up hair. Gisele went behind the counter and poured Emma a glass of cool cucumber water. Emma said, "I'd like to settle the bill now."

"Ma'am, you already paid," said Gisele.

"I know but it was worth double the price." Emma put her credit card on the counter. "Hit it for another five-hundred." Gisele ran the card and gave her back the receipt.

Emma walked over to David in a slow motion exaggerated strut like a model on a catwalk. She bent down and kissed him right on the mouth. "Get ready, Darling," she said. "This place is going start hopping like Studio 54 in 1978. I'm telling everybody."

As soon as the door closed behind her, Gisele said, "We're charging a $1,000 a pop from now on!" She held up both receipts totaling a $1,000. And they did exactly that. Emerald Ferrari must have been much more influential than either of them ever imagined. Television personalities, A and B list movie stars, lingerie models, professional athletes, dancers, and a slew of women "in show business" booked David's services. Most of the women paid in cash to keep it off the records and they all tipped generously.

David and Gisele conspired to "book" half of the cash and keep the rest off the ledgers. David hadn't seen money like this since his carnival days. Things were good.

Chapter 62

Some Surprises

In the fall of 2007, Emerald Ferrari visited David's spa for the last time. She had been the best unpaid partner in the world. Her word of mouth literally generated millions of dollars of revenue over the last five years. She visited at least once a year and all services were free. Emma was in her sixties now and said she was going to retire and move to Montana. She was nominated for a fourth Oscar but didn't win and she just lost her drive to compete in Hollywood. She sold her shares of her clothing business and had more money than Carter had pills. She suggested to David he needed to start thinking about retiring also.

In the late hours, after closing the spa, Gisele and David sat discussing plans. David was fifty-four years old and hadn't once thought about the future because he spent most of his time trying to get away from the past. Gisele was much younger than David and didn't spend any time planning for her future either. She thought the gravy train they were on would last forever, after all, it did survive 9/11.

Gisele finally came out as a lesbian and told him she had a beautiful new significant other. The "Other" was an out of work actress but both of them had been living high on the hog and hadn't saved anything. Their favorite weekend pastimes were going to $300 Broadway plays and eating at Keens Steakhouse. David paid Gisele over six figures a year to clean up, do the laundry, and make appointments, a ridiculously high salary for that level of responsibility but even a salary like that couldn't withstand expenditures so frivolous. David could tell that Gisele was in a mild panic thinking that he might bail on her soon and without warning. He reassured her that he had no intention of retiring and shutting down the spa any time soon but he would develop a personal retirement plan immediately. He suggested she do the same.

Later that week, Gisele found an unusual letter in the office mail. It was postmarked from Oregon. She brought it to David who opened it standing in the middle of the lobby. Gisele stood, looking over his shoulder, curious like all women, even gay women. He told her that the letter was from Janice Goldberg, his former Las Vegas manager. Janice wrote she was reading a gossip column in a trade journal and one of the women in the article mentioned a magical place in New York where "you could get the highest level of sexual satisfaction in a room by yourself" and this "wonderful and handsome guide" would take you to the "promised land". Janice said she immediately recognized the "guide" as Mister Orgasm.

Janice spent several days trying to track down David. She finally found the name of his spa, Day Dreams Spa, on line in a chat room. In her letter, she stated that she was reasonably happy. Of course, she wished things had turned out differently but she met a man and married him even though he was in the cheese business. He was affiliated with the Tillamook cheese production farms and she was never so sick of eating free cheese.

Her husband, Clay, was a kind and gentle man who treated her like she was the only thing that mattered in the world, except cheese. David smiled and teared up at the same time while he was reading. She went on to say that her legs never healed right and she had to have additional operations, two on her left leg and one on her right.

She said her kids never came to see her and she hadn't heard from them in years. However, Clay had a big family and she liked all of his kids and grandkids except one. The poor kid's name was James and he was really a great kid but he was big, wore plaid shirts, had a beard and looked just like he was a member of Rough Lumber. She never really let on she was afraid of him but she was always uneasy around him. She finished her letter with some other trivial things about her life, living on a three acre ranchette, having two dogs and a pending trip to Hawaii. It sounded like Janice had finally found a good life, thank God. David was actually happy for the first time in, he couldn't remember when. He had to wipe a tear off his cheek. Gisele put her hand on his shoulder and gave a supportive squeeze.

In between clients that day, David contacted his banks in Las Vegas for the first time in years. He had been sending money every month for them to invest but he never cared about how much he had, until now. To his surprise, he had a little over a million in cash. The investment brokers liked to keep at least a million in liquid assets for emergencies or for instantaneous investment opportunities. The real surprise was that the brokers had been investing all the other money he sent over the years in tech stocks that were increasing in value at astronomical rates. He had over 200,000 shares of Microsoft, Amazon, Yahoo, Hewlett-Packard, and Dell, plus some other more stable blue chips. His portfolio was worth over $7,000,000.

David was amazed at his wealth. Sending off most of his money for investment, he pretty much lived paycheck to paycheck in his daily life. He decided to do the most stupid thing he had ever done or the smartest, only time would tell. He asked his brokers to cash out everything! They tried to talk him out of it but David wouldn't listen. He wanted all of the money in his hands under his control, right then. His brokers had no choice but to comply and cashed out the whole lifetime of investments.

After all the fees, taxes and other extraneous expenses, David had 4.8 million dollars in his New York account. He couldn't even fathom it, nearly five million dollars! So much for worrying about retirement. He needed to start worrying about spending some before he died, so he started a list.

The first thing on the list was to hire the best private investigator money could buy. The investigator's job...track down all six members of Rough Lumber. David would figure out the rest when the private eye found them, if he could. The second thing on the list was buy a brand-new Cadillac and send it to Janice. She was financially stable and didn't really need it but he thought she would appreciate the sentimental gesture. Lastly, he was going to talk to Gisele about helping her manage her money. Since she had been living with her new girl-friend, she had been spending more money than she was making and acting all high and mighty. Gisele's personality was starting to change for the worst. She was becoming greedy and mean. He wanted to try to stop her from turning into a greedy, mean lesbian bitch.

He started with the Cadillac. All it took was visit to a Cadillac dealer in New York, a couple of phone calls to a Cadillac dealer in Oregon, writing a sizable check and it was done. The retirement planning for Gisele was also easy. He arranged a meeting between a high level personal finance consultant and Gisele for some advice. After talking it over with her significant other, Gisele declined to start investing or saving. They felt like they needed all the money they could get right then. David also wrote out a Last Will and Testament with the aid of a very expensive lawyer.

Finding someone to track down Rough Lumber was much more problematic. He knew nothing about the private detective business and wondered if he should try to do it himself. After he came to his senses, he decided to hire a guy to find them. He went to the police department and started asking if they knew a private eye that was any good. After about a dozen "Get the fuck out of here!" remarks he finally ran into a person who recommended former Detective Lawrence Spignoli.

Spignoli's detective agency was called The Night Ranger Detective Agency. The agency consisted of two employees, a big busted receptionist and Detective Spignoli. When David visited the office, the Detective was out. He visited again the next day and the receptionist said he was out to lunch.

"At ten in the morning?" David asked.

She just shrugged her shoulders.

David came back the third day and found him in his office with his receptionist under his desk giving him head. Doubts about choosing this guy surfaced. David went back for the final time. The detective was in his office and was ready to talk.

David and the detective discussed the situation for hours. The detective agreed that these guys needed to be found and if anyone could find them, it would be him. His rate was $450 per day plus expenses. David agreed to the terms and gave him a $4,500 retainer for the first ten days. The detective would send additional bills as needed and a final bill after the mission was completed.

In the office the next day, Gisele apologized to him for acting ungrateful about the help with the retirement account but she really felt that she "wasn't making enough money" to be able to invest any amount at the moment. She went in for a hug as part of the left-handed apology and their eyes accidentally met and she started to cum while she was hugging him.

She was built a little like a fireplug, putting on twenty pounds since she went to work at the spa, and squeezed the breath out of him while she was cumming. She didn't recover very well and he had to help her over to chair in the lobby. He got her sat down and went to get her a bottle of water. She drank a little and asked, "Is that what you do to those women in there?"

"Pretty much," he said. "But it's dressed up in a nicer package. I'm sorry I let that one get away from me."

"It's on me," she said. "I was all over you and I'm sure you couldn't help it. You know I'm gay, don't you?"

"Of course I know, but the hypnotism works on women. All women. I'm really sorry and I hope this doesn't effect our working relationship."

She took another drink and shook her head "no" and said, "You better be thankful I'm gay or I'd have that shit tied to the bed post in my apartment." David laughed a little.

They started the work day but Gisele smiled a little broader every time a woman walked out of the exam room. David smiled a little less because in his experience, he knew things would not be the same.

Chapter 63

A Detective Story

After exposing Gisele to his prowess, things in the office for the next few days seemed a little tense. When the last customer finally left, David sat down with Gisele to clear the air. Gisele said things were "all strange" at home because of what he did to her the other day.

David apologized profusely and said he had no idea that it was affecting her personal relationship with her significant other. She shook her head and said, "No, no, it's not what you think. I told my girlfriend what happened and she's not jealous or pissed but she wants you to give us both a treatment at the same time. I haven't been able to work up the courage to ask you but she won't let it go. It's a nightly argument." She started to cry and David handed her a tissue. She continued, "I'm sorry to put you in the middle of our relationship." She wiped her eyes waiting for David to say something. David was ominously silent thinking he was about to be played.

She could tell he was wrestling with his conscious. He rubbed his forehead like he had a headache. After what Gisele thought was an interminable amount of time, David said, "Okay."

"Okay, what?" Gisele perked up and David was fearing another hug.

"I'll meet with you and your partner and you can have a session on the house. One session and one session only. One and done, got it?"

She flew at him again and grabbed him around the neck showering him with appreciation.

David put out his hands and tried to block her saying, "Hey, wait a second, remember how all this got started."

"You're right." She backed off, put out her hand and said with fake formality, "Thank you Mister Gideon for the generous offer." David shook her hand, told her to go home, talk to her other half, and let him know what day, after workings hours, would be good for them and he would take care of business.

The next day Gisele announced that this next Friday would be the night. She was all excited. David said Friday would be fine and he was as apprehensive as Gisele was excited. He was thinking of the many more things that could go wrong with this than go right and he was pretty sure he had just been handled.

About two in the afternoon, Gisele announced that he had received a call from a Detective Spignoli and handed him a message with a 702-area code phone number on it. David called and got the Golden Nugget Hotel and Casino in downtown Las Vegas. He asked for the room number on the message. After three rings the detective answered the phone.

He informed David that he had already found two of the Rough Lumber crew. He said he had a plan to ferret out the others by concocting a fake TV show making a documentary on pioneer boy strip groups like the Chippendales or Thunder Down Under. The detective would offer Rough Lumber $50,000 for an interview if they could get all six members back together. The detective said, "Let's let them do our work for us."

David thought it was an ingenious idea. The detective would rent a suite at the Golden Nugget, make contact with the two Rough Lumber members he had already located, and have them reach out to their buddies for an initial interview. They would get $500 each for the interview with the big money for shooting the documentary. Once he had them all in the room together, David could have his way with them. David agreed to the plan and wired the detective his expenses and the money needed to pull off the plan.

David spent the rest of the week thinking of what he could possibly do to exact revenge on the bunch of nearly sixty-year-old men in Rough Lumber. He imagined everything, but really came up with a big zero. Before he knew it, it was Friday. Gisele was giddy with excitement. David was less than enthusiastic.

At 6:00 pm, the appointed time, Gisele and David sat in the lobby waiting for Andie, Gisele's partner, to show up. Thirty minutes went by and Gisele showed concern. An hour went by and Gisele started to get pissed. Finally, at 7:30 pm Andie walked in like nothing had happened. Gisele jumped up and started yelling at her in a loud whisper. "Where have you been? We've been waiting for an hour and a half." Andie was a tall, thin and extremely attractive woman. She bent down and kissed Gisele on the lips with a voracious amount of tongue. Gisele just melted and all was forgiven.

Andie strolled over to David, flipped her long dark hair to one side of her face, posed with her hand on her hip. "Andie Devine Domino," she said. An obvious stage name. He was hoping that Andie was not a well put together she-male. He'd been down that road before.

David said, "David Othello Gideon."

"Cute," she said as she folded her long body into one of the chairs. "So, what are you going to do for me today?" David didn't like her attitude.

Gisele was just standing, mesmerized by Andie's presence. David started to explain, "Usually the clients...."

"Client! Is that what I am, a client." Andie was looking at her nails and never looked at David.

David started again, "Usually our guests go into the exam room...."

"Exam room? This is starting to sound like no fun at all." She turned to Gisele, "Sugar, are you sure this is what you want for me?"

Gisele answered, "It's really fun. He's such a nice guy and makes you feel special."

Andie reached out and touched Gisele's thigh, "I know Sugar. I have no doubt that he makes *you* feel special."

Condescending bitch. "Okay, it's late..."

"Late! It's only eight o'clock." Andie looked disgusted with him.

"Do you want to do this or not?" he asked.

"We do," interjected Gisele. "Let's go to the back room." Gisele put her hand on Andie's shoulder.

"Oh, now it's the back room," Andie said as she got up.

The three of them went to the exam room. David wanted them on the bed but Andie immediately sat down in the "coach's" chair. That left David and Gisele on the bed which was awkward.

David started off, "Usually the women..."

"Usually! You may have noticed that I'm not your usual guest. Have you ever heard the term "Diva"? That's what I'm used to, so you can start again." Andie smiled at Gisele and Gisele nearly swooned.

David rolled his eyes. He was cursed with another mean lesbian bitch. "I don't have time for this. Here's what is going to happen. You two are going to take off your clothes and lie on the bed. I'll do what I do and you will fall into a pile of orgasms. Now get undressed." Andie didn't move. "Now!"

Gisele stripped off in a matter of seconds. Her short, strong, thick body looked attractive and natural. Gisele got in bed urging Andie to do the same. When Andie stood up to disrobe, David sat in the "coach's" chair. She was tall, long legged and big busted. She was thinking that David ought to be counting his lucky stars he gets to see her naked. She pulled off her heels and threw them in David's lap. He put them on the floor beside the chair.

She then dropped her short skirt and blouse to the floor. Standing in bra and panties she struck another pose. Gisele's eyes widened while David's rolled again. She unhooked her bra and flashed Gisele a few times before she finally took it off. She tossed her bra at David too. She'd obviously had some work done. He could see smalls scars underneath her breasts. Looking further, he could tell her nose and lips were also a product of a doctor's imagination.

She started to remove her lavender colored panties. Gisele raised up in anticipation while David prayed there wasn't a dick jammed up in there. She shimmied out of her panties and threw them to Gisele who stuck them to her face and inhaled the aroma. David automatically crinkled his nose at the same time.

Andie posed again making sure he saw her cleanly waxed pussy before she moved to the bed. A couple of hip wiggles, a hair flip to one side of her head and a slow-motion crawl on to the mattress and finally, they were both on the bed. Andie maneuvered Gisele to a place between her legs. Gisele's head rested on Andie's belly. Gisele was hugging Andie's hips and Andie had her long legs wrapped around Gisele's short frame. This appeared to David to be the starting point for most of their love making sessions. It was an Andie dominant position.

"Ladies, would you like to experience it simultaneously or individually?"

Gisele looked at Andie for the answer. Andie just said, "Whatever."

"Simultaneous it is," said David

Chapter 64

Couples Retreat

David stood by the bed and looked at both women as quickly as he could. Andie went off like a bomb and shoved Gisele's head all the way down between her legs. Even though Gisele was cumming too, she tried to perform cunnilingus but mostly just got her head mashed into Andie's twat, a place she had been many times before, but suffocation looked like a real possibility this time. Andie trapped Gisele's head by wrapping her thighs around it and hooking her foot under her other leg in a Mixed Martial Arts submission choke hold. Andie had two fistfuls of Gisele's hair and was fucking the shit out of Gisele's face.

Andie looked up at David and screamed, "Give me some more, she hasn't had enough." David wasn't sure if she was referring to herself in third person, her pussy or if she was calling Gisele "she". David looked at Andie and her grip tightened on Gisele who just made a muffled noise.

Andie finished cumming and released Gisele from her grip. Gisele didn't move. She's been choked out! David jumped up and rolled the little woman over. Her face was sticky with Andie's juice and her lip was bloody. "Good God, Gisele." She started to wake up. She wiped her face with her hand and tried to sit up. David helped her. Andie scooted to the head of the bed leaned back against the wall. David got Gisele up sitting on the end of the bed and said, "I think you got choked out. Is it always like this?"

Gisele looked at Andie before she started to speak. "She doesn't mean to do it. It just feels so good that sometimes she gets carried away."

"Bullshit, that's just not right."

"What the fuck do you know?" Andie said getting up on her knees.

"I know you're a sadistic bitch."

Gisele grabbed David's arm, "It's Okay."

"It's not Okay! Its abuse."

"She likes it, don't you Babe?" Andie was looking at Gisele.

Gisele turned around with a renewed confidence. "I really don't like being hurt."

Andie sat back on the bed and spread her legs, exposing her smooth hole. "You never complained before. It's just because your boss is here." Andie started massaging herself with her fingers, her pussy glistening with wetness. Gisele actually licked her lips. David had never rolled his eyes so many times in his life.

Gisele said, "Can we start over?" David didn't know exactly which one of them she was talking to, maybe both. Gisele moved up and started eating Andie's pussy. Andie smiled like the cat that ate the canary. David thought, *what in the world am I doing here? They don't need me.*

David said he should just excuse himself and let them have at it but Gisele convinced him to make them both cum again. Gisele sat up next to Andie at the head of the bed. They were holding hands, "We're ready."

David looked at them both and they fell against each other. Andie started to shove Gisele's head back down between her legs but Gisele wasn't going for it this time. Gisele stood up and stuck her pussy right in Andie's face and Andie didn't like it one bit. David thought it was funny. Gisele grabbed Andie's long hair and rode her face like a bucking bronc. Andie's head even banged against the wall a few times. David thought that was even more funny.

When both of them were done, they sat down leaning against the back of the bed. Gisele was caressing Andie's ample boobs. "Have you had enough?" asked David.

"From you?" Andie said.

"You guys are the ones dripping with sweat and blood." Gisele put her hand to her lips to see if she was still bleeding.

Andie said, "I'm not done. I haven't had anything I couldn't do for myself yet. And if I can't do it, I'll get this little cunt to do it for me. Watch this."

Andie got on her hands and knees and told Gisele to eat her ass. Gisele did! Andie looked back and said, "See what I mean. Now if you wish to indulge yourself in your fantasy, quit staring at this cunt eating my ass and look at me." David looked at her and Andie had a wonderful orgasm while Gisele licked her back-door hole.

David just turned and faced the wall, throwing his hands up in frustration. He turned back around when he heard them finish up.

Andie assumed her position against the wall at the head of the bed. Gisele laid beside her and fondled Andie's breasts just like before. Gisele looked at Andie and asked if she could have another one. Andie took Gisele's face in her hand and said, "If you want one, go ahead. It's free."

David loathed this mean lesbian bitch. Why did all mean lesbian bitches have to be so...mean?

"You ready?" David asked. Gisele nodded. David looked at her and she started to cum. She tried to clutch Andie but Andie pushed her away and stood up saying, "Is that the bathroom? I need to pee."

Gisele tried to ask her to stay with her during her orgasm but she couldn't form the words. It was a particularly strong orgasm. David went over and put a reassuring hand on Gisele's back. She was face down muffling her moans in the pillows.

Andie flushed the toilet and walked out of the restroom still naked, wiping her pussy with a tissue. She threw the tissue in the corner of the exam room. *Bitch*, he thought. She saw David with his hand on Gisele's back and took great offense. "You fuckin' asshole! Nobody touches my whore unless I say they can." She took two giant steps toward him. He looked at her in the eyes on the third step.

She started to have an orgasm right when she tried to throw a round-house kick to his head. Half-way through the spin the orgasm gripped her. She folded up on the floor but still had the where-of-it-all to continue to crawl toward him. David assumed a fighting position that looked more like a Tango dance step than a fighting position. As he was standing *en garde*, a strange realization went through his head. His life was like a Salvador Dali painting. It was real, but some how it just couldn't be this bizarre.

The scene: He was in a room fighting off a naked, whirling, kicking, mean lesbian bitch in the throes of orgasm while her naked, halfway normal lesbian lover and mostly decent employee until recently, laid on the bed screaming in ecstasy into a pillow. All the while he was wearing a suit and tie and doing this shit for free. He promised himself, in that mad moment, he would try to lead a more normal life in the future.

Andie ceased her attack and slithered back onto the bed and they continued the session. At two in the morning, David walked out of the exam room after giving them no less than thirty-five orgasms between them. A new record. Both women were naked and asleep on the bed soaked with female cum juice. Their lips and eyes were bloody and swollen from such rough sex and they were exhausted from all of the strenuous orgasms and other pugilistic activities.

The exam room was a wreck but David felt sure that Gisele would have it all put back together by Monday morning. He locked the front door behind him and went to his apartment for some soul searching and much needed rest.

Chapter 65

The Vegas Plan

At eleven in the morning on Saturday, David got a call on his new cell phone. It was the detective telling him that the two known members of Rough Lumber agreed to round up the others for the initial interview which would take place the following Saturday. It seems that none of these idiots ever left Vegas.

The detective explained if all of them showed up, he would make a date two weeks after that for them to meet for the taping of the documentary. He told them this was a TV documentary and it lasted six weeks, one episode airing each week. "Rough Lumber" would be the name of the second episode and of course all of them would be featured. He told David they tried to beat him out of more money and he agreed to pay the group $100,000 for the interview instead of the initial offer of $50,000. The detective said he put up a big display attempting to reject the offer but eventually caved in to their demands. The detective laughed on the other end of the phone, "I guess I could have promised them a million each since we're not going to pay them anyway." David clicked off his new cell phone and thought Detective Spignoli was enjoying his job way too much.

David spent his Saturday lying around the apartment trying to recover from the previous night's fiasco. He hoped that he and Gisele could continue their good working relationship. He watched college football and ordered Chinese take out from down the street. On Sunday, he went to MOMA, the Museum of Modern Art, which took the biggest part of the day. He felt almost normal by Sunday night.

As he lay down to sleep, he kept thinking about what his purpose was for finding Rough Lumber. He knew revenge was the biggest part of it but he just couldn't put a handle on how to exact it. Maybe he should seek some advice. He grabbed his new phone and called Janice in Oregon. It was several hours earlier on the West Coast so he didn't disturb her sleep.

He explained how he had Rough Lumber in the crosshairs but didn't know what to do with them. He asked her if she had any suggestions. After the initial shock and apprehension passed, she said she would like to see them castrated. David didn't know if she was kidding or not. Finally, she said for him to tell her when Rough Lumber would be all together and she would meet him in Vegas to form a plan. She would consult her husband on the matter. David didn't know if that was a good sign or not.

On Monday morning, Gisele and David sat down to have a little talk, again. She apologized over and over for Andie's behavior and thanked him just as many times for the service he delivered. Gisele came in on Sunday and cleaned the office to a point where it looked better than it had ever looked. David was pleased things were once more right as rain.

David could hardly stand the anticipation of the upcoming weekend when all of Rough Lumber would be together for the first time in years. Friday took forever to roll around and when it did, he couldn't sleep that night. On Saturday at four in the afternoon, Detective Spignoli called. He reported that all six members of Rough Lumber attended the preliminary interview and he paid each one $500 in cash. He told them to buy some new clothes with the money but they went to drink it up, gamble and pay for hookers.

The next two-week period moved even slower than the first week did. David closed up shop on Wednesday before the target Saturday. He gave Gisele time off and he flew to Las Vegas. He was staying at the Golden Nugget in a different tower than Detective Spignoli.

Janice and Clay had a room at the MGM Grand on the Strip. They agreed to meet David and the detective at the Nugget in the suite set up as a TV studio. Detective Spignoli had purchased a music mixing console, two microphones, an amplifier, lights and cameras to make the room look official. He got most of the equipment from the Gold and Silver Pawn Shop for which David would reimburse dearly.

David and the detective occupied the fake studio suite anxiously awaiting the arrival of Janice and Clay or at least David was anxious. Spignoli told him several times to sit down and quit pacing. Finally, a knock on the door. The detective yelled, "Come in!" before David could respond. Janice burst through the door, ran and hugged David around the neck. She wouldn't let go. Clay followed her through the door. He was a tall distinguished looking gentleman with grey hair, about seventy years old wearing what looked like might be a golfing outfit.

Janice let go of David and wiped away a tear. She grabbed Clay by the arm and pulled him over close, "This is David," she said. Clay shook hands with him and announced his name. David introduced Spignoli and they all sat on the ample couches and stuffed chairs in the suite.

Janice said that Clay knew everything. She emphasized, "everything" and looked into Clay's eyes. David let Detective Spignoli tell the story of how he set up the sting then Janice asked, "Why now?" David told her he had just come into a substantial amount of money and he could afford to find them, so he did. "And," he said. "It's finally time."

When the question came up, "What do you want to do to them?" they just sat around scratching their heads. They made a few jokes, but in the end, it was left up to Janice and Clay to figure it out. Detective Spignoli would gather Rough Lumber in the makeshift studio and hire some girls, David would pay the expenses and Janice would drop the hammer. Those were their roles but David still had no idea what Janice was going to do.

Janice closed her eyes and kissed David on the cheek, shook hands with Spignoli and they all parted ways until Saturday at 7:00 pm. David spent his time like he used to, playing blackjack and going to the movies. By noon on Saturday, he had amassed four grand. Making money was never a problem for David. However, sustaining happiness was impossible.

Chapter 66

The Sting

Detective Spignoli hired a couple of good looking young women to play "studio employees" to make the sting look more plausible. He auditioned the girls which meant whomever was willing to have sex with him got the job. Out of the nine hopefuls, one girl hiked up her dress and he got her from behind and another agreed to a blow job. A third one gave him a hand job but she didn't get a part. The other six interviews resulted in five rejections and one rejection with prejudice after the girl slapped Spignoli across the face.

At 6:00 pm, David, Clay, Janice, Detective Spignoli, and the two girls met in the studio suite. They finalized their plans and sorted out the equipment. Janice and David would hide in the second bedroom while Detective Spignoli and the girls would greet the members of Rough Lumber as they came in. Clay would be in the master bedroom and act like a TV executive.

At 7:15 pm, four of the Rough Lumber crew knocked on the door. The girls escorted them into the "studio" and had them sit in four of the six straight back chairs lined up in a row. The girls kept the guys entertained by serving drinks and sitting in their laps. These guys were around sixty years old and the girls were in their twenties. The whole scene was disgusting. At 7:30 pm a fifth member knocked on the door. At nearly 8:00 pm the last member showed up. He was already drunk.

When the last member sat in the chair, Clay came out and said they would like to start the interview. The girls went to the side of the room and Spignoli positioned himself behind a camera. Clay had a script in his hand and started asking questions, "How did you meet? Why and how did you decide to start dancing? What kind of paydays did you have? How did it feel to be pioneers in the field of male exotic dancing? Would they be willing to dance for them on film?" Clay made a motion to Spignoli to turn the camera off, which he faked with flare.

Clay said, "We didn't tell you, but if you are willing to let us record you dancing one more time, another $100,000 payment is in it for the group. That's a hundred grand for the interview and another hundred grand for the dance. So, what do you say to $34,000 a piece for the interview and dance?"

They all looked around at each other and agreed. Even at nearly sixty years old, they were all so conceited they thought every woman would still want to see them naked. Clay explained they would shoot the dance scene first and finish the interview after. Clay told them they would have an hour to work up a thirty second routine. They assured Clay it wouldn't take that long. The girls stayed with them to help out and give them compliments to keep them distracted. Clay and Spignoli went to the second bedroom where David and Janice were hiding. They giggled for a minute or two as they peeked out the door and saw them line dancing to Rod Stewart's *Hot Legs* playing through the studio boom box.

In forty minutes, the crew stated that they were ready. Clay and Spignoli went out to meet them. Spignoli assumed a position behind the camera and Clay sat in the "director's" chair. "Okay," Clay said, "Strip." Rough Lumber stripped off their clothes faster than greased lightening. Each man was playing with his cock trying to get it to fill out a little for the camera. Clay, acting his role perfectly said, "Gentlemen, we have fluffers to help you with that. " Clay snapped his fingers and the hired girls moved in and started working their dicks. When each one was half hard, Clay said, "Start your act." The girls moved away, Spignoli turned on the boom box and started his fake filming. The guys lined up and began a really simple routine. About a minute into the routine, Clay cut them off and said he filmed enough dancing. "Congratulations, you just made $100,000." Clay took out a brief case and opened it up. It looked like it was full of money but it actually had a dozen hundred dollar bills stacked on top of cut copy paper. To the greedy, naked members of Rough Lumber, it looked real. Clay shut the case after allowing a short glimpse.

"Now sit in the chairs. We're going to do some artsy shots," Clay said nonchalantly. The guys asked if they were supposed to put their clothes back on but the answer was no. When they sat down, they were instructed to put their hands behind their backs because they were going to be handcuffed. Four were willing but two didn't want to do it. Clay snapped his fingers and Spignoli began handcuffing the compliant dancers. As soon as they were cuffed, the girls started trying to get them hard again by sucking their dicks. When the dissenting two saw the reward for being handcuffed, they complied.

Big, hairy, old, naked Rough Lumber sat in the chairs, hands cuffed behind them with the cuffs woven through the chair seat. The girls tied each of the dancer's legs to the legs of the chair. They willingly let their legs be tied because each man got a quick dick sucking when done. For a finishing touch, the girls put a piece of duck tape over the guys' mouths and gave it a big sloppy kiss.

When the stage was set, Janice and David revealed themselves from the second bedroom. Rough Lumber showed no signs of recognizing them, of course, it had been thirty something years and none of them had a conscience. They thought Janice and David were more studio representatives. Janice, in a booming professional sounding voice, "Okay boys! Drop your cocks and pull up your socks!" Rough Lumber looked around at each with their taped mouths and wondered what the hell she was talking about. "Anybody recognize me, bitches?" She paused for a long time, turning her face from side to side slowly so they could get a good look.

"Nobody recognizes me? How about this guy?" She pointed to David. There was no sign of recognition in their eyes. Both David and Janice were thinking, *how could they do what they did to us and not be haunted by it?* David stepped forward to give them a good look.

"Well boys, my name is... well, it doesn't matter. Let's just say that my name is your worst nightmare." She looked at each one and still no recognition. "You guys are a bunch of cold-hearted bitches, aren't you?" She looked at them handcuffed and mouths taped. "With really limp dicks." She laughed at them.

She grabbed David, shoved him up close to the naked guys, and said, "You don't remember him?" None of those assholes even had a glimmer of memory. She shoved David back behind her. "I can't believe this." She was wondering what despicable things they had done in their lives that could completely erase the memory of robbing, maiming, raping, and sodomizing an innocent couple in a Las Vegas parking lot.

"Girls," she said to the two hired starlets. "Start with the first one and get him back up. I want to see what he's got." The two helpers went over and started working on the man's dick. Within a few minutes, he had a spectacular hard-on. Janice thought, *What a waste of an incredible dick.*

"Okay girls, my turn." Janice reached into her oversized purse that was sitting on a table in the studio and pulled out a simple, old fashion, sand paper covered ping pong paddle. She walked over to Rough Lumber No. 1 and without hesitation, bashed the living shit out of his enlarged cock with the ping pong paddle. Janice was in her mid-sixties but was as strong as an ox because she had been doing physical therapy for thirty years and walking on crutches for most of that time. Her upper body strength was tremendous.

Rough Lumber No. 1's eyes went wide with panic and pain. Janice had split the head of his dick open. He was bleeding profusely from a one-and-a-half-inch wide gash. His dick shrank in seconds and hung between his legs looking like a noodle with a plum gushing blood on the end of it. Rough Lumber Numbers 2 through 6 were trying desperately to escape their bindings. The best they could do was inch their chairs around in different directions by hopping like rabbits. Rough Lumber No. 1 nearly succumbed to the pain. He slumped over moaning into his duct tape while he continued to bleed profusely on the floor.

Janice walked over to Rough Lumber No. 2. She ran her hand through his greasy hair and jerked his head back. She looked him in the face, "Remember me now?" Still nothing. "Girls, do your thing." This time the young starlets were a little hesitant. "Girls," she said more sternly, snapping her fingers. They went to work on Rough Lumber No. 2.

He fought it the best he could but in the end, it was just a physical reaction that he couldn't help. His rod grew to its full glorious length. "Move girls." Janice stepped in, wound up and smacked the ever-loving hell fire out of his cock. He jerked uncontrollably in his bindings, screaming into his duck tape. "Look at that!" She pointed to his dick. It was poking out in a right angle half-way down the shaft. She literally, broke his dick in half. It started swelling and turning purple at the break point. David's little cock retreated up into his chest somewhere.

She moved to Rough Lumber No. 3. "I remember you." She bent down and whispered in his ear. "I'm the woman you raped in the parking lot, after breaking my legs. Remember me now?" He recognized her and went hopping off towards the door in his chair. He hopped ten or fifteen times, but he only moved about an inch with each hop. She laughed at him.

"Girls, get this man up so I can do my work." They were extremely hesitant but were afraid not to try their best. Rough Lumber No. 3 refused to get hard. "That's Okay. I didn't think he would prove to be much of a man." She reached into her purse and pulled out a pair of vise grip pliers. Rough Lumber No. 3 went hopping toward the door again.

Janice got in front of him, kneeled down and stretched his cock out as far as it would go. "I hate touching your nasty dick and I resent you for making me do this." She put the head of his cock into the vise grips, squeezed them completely shut, locking them into place. Rough Lumber No. 3 nearly passed out from the pain. The vise grips were locked on him and hanging heavily between his legs. The pliers weighed about two pounds which increased the amount of painful pressure on his dick. It was a constant pain showing on Rough Lumber No. 3's face. Janice slapped the dangling pliers back and forth a few times causing black-out levels of discomfort. Satisfied with her work, she went to Rough Lumber No. 4.

"What can I do for you?" she asked sarcastically. "How about I just cut it off. Get this over with quickly. What do you say?" Rough Lumber No. 4 was shaking his head. "Okay then, I'll give you a special treat, since you were the second jackass to climb on me." She went to her purse and retrieved a six-inch-long glass tube. "Hey, Honey," she said to him. "I'm going to stick this up your miserable, foul smelling dick and then hit it with my paddle. Won't that be fun?"

"Girls, get over here and see if this asshole is a man." The girls only got him about half way hard but that was good enough. Janice greased the glass tube with some kind of red lubricant. David thought it might have been iodine or Betadine solution but it was actually habanero sauce.

Janice worked the glass tube and slid it up his dick until nothing was showing. She stood up and watched him for a while to see if the pepper sauce would have any effect. Within seconds it started burning. A few more seconds passed and it was burning badly. When he started screaming into his duck tape she smacked his cock with the paddle using a forehand stroke. She returned serve with a back hand and then another forehand smash straight down. Three tremendous blows in a second and a half. The glass tube was shattered inside his dick. Pepper sauce seeped into each cut. Rough Lumber No. 4 had lost his mind, truly. He was conscious but somehow psychologically disassociated.

She turned around and said, "Number five, you're next. One of you guys, stuck something up my best friend's ass back then in the parking lot. It's only fair we return the favor." She reached in her purse and pulled out a small seven-inch flexible dildo. "This doesn't look like much." She held it up and wiggled it at his face. "But, I modified this one. It's got two razor blades in it. You'll barely feel a thing."

She kicked Rough Lumber No. 5 over and lifted the chair so she could get to his ass. He was wiggling so much and his butt was smashed against the seat of the chair so tightly that she couldn't get it in. "Hold still, bitch." He kept squirming. Spignoli walked over and kicked him in the face. "Oh, by the way, Number Five, I put pepper on this too." She shoved it in his ass, pulled it back and forth a couple of times and then used her thumb to push it in beyond sight. "There," she said. "Enjoy that." He was crying as blood trickled out of his hole.

"Okay, Number Six, I have many more tricks up my sleeve, but you'll get what Number One got. A quick smack to the head of your precious cock and we'll be done for tonight. Okay?" He actually shook his head in agreement. "Girls get him up." They went to work on Rough Lumber No. 6. The asshole almost looked like he was enjoying it. When he had a full hard-on, Janice whacked it with the paddle. It didn't split open or break like the first two so she smacked it again. It still didn't split or break but a huge goiter like swelling came up on the side and ran half way down his dick. She stared at it for second trying to decide if that was good enough. David was watching in anticipation. She must have flashed back to the parking lot so many years ago because it became apparent what she had done to this man was not enough. She reached way back with the paddle and slapped his swollen dick with a vengeance. The goiter swelling burst, splattering a bloody liquid all over Rough Lumber No. 6's chest. He took one look down at his burst dick and passed out in the middle of a scream.

Janice went back to No. 3 who had the vise grips clamped on the head of his cock. She kneeled down between his legs and said, "I'm certainly not going to leave a good pair of pliers with you. You fucking sadistic rapist. You broke my goddamn legs!" She stood up, jerking the vice grips with all her might. Half the head of No. 3's dick came off in the pliers. She stood there with them in her hand for a moment watching his dick gush blood like a water hose.

Janice dropped the vice grips and ran to Clay, falling into his arms exhausted, ashamed, but avenged. Spignoli said "Go on get her out of here." Janice and Clay left the room never saying another word. Spignoli told David to leave also and he would pay off the girls and sterilize the room. "We committed about ninety different crimes here today," he said not exaggerating at all.

David handed Spignoli a small stack of business cards. Make sure each one of them gets one of these. The cards were white with bold black letters. MISTER ORGASM was all it said. "Sure boss." David looked around the room one last time. He noticed Janice's purse on the counter. He grabbed it and ran. Going down in the elevator, he looked inside to find a cork screw, a bottle of sulfuric acid, an ice pick, the habanero sauce and five more glass tubes.

David flew back to New York that night. In six days, he received a final invoice from Detective Spignoli. It was the best and worst $119,000 he had ever spent.

Chapter 67

Living a Normal Life, Not

Three weeks after his Vegas trip, his life was getting back to normal. He worked the spa, servicing the older, richer ladies who foolishly tried to find fulfillment with his services. Gisele's life was in turmoil which meant nothing had changed except she was getting a little pushier with the clients. Gisele could also tell David was acting differently but he told her it was because he lost a lot of money in Vegas. She suggested he try Atlantic City next time because she always had good luck there.

About a month after the Vegas trip, David received a letter from Oregon. It was from Clay. He said he regretted that they had to meet under such strange circumstances and Janice was happy to see him again. He went on to say after they had returned to Oregon, Janice went to the synagogue every day and prayed for hours. She nearly wore out the rabbi. In a couple of weeks, she was whole again, happier than she had ever been. Clay went on to thank him for setting up the "sting" and taking all those risks for her.

After reading the letter, he felt so much better but he still wasn't sure if he had done a good thing or not. In God's eyes, there was no doubt what they had done was an abomination, but for Janice, it brought closure. David knew it was wrong but, deep down, he thought that big tough Rough Lumber got exactly what they deserved. He was surprised that something in his life turned out right.

David's heart was no longer into operating the spa but it was safe, profitable and worked well for his circumstances. He and Gisele had a discussion and he told her that he was going to increase his prices. That way he would only have to work a day or two a week. Gisele was concerned about money and David assured her that she would still be well compensated.

The prices were going up from $1,000 a visit to $2,500 a visit. They sent out emails and texts to all customers who chose to leave their contact information with them. The prices would change in two months. The spa was flooded with women trying to get the bargain price of only $1,000. He had about ten customers a day. He was working harder and making more money than he'd ever done before. His price increase warning was counter-productive to the outcome he wanted which was to slow down a bit.

At the end of the two months, they shut the spa for a week just to rest from the madness. When they reopened, they were going to try to have the spa open on Tuesdays and Thursdays only. On the first Tuesday, they had three customers and on Thursday they had two. It was a far cry from the fifty or so customers they had each week during the "sale".

They worked out the math and decided that Gisele could keep her salary and David could pay the bills and still have a quarter of million in profit a year. This would be acceptable as long as they could average five customers a week.

Then the unthinkable happened in the year 2008. The market collapsed and all those ladies with a bad love life, time on their hands and money to burn, no longer had money to burn. Their customer base dropped from five a week to two a week which wasn't enough to pay Gisele, the rent and other expenses.

David was in great financial shape because he converted all of his stocks to cash the year before. He was always lucky when it came to making money. He was just 'snake bit' when it came to love and happiness. Gisele and David huddled up again and decided to lower the prices to see if they could get some of their customers back. "Fire sale! Five-hundred bucks!" said Gisele and the advertisements went out. After a couple of months, they could only get eight to ten customers a week with any regularity. They were making less than when they charged $2,500 a service so they changed the price back. Gisele was smart enough to see the writing on the wall. If business didn't pick up soon, the operation would fold.

Chapter 68

The Customer

On a cold February morning in 2009 a lady they had never seen before walked into the spa. She looked familiar. She wasn't tall, nor short, her hair was brownish and hung wavy down to her shoulders. She was fit and looked to be in her forties.

"Am I in the right place?" she asked holding out a business card with Day Dreams Spa on the face of it.

"Yes, you are," said Gisele. "What can we do for you today?"

"I'm not sure. Some friends recommended this place to me. They said it was a spa that could help you...you know, uh?" She started rotating her hands trying to get Gisele to finish her sentence.

Gisele said, "Have an orgasm."

"Yes"

"Well you have come to the right place. No pun intended." Gisele explained what was going to happen and how much it would cost. The lady forked over the cash without batting an eye. The lady was directed to the exam room and David went in seconds later. He explained how things worked and sat in his "coach's" chair while she sat on the edge of the bed. David went through the procedures in more detail.

"So, I can take my clothes off or not, it doesn't matter?" she asked.

"That's correct. The orgasm is an auto-orgasm produced by the hypnotism. I never touch you but the onset is very fast. Most women receive the service with their clothes off. But it's entirely up to you." David sat back in his chair with his fingers steepled at his chin.

"I think I will take my clothes off." She started to disrobe, her jacket first, then her shoes. She took off her slacks and underwear but hesitated with her blouse which hung down to her thighs. David could see she was struggling.

"Do you want me to leave the room while you finish?"

After a moment, "No. It's alright. It's just me." She looked like she was about to cry. Slowly she turned her back to David and took off her blouse. She wasn't wearing a bra. He could see her run her hands up and rub the back of her neck like she was trying to alleviate the tension. Then he could tell she crossed her arms in front of her breasts.

She turned around and dropped her hands. A giant, beautiful rose bush covered in roses was tattooed across her entire chest. Both of her breasts were gone. Surgically removed. "I'm very self-conscious about this," she said as she laid down on the bed.

"It might be the most beautiful thing I have ever seen." He knelt down beside the bed and took her hand. Something he did on rare occasion. "Are you ready?" She shook her head "yes". "Then look at me."

She looked and started having an immediate orgasm. She clasped both her hands on his, rolled to her side facing him and pulled her knees up. In a minute when she finished, she rolled over on her back still holding his hand. She was breathing hard and slowing flexing one leg up and then the other.

"When you're ready, you can look at me again."

"I really don't think I was ready for that one let alone the next."

"When you're ready."

She took a couple of deep breaths, turned on her side facing him again and looked. As so often was the case the second one was stronger than the first. She let go of his hand and reached for his shoulders. David hugged her forcefully in return with her flat tattooed chest up against his. She felt so...vulnerable. She squeezed him and released a little and squeezed him again in a pulsating manner. He tried to time his caresses with hers.

When finished, she fell onto her back on the bed again, holding her forehead with one hand and rubbing her pussy with the other. Her legs kept undulating. "I never knew," was all she said. David was hoping that it was a good expression.

"When you're ready," David said again.

"How many of these do I get?"

David explained, "It's like a buffet. All you can eat."

"As many as I want?"

"All you can handle."

"What a good service. Can I go on line and give you a review?"

David chuckled a little, telling her that they tried to keep a low profile and although he appreciated it, reviews were not necessary. "We just like satisfied customers."

"Well I may be here all day then."

"You're more than welcome." She got into her side position holding David's hand and they looked at each other. Once again, she wrapped her arms around him but pulled him down on her this time. Her flat chest smashing into his. This one lasted longer than the first two.

When she was done, she put her hands between her legs. "Do you have a tissue or rag? I'm dripping wet"

"That's a good thing, isn't it?" David said as he got up to get one of the hundred hand towels from the cabinet.

She took it from him and started cleaning herself up. She had no inhibitions now. It was as if they had been married for a dozen years. "Ever since I got cancer, I've been miserable. My husband left me for a newer model without any dents or scratches. My kids moved off but not before they let me know they were ashamed of me. Then I started feeling the same way."

"About what, the tattoos or losing your breasts?"

"Both," she said. "At first there was denial, then anger and all of the other phases of grief. I didn't know what to do. I listened to all my friends who really aren't my friends anymore. Once I couldn't get a job, they all abandoned me."

"What kind of work do you do?" David stared as she sat on the bed with her knees pulled up to her chest.

"I'm an actor. Was and actor I should say. They dropped me like a hot potato when I got sick."

"I thought I recognized you but, I can't seem to remember any of your movies."

"I was in the Season Series movies. You know, Autumn in New England, Winter in Prague, Spring in Paris, Summer in Malibu."

"I remember those, I think."

"The Autumn movie was the best. We made millions. The Winter movie grossed less than half the Autumn movie, the Spring movie was selectively released in regional theaters and the Summer movie went straight to video. We probably shouldn't have made the last one but the contract called for all four movies. Making the fourth movie was cheaper than fighting the lawsuits." She hesitated, "Listen to me, I'm talking too much."

"A famous actress in my spa. How 'bout that. When you're ready, we can go again."

"I think I'm ready now. But, can you lie on top of me?"

"I suppose I can." David awkwardly got on top of her. She wrapped her arms and legs around him.

"Now," she said. David looked at her. She clinched and squirmed beneath him like she was having the best orgasm of her life. David couldn't help but get hard and dry hunched her through his slacks. He was fifty-six years old and was dry hunching like a teenager in the back seat of a Ford Fairlane.

Even when she finished, she kept squirming underneath him, squeezing and caressing. He kept hunching. After a few more strokes, he said, "I think I'm going to cum in my pants."

"Oh no you're not," she said. "Stand up, hurry." David jumped up beside the bed. She sat up with him standing between her legs. "Don't cum yet," she instructed as she unzipped him. She pulled out his little rock hard cock and expertly stroked it half a dozen times before he exploded all over her beautiful rose bush. His knees gave way and he had to sit down in his chair.

She rubbed the juice into her tattoo. "That was not very professional of me," he said.

"Are you kidding?" she said not really asking a question. "This was perfect." He didn't know if it was perfect or not but it was about as good as it ever got for him.

She asked if she could get a shower and he directed her to the little three-quarter bathroom in the corner. She moved around the exam room, still naked and seemed to be comfortable in her own skin despite her obvious surgery. She closed the door behind her and he listened to the water running while she showered. She came out drying herself off, not trying in the least to cover her nakedness.

She sat back on the bed with her knees up, arms wrapped around them. He could tell there was something on her mind. Finally, she asked, "Have you ever..." she never finished the question.

"Have I ever, what?" asked David.

"Do you ever have relationships with your clients?"

"Every now and then, something like what we just did happens but I have never had a relationship with a client. As a matter of fact, I'm not very good at relationships at all."

"I can see how it would take a strong woman to be able to tolerate what goes on in here."

"That's why I gave up years ago. I can barely tolerate what goes on in here myself. Just imagine the ugliest, fattest, smelliest, hairiest, most obnoxious man you can imagine, got him in your mind? Then imagine you having to make him cum until he doesn't want to cum anymore. He's paying big money for the service so he thinks he's entitled. Then he asked you to lay on top of him and then he wants to squirt his cum on your chest or in your face. That's what it's like most of the time. Not everyone is as beautiful and intriguing as you."

"It's kind of like being a whore, isn't it?"

"Now that you mention it, I guess that's what I am. Although I've always thought I was helping women. At least that's what I thought."

"You helped me. Maybe too much. I don't want to leave." She raised her shoulders as if to say, "Oh well" and then she laughed a little. She got up and started to get dressed. When she was ready to leave the exam room, she stuck out her hand and shook his. "It's been one of the best and most unusual experiences in my life. I know you hear that all the time."

"This is what I had in mind when I started this business. Mostly I service the "My husband doesn't get me" types or the "I'm so homely I can't get anybody" types. You might be the most singularly unique and sexy client I've ever had."

She reached out and touched his arm, "It's only because I let you shoot your wad on my rose bush."

"I know you are kidding but you may be right."

She turned to leave the room. "I'll see you soon." She stopped at the reception counter and dug through her purse. She handed Gisele a $1,000 tip. She looked at Gisele and said, "He's special."

When she left the office, David told Gisele to Google up Autumn in New England, the movie. Gisele did and was surprised to see the lady on the monitor. "She's a movie star!"

David asked, "What's her name?"

"Olive Lancaster."

"Google her name, would you?" Gisele Wikipediaed her, found a rather long list under filmography, and a just as significant list under stage and TV. David walked behind the counter and looked at the screen. "She was something special wasn't she."

Gisele held up ten one-hundred dollar bills, "You must have been something special too."

David grabbed the fanned-out bills and handed her one. "For once, I guess I was."

Chapter 69

Winding Down

After a few months of slow business, two to three customers per week, David received a letter from Clay, Janice's husband. He said she had a prolific change in personality. He said Janice cried every day for a month and then found a deep and profound alternate religion. He said she spends most of her time in a commune in the hills near the Washington border growing vegetables and singing Kumbaya. Clay said he filed for divorce but the only one sad about it was him because she didn't give a shit anymore. In so many words, Clay said, "Thanks for nothing." He concluded the note with telling David that Janice sold the Caddy and gave all the money to the head "Ass-holy Man" at the commune. The commune needed the money because smoking butt-loads of weed was a common practice of the new religion. It sounded like Janice finally had to disassociate herself from everything that happened in the past. David hoped she had found peace at last but really suspected she just found a new means of screwing up. It was another monumental relationship failure in David's life

David also struggled with getting some of that Rough Lumber imagery out of his head. He wouldn't call it PTSD but some things a male human just shouldn't see or endure. Besides the first atrocities that Rough Lumber inflicted on them there was the revenge... Six naked men, each man with an abnormally large dick standing erect. Intimidating enough. Then there was the imagery of each of those dicks broken and bleeding and those big burly guys reduced to sniveling little bitches. David's dick shriveled up every time he thought about it and he thought about it a lot. Maybe *he* needed to run away to an ashram and smoke weed all day.

David began to dread going to the office and pleasing the rich spoiled women that could afford his service. He had priced himself right out of what he originally intended to do, which was help people. Now he was just the whore that Olive said he was. His only pleasure at the spa was Olive's once a month visit. He enjoyed her company immensely.

Eventually, Olive decided to let him have her. She said, "I'll let you in me but you have to get it really wet, because you're so big." David hadn't been considered too big since his Senior Prom date thought he was huge just because he shared company with Big Cindy.

"You know how big I am. You had your hands all over me and you even put it in your mouth last time. I'm not even average size let alone too big."

She was naked on the bed with her beautiful rose bush tattoo exposed. "That's how I know you're going to be too big. The mouth test. Touching you, I thought maybe it would fit. But when I gave it a good suck last time, I knew, it would really be a struggle."

David walked to the small closet in the exam room and opened the door to expose several shelves filled with linen, lubricants and lascivious instruments of pleasure and pain to include dildos, butt plugs, vibrators, whips, gags, restraints and other erotica. Olive took one look and said, "Now that's a pantry."

"You never know what a client might want." He pulled out a small squeeze bottle of a lightly scented and flavored KY oil which he held up next to his face. "Guaranteed to increase the pleasure of both the woman and the man. Says so right here." He pointed to the words on the bottle.

"Well get over here and get you clothes off. We're going to get slick."

David took his clothes off and laid them across the back of his "coach's" chair. He stood at the edge of the bed. He was about three-quarters hard from anticipation. She said, "Let me just take one more measurement before we get started." She gabbed his balls and pulled him close, taking most of his cock into her mouth. She made deep, slow strokes down her throat, burying her nose in his pubic hairs at the deepest point. All the while she was making lightening quick circular motions with her tongue around the head of his dick. The sensation of fast and slow combined was overwhelming. He was as hard as he had ever been. When she sensed he couldn't get any bigger, mostly because the head of his dick was throbbing and nearly purple, she pulled away and visually inspected it. "Yep," she said. "Too big."

David stood dumfounded. She laid back on the bed, took the bottle of KY out of his hand and squeezed a little right on her groomed pussy. She rubbed it in and handed the bottle back to him. "I'll bet you $2,500 you can't get it in."

David snapped out of it and lathered up his cock with generous amounts of the KY. He got between her legs and, with no other fore-play, began to insert himself. Her pussy was so tight that try as he might, he couldn't get it in more than half way. He moved her around in several positions but none proved any more successful than the original "man on top" position. He finally got her to squat above him and use all of her weight to try to drive his shaft home. She was literally sitting on his dick, impaled, bearing down with all of her weight and still she was two inches away from taking it all in. Two inches doesn't sound like much but when there is only five inches to work with then two inches is forty percent of the whole. The pressure on her little pussy was so great that she was grimacing. He finally thought, *this has to hurt*, and he rolled to his side.

They both just laid quietly for the moment. After an awkward pause, David said, "I guess I owe you $2,500 and I bet an "I told you so" is somewhere in a near conversation."

Olive was rubbing her pussy, trying to massage the pain out of it. David watched for a while and asked, "How did you and your husband of twenty years ever do it?"

"He was a petite man," was all she said.

"He must have been."

"Just how petite was he, you ask?" David didn't ask, but she wanted to tell. "Can you imagine half a pencil?"

"You're making that up." David didn't believe it.

"You're right. Stick out your middle finger like you're shooting me the bird." David did. She grabbed his hand and jacked on his middle finger a few times. "That's about the size for real."

"That must have been terrible for him."

"Why?" she responded. "He got to stick it in me all the way to the hilt every night. Why is that so bad?"

"Now that you put it that way, lucky bastard."

"It could have been really good but he couldn't control himself."

"What do you mean?" David raised up on one arm and faced her rose bush.

"He was little, which didn't bother me because as you know now, I can't take a big one. He got an erection easily and he liked it every night, he just came too fast. I remember once he was going down on me. His head was right between my legs. We were both naked and I put my feet down to play with his dick while he gave me head. The next thing I know, I felt something wet on my feet. I had to look to make sure but he came on my feet after I just touched him. He was done that night right then and there. On other nights, when he went to put it in my pussy, he'd squirt on me before he got it in. Sometimes he actually got it in and pumped a few times before he came. If I ever sucked him to get it up, I'd get a face full before I even got started. Most of the time we just settled on a hand job because when I manipulated him to get him hard, he'd cum anyway, making it a hand job by default"

She paused to catch her breath. "The best times were when he'd let me get him up a second time. He could actually fuck me long enough for me to cum. But that didn't happen very often. He came pretty quickly the second time too and he said the second time hurt so he didn't like to do it. It was pretty much a sexual hell, but that's the way it's always been with me."

"I know the feeling," said David. "My whole life has been one long sexual tragedy."

"You want to make another bet?" she asked staring at her feet, not daring to look up.

"I didn't do too well with the last one. I already owe you $2,500 or a free session I suppose. I've got a five-inch dick, so who wouldn't have taken that bet. It was a trick."

"Do you want to make another bet or just whine, Tiny?"

"Oh you're asking for it now. What's the bet?"

"I'll let you get in me as deep as you can, then you look me in the eyes and I bet you can't keep your dick in me. No tricks. I won't squirm or wiggle around. As a matter of fact, I'll wrap my legs around you and try to hold you in. But...I bet you can't keep your dick in me."

"I don't know if I understand the bet but you're on."

"Okay, let me get you hard again so you won't say I was cheating." David moved around so she could suck his dick, tasting the strawberry flavored KY. When it was stretched to its limits she said, "Keep it wet and get on top of me. Stick it in." David got on top of her and inserted his dick as far as it would go. "Deeper," she said teasing him.

"Bitch," was his snappy comeback.

She wrapped her legs and arms around him. "Now just fuck me." David complied wondering what part of this was the trick. He was getting into it even though he could only muster half a stroke. When she could tell that he was about to cum she said, "Look at me."

David raised his head and they locked eyes. She started cumming and instantly, when she did, her pussy tightened up and she Kegeled him right out of her. David was stunned for a second. "Oh no you didn't," he said while trying desperately to reinsert himself. Olive laughed while she was cumming. Somehow, she was getting the best of all worlds, a laughing orgasm while winning $2,500.

David, on the other hand, was paying $2,500, while being laughed at when trying to stick his dick back into her pussy that was shut tighter than a Mississippi River mud mussel. He was also so close to cumming that he was now dribbling his juice on the sheets.

When she finished, he rolled off her and laid beside her on the bed. "What just happened?"

She started giggling again. "I'm sorry. It's just that you're so easy. I'll make it right." She started giving him head again while he was lying beside her. "This will be a good one, I promise."

While she was sucking on him, he asked, "How did you know you could push me out like that?"

She continued working on him as she talked. "I've always been able to do that. I have to concentrate really hard, not to do it." She stuck his dick back in her mouth.

"In about two more minutes, I'm not going to care that your rose bush has a few thorns."

She worked him up with an expertise acquired through years of wanting to please. She was fondling his balls and when they drew up inside him she knew it was almost time. She pulled her mouth away, jacked just the head three more strokes. He shot like a water hose, two huge squirts and many more lesser convulsions. Somehow, she had aimed right at his face and she hit the target. Both squirts got him. The first one hit him flush in the face. He quickly turned his head and the second one hit him in the right ear. He couldn't believe it. He just fucked himself in his own ear.

When he caught his breath, she said, "Let me start off by saying, I didn't know an old fart like you was going to shoot so far and..." She started laughing so hard she couldn't get the apology out. When she finished laughing at him, she leaned forward, kissed him on the left cheek, the only spot that didn't have cum on it, and said she had to run.

She got dressed and as she was leaving she said, "I'll expect a refund for this one and I'll collect the rest of the debt in the form of a free one next time." Then she laughed some more shutting the door behind her.

David stayed in the bed, smiling.

Chapter 70

The Declaration

The next days proceeded in a blur. After thinking about Olive continuously, he decided that he was going to ask her to start a relationship with him. He didn't know much about her. He didn't even know where she lived but, in time, he would learn all there was to know.

She always scheduled a monthly appointment one day ahead, usually sometime during the third week of the month. He wanted to turn back the clock and feel like a teenager again so he decided he was going to ask her to go to Coney Island. He was excited.

Gisele noticed his positive change in attitude and asked him, "What's up?"

He told her about how she made him feel and what he had planned. Gisele thought it was a great idea. She said a former A-list actress had probably been wined and dined all over New York but, "I'll bet nobody ever ask her to Coney Island."

David was floating around on wings. He gave all the customers that added touch. They loved his service and showed their appreciation with enormous tips. While the rich women writhed on the bed in full blown orgasm, David's mind was on riding the Cyclone, eating a Nathan's hot dog and staring at the ocean from the top of the Wonder Wheel, all with Olive by his side.

The third week of the month rolled around, finally, and David anxiously awaited the call from Olive to make her routine appointment. She didn't call on Monday, but that wasn't unusual. Then she didn't call on Tuesday and Gisele could see David slowly start slipping into worry. No call on Wednesday and David was obviously concerned. Thursday and Friday passed without a call and David was convinced something was wrong. Gisele had her hands full trying to keep him focused on the business.

At the end of he month, David was panicking and called his old partner in crime, Detective Spignoli.

He told the detective he was worried because she had made an appointment every month for the last six months and she said she would be back for her free session next time. This was the "next time" and she wasn't here. Detective Spignoli spent thirty minutes listening to his story and trying to calm him down. The detective promised he would find out what was going on for the usual fees, of course.

David didn't have to wait long, Detective Spignoli called the next day. Gisele answered the phone on the reception counter and put it on speaker. David was sitting in one of the lobby chairs. He didn't even get up, just held his head in his hands.

Detective Spignoli started off, "First of all, I want to say, no charge on this one, Okay? Have you ever been to her website?"

David said in a barely audible voice, "I didn't know she had one."

"Most public figures do these days. Just go to OliveLoveLancaster. com. Her real name was Olive Love. Her stage name was Lancaster. Got it? OliveLoveLancaster.com. I'll talk to you later." Spignoli hung up the phone.

Gisele was typing in the URL before the phone even went to dial tone. The hyper-fast computer with which David had equipped the office pulled the website up in less than two seconds. David and Gisele both fell silent.

"This website will no longer have any active posts. After years of remission, cancer has resurfaced and Ms. Lancaster would like to spend her time in peace with her family. Any well wishers are asked to respect her privacy."

Gisele stared at David and David stared at the screen. She wasn't sure if he was going to collapse or go on a rampage. Fortunately, he did neither. "What do I do?" he asked no one in particular. Gisele's only response was one motion-picture-perfect tear rolling down her cheek.

They canceled all appointments for a week while David tried to compose himself. He had the strongest urge to track her down and go visit, but Gisele talked him out of it. What stopped him cold was when Gisele said, "She doesn't want you to see her like this."

On the way home that evening, he decided to walk through Chelsea Park. He sat on a bench watching some kids play basketball in the distance. He was lost in his thoughts when he felt a strange sensation on his leg. He looked down and a small white and brown dog was just sitting by his side. It had the looks of a Jack Russell Terrier but he could tell it wasn't a purebred.

He petted the dog's head and the puppy leaned into it. "A dog who knows what he wants." David looked for a collar but found no signs of identification. He thought maybe there was a micro chip. He'd heard of dogs being chipped these days. He made himself a deal, when he got up, if the dog followed without him giving it any encouragement, then he would try to figure out who owned it and if no one did, he would keep it.

"Okay, here we go." David got up without a word and started walking towards his apartment. The dog stood up with him, spun around twice and followed him all the way home. David got the dog up in his apartment and fed him some hickory smoked ham that he had gotten at the deli. His apartment rules did not allow pets so he was going to have to figure something out.

It didn't take long, the very next day in the apartment lobby, the apartment manager caught him with the dog. David lied through his teeth. "It's a friend's dog. They went to Europe for two months and I promised to watch their dog." David sat on a lobby sofa and the dog jumped up on the cushions. The manager was looking sternly at them both. "You can tell any of the other tenants asking about her that it's only temporary." The dog moved over the cushion on the sofa and put its head on David's leg.

"What's your little sofa dog's name?" asked the manager as he reached out to pet the animal.

"Well you almost said it yourself, you must be psychic."

"What do you mean?" The manager was still scratching the dog's ear.

"Her name is Sophie Dog. See, you almost said it yourself, Sofa Dog."

"Well I guess. But I want this dog out of here after two months." The manager huffed off like he was large and in charge but David could care less what he wanted. David was keeping this dog even if he had to move.

David rarely got a call on his cell phone and he received texts less often. The only texts he ever got were from Gisele, telling him he had an appointment in 30 minutes and he better get his butt back to the spa. But this day he got one from and unknown source.

{Hey u little cum squirtin, can't keep my dick in, bet losing bastard. How the hell r u?}

It was from Olive. David texted back...{Well if it isn't the tiny pussy, make me shoot cum in my own face, bitch.}

{Sorry I haven't been in touch. Preoccupied I'm afraid.}

{How's it going?}

{Not well, bone and lymph cancer this time. Don't see any way out.}

{What can I do?}

There was a really long pause. {No one can do anything. This is my last text. I'll be doped up too much after this to make any sense.}

{I was going to ask you to go to Coney Island with me on your next visit.}

She didn't respond. David texted again. {I was going to ask you to be with me.}

She still didn't respond. He sent {I think I love you.} He waited, every heart beat a lifetime.

She started typing, {I know you love me, I wouldn't have it any other way.}

He texted back a dozen times but all in vain. She never responded again.

Two months after the last text, Gisele showed him an article in the entertainment section of the paper. "Olive Lancaster passed away last night after a long fight with cancer. She was surrounded by her...." David didn't finish the article. He told Gisele to cancel the appointments for a week again and he would get back to her soon.

Gisele was worried about all the cancellations. It was not good for business. David didn't care about business. Life was eating him up.

Chapter 71

Assessing a Life

David took a complete month off before he felt like going back to work. His greatest pleasure in life was spending time with his little dog, Sophie. Their favorite place was Chelsea Park where they found each other.

David could barely drag himself into work. He only went twice a week but it seemed like such a waste. All he ever wanted to do was help women but what he was really doing is what Olive said, whoring himself out. His whole life now consisted of a before work bagel at Murray's, a movie at Cineopolis every Friday night, walks in Chelsea Park with Sophie, and an occasional Yankee game in the Bronx. A simple life for a very complicated man.

David contemplated why he was still working. He had nearly five million dollars in the bank. He didn't need to work, ever again. He wasn't doing anything that helped society except employing Gisele at an astronomically high salary and paying taxes.

On a particularly cold December morning, while David and Sophie strolled the sidewalks of his Chelsea neighborhood, he had one of those dreaded epiphanies. He would move out west to Montana, Wyoming or Colorado and live in a large country estate where Sophie could run free. That little dog had become his whole world.

When David arrived at the spa the next day, Gisele could tell that he was in an excellent mood. He had three customers that day which was two more than usual. The first one was a regular who liked the same treatment every time. She brought her vibrator with her that looked and sounded like a weed eater when it was revved up to full throttle. She would lie nude on the bed, cram the gigantic vibrator up between her legs and asked for the look. For the next thirty minutes, she would request more "looks" and weed whack herself until she had nothing left. When finished she would let the vibrator slide out of her hands and sleep or pass out for about an hour. David would turn off the vibrator, cover her up with a blanket, and then go out and visit with Gisele. Today, he would do research on real estate in the Rocky Mountains.

Gisele talked incessantly about her flawed, yet wonderful love life with her mean lesbian bitch partner, Andie. David heard, "blah, blah, blah." After an hour and fifteen minutes, the customer came out of the exam room. She walked over to David, dropped four one-hundred dollar bills on the counter, touched his cheek and said, "Thanks, Babe," making him feel just like the whore he was. Gisele rolled her eyes.

The second customer came in a little before noon. She was a rookie, hadn't had an orgasm in years and paid Gisele in twenty dollar bills. She had been saving for this for as long as she had not been having orgasms.

Her name was forgotten by David as soon as they were introduced. She was as average as average could be like most of his customers. The only thing that set her off from all the other thirty-year-old desperate housewives was this lady was poor and she was wearing a Burger King uniform. She had just finished her shift.

As David walked into the exam room with her, he couldn't help but think that one of the two of them was the most pathetic thing he had ever seen before and he wasn't sure which one of them it was. The customer, whatever her name was, started to cry as soon as she sat down on the bed. "Oh good grief," David said under his breath. They sat together and talked for twenty minutes. After he boosted her confidence enough to continue, she began to disrobe. She cried some more during the process. She jumped under the covers and pulled them up to her chin. David got a glimpse of her body and would describe it as ordinary.

Between sniffles David ask if she was ready. She said it had been so long she couldn't remember what it felt like. "Just like riding a bicycle," he replied. He walked over to the bed, looked down at her eyes which were barely poking out from underneath the covers. "Enjoy yourself," he said as she started to cum.

He tried to make her visit as special as possible so he kept her cumming continuously for an hour and half. The sheets were soaked with sweat and juice when she was done. She had gotten hot and thrown the damp sheets to the floor and was lying on her stomach with her legs spread. She had her head on her arm and the other hand was between her legs holding herself.

David said, "I see that you've still got it. You just think you forgot how to have an orgasm." When she didn't respond, he said, "I counted and you had fourteen orgasms. Is that what you counted?" She mumbled something this time but he couldn't understand it. "We have a money back guarantee if you're not satisfied. Are you satisfied?" She shook her head affirmative and mumbled again. David covered her up and left the room.

David joined Gisele out in the lobby. He picked up a copy of a *USA Today* and started reading. More like he was pretending to read. His mind was going too fast to really read. He was wondering when the last time he had an erection during bone of these sessions. He'd just witnessed an average looking thirty-year-old woman have over a dozen orgasms and he didn't feel a thing. The last woman that could get him going was Olive. That had been a couple of years ago now. My how time flies.

When the Burger King girl came out of the exam room, David handed her $2,500 and said it was on the house. "It's advertising," he said. "Every so often someone comes through the door that gets a free session so they will spread news about our services through word of mouth. You were the 500th customer since we did this last so, you get the freebie. How was it?" She started to cry again. "Oh good grief."

Gisele chastised him severely. "You can't be giving that shit away. How am I supposed to pay the bills?" Meaning her exorbitant salary. David put his finger to his lips to shush her. "I needed to do this," he said.

"Punk," she responded.

Gisele said that his next appointment was at 4:00 pm that afternoon so he could go somewhere for a couple of hours if he wanted. He definitely wanted. Since he worked through lunch he was hungry. He hailed a cab and went to Katz's Deli to get a hot pastrami sandwich. They always piled on so much meat that he could take half of it home to Sophie Dog. Between the cab, the sandwich and drink, lunch ended up costing David $62.89. Thank goodness, he was stinking rich.

Back at the spa by 3:45 pm he was ready to take on his last client of the day. Standing outside the door of the spa he was wishing beyond hope that his last client would be routine. He said to no one in particular, "Let's get this over with."

Chapter 72

A Shock

At 4:15 pm the front door started to open. Then it closed. Then it started to open again. Then it closed. Gisele got up from behind the counter and opened the door. A thin, old black lady was standing there with a piece of paper in her hand. The old lady asked Gisele if this was the right place. She showed Gisele an address on the paper. It was the address of the spa. Gisele and the old lady entered. Gisele positioned herself behind the counter and asked, "How can we help you today?"

"I'm here for a service." The old lady sat in the lobby chair.

Gisele turned to David and whispered, "This better not be another fucking charity case."

David stepped around the counter. "Ma'am, do you know what we do here?"

"Of course I do."

Gisele was as blunt as usual, "But you're eighty years old!"

The lady looked Gisele up and down, "I'm eighty-one."

Gisele crossed her arms, "What could an old, ancient, dried up woman possibly want here?"

The old lady looked at Gisele with daggers in her eyes. "I'm here to get Mister Organism in a room alone."

"Orgasm, lady," Gisele said with contempt.

David got goose bumps all over his body. "Ma'am, do I know you?" She didn't say anything. "Have we met?" She still didn't say anything.

"Are we doing business or not?" the old woman asked.

Gisele was quick, "You got the money?"

The old lady took a minute but she unsnapped her purse and pulled out a roll of hundreds and handed it to Gisele. "Now do I get in a room alone with Mister Organism?"

Gisele shook her head, "Orgasm, are you dense?" and busied herself with counting the money. David gave Gisele a "shut up" look and escorted the lady to the exam room. As they went through the door, the old lady hollered back to Gisele, "Enjoy that money now. Everything comes to an end sometime." Gisele never looked up but David got goose bumps again.

David sat in his "coach's" chair and the lady sat on the edge of the bed. For eighty-one years old, she was attractive. "How do you know the term "Mister Orgasm"? I haven't used that for years."

"I've known you all your life, every name you ever had, boy."

"You're scaring the crap out of me."

"You better be scared boy. Look me in the eye, right now."

David did as she directed. They stared at each other and not a damned thing happened. This only occurred once before, over thirty years ago in New Orleans. "Who are you?" he asked.

"I'm who you know I am." What kind of crazy answer was that? David stared at her searching the dark recesses of his mind trying to remember where they had met. He was always afraid of the past coming back to haunt him.

"Please tell me you are not from New Orleans." He leaned back in his chair symbolically trying to distance himself from her.

"Boy I ain't been a subway ride away from Harlem all my life."

"What's your name?" he asked not really sure he wanted to know.

"They call me Sister Louisa."

"Sister Louisa," he repeated. "What do you do or did you do for a living?"

"I lived boy. What kind of stupid question is that?"

David was not going to get ahead in this discussion. He gave up. "What can I do for you today?"

"Are you dumb boy? I came here to get me some of them organisms."

David almost laughed. "You mean orgasms?"

"That's what I said and I done paid twenty-five hundred cash money for you to give them to me. I heard you did it just by looking the bitches in the eye. But there must be something else. You give them drugs boy?"

David was shaking his head. "Usually I just look them in the eye and they have an orgasm. But it didn't seem to work on you. Maybe...."

"Maybe what? I'm too old. I have you know when Eldridge was alive, he'd get on top of me and I'd collect those organisms by the handful."

David was trying to be professional but this lady could have been comedian. "How long ago was that?"

"He's been dead since eighty-five."

"That was twenty-eight years ago. Have you had an orgasm since then?"

"I ain't needed one until recently."

David was dying of curiosity. "Why didn't you need one until now?"

"I done read me a book and it got me all stirred up again."

"A book? Like the Joy of Sex or something like that?"

"You from another century boy? I done read me Fifty Shades of Grey. Hoowee! that boy can whup an ass."

David could hardly keep a straight face. "Well, what can I do for you?"

"You can start handing out those organisms like I paid for."

David shook his head. "It doesn't seem to work on you. When I look you in the eye, nothing happens."

"Then it looks like you got to do it the old fashion way."

David drew back, "What do you mean?"

"You pull out that white pecker and give Sister what she needs." David was stunned. She continued, "What? You gonna tell me you ain't got no dick now?"

"I got a dick," was his retort.

"Then get yourself up on top of Sister and get busy. I need it just like my Eldridge give me. I need ten inches and I want it to hurt."

"I don't want to disappoint you, but for me to give you ten inches and make it hurt I'm going to have to stick it in twice and slap you."

She snorted. "Then I was right the first time. You ain't got no dick." She took her shoes off, stood up and dropped her shift dress right to the floor and laid back on the bed with her legs spread. She wasn't wearing a stitch of underwear. For an eighty-one-year-old woman, she wasn't bad looking. Her tits had given up on her but the rest of her body was reasonably tight and still shapely.

"Time to do your business boy."

David was still astounded. "Look, it's a money back guarantee. If you are not satisfied with the service then I'll give you your money back. So why don't I just give you your money back and we call it even."

"I ain't even had no service yet to tell whether I'm satisfied or not. So, get on up here and get to servicing, then I'll tell you if I'm satisfied."

David was trying to decide if he should call Gisele for help. He looked lost.

Sister sat back up on the edge of the bed and motioned for him to come closer. "You just a little embarrassed about that short white dick. Ain't no worry. Sister take care of that just fine." David moved closer until she could reach out and grab him. She pulled him up to her and started unbuckling his belt.

She was mumbling to herself and licking her lips. "Sister gonna make this alright. Everything gonna be good now. That little white dick gonna get some black and it ain't never goin' back." Then she laughed a little. She got his pants down to his knees and started pulling down his navy-blue Fruit of the Looms.

She held his flaccid, little penis in the palm of her hand, staring at it. Then she looked around on both sides of his hips and said, "Well I got this but where's your dick?" Then she laughed like a hyena. When she quit laughing, she said, "Let's get this stretched out as far as it will go and see what you can do with it." She took it all the way into her mouth. Even as it grew to full length, she could deep throat it with every stroke.

It had been a very long time since David had seen any action and even though he was sixty years old, and she called him 'boy', he was going to cum quickly. When she performed about half a dozen more of her deep throat strokes, he announced that he was going to cum. He made the announcement as a courtesy so she could pull it out and give herself a pearl necklace or spend it on the floor if she didn't want to catch it in her mouth. However, Sister just kept going.

He exploded down her throat with what he thought must have been a tremendous load but she swallowed twice in quick succession and kept going. David was about to collapse and jerked in pain every time she hit the sensitive head with her lips.

After he slowed his heart rate and got his senses about him again he realized he never lost his hard on. She just kept sucking it. She finally pulled her mouth away but kept jacking him and cupping his balls. "You know the secret to eating cum boy?" He didn't know if that was rhetorical or if she thought maybe he ate a lot cum. Before he could even begin to form an answer, she continued. "When the man start to squirt, you just swallow as fast as you can."

"Now it's time to make Sister feel good." She laid back on the bed and spread her legs again. David didn't even think twice this time. He'd pretty much gotten over the fact that she was eighty-one years old. He peeled off all his clothes, got down between her legs and started to slide it in. David wasn't sure what it was going to be like, he thought maybe when one was that old it worked differently but she was dripping wet and he slipped in like cream in coffee.

She wrapped her legs around him and wiggled and squirmed like a woman half her age. She scratched and pulled, kicked and bit, slapped, grunted, and screamed obscenities. She got on her hands and knees and David plunged into her from behind with everything he had. He reached around and felt her flat little pancake tits. Her nipples were thick and black like Hershey's kisses. She moaned when he pinched them. She moaned even better when he pinched them really hard.

She reached between her legs and raked his nuts with her fingernails so hard that he thought he was bleeding. They ended up where they started with David on top when he began making the last sprint to the finish. She could tell he was about to go off again and started calling out encouragement, "Come on boy, put it on me. Give it to me."

He pulled it out and before he could get his hand on it, she grabbed it and expertly brought him to a finish. He came a small amount of rich, thick cum. He fell across the top of her panting like a bulldog after a hundred-yard dash. She petted him and praised him in a low whisper, "That's a good boy. You made Sister feel real fine. Real fine."

"I didn't squirt very much," he said.

"That's okay, Sister would rather have a cup of cream than a gallon of milk anyway."

David's mind was racing. All of his previous thoughts about the elderly, not that he thought about them often, were misconceptions. He always thought that somewhere in life, the woman would age out and just admit, "I'll never suck another dick." David wasn't sure what age that was but he really thought eighty-one was beyond it. Was he ever wrong. Sister Louisa could match sex sessions with any woman he'd ever known. He couldn't imagine what she must have been like as a young woman.

Still lying on Sister, feeling her warmth and the wetness left from his ejaculation, he just drifted in thought. Every woman, no matter what size, shape or age can fuck. He didn't know where they learned it, if it was taught by the mother, siblings, cousins, friends at school, from pornography or by trial and error, but every woman knew instinctively how to fuck. Some of the fattest, biggest most enormous woman he had ever serviced could pull their feet up over their heads and expose themselves enough for a man to fuck. What a marvelous thing, sex. If one could put love with it, there probably wouldn't be anything better.

Sister tapped him on the butt twice snapping him out of his enlightenment and said, "I gots to go."

David stood up and looked down at the old woman. "You're a good fuck Sister Louisa."

"I know that," she said with no kind of conceit, just confidence.

She sat up on the edge of the bed. David stood with his junk right in front of her face. She reached out and played with his little flaccid dick for a minute and then pulled on his balls a bit. She looked like she was thinking. Then she said, "Did you know that I could tie Eldridge's dick and nuts together? I could just wrap that big ol' black cock right around those bull nuts and cinch 'em up." He didn't know how it happened but his dick shrunk even more and his balls drew up tight. She laughed and slapped his stuff away from her face.

After they both showered and dressed David asked her if she wanted a refund because satisfaction was guaranteed.

"You was like warm vanilla sugar," she replied. David took that as one of the highest compliments he had ever gotten. She took his face in her hands and kissed him, tongues swirling. He closed his eyes feeling his cock twitch again. He liked this lady.

They walked out of the exam room together, jibing each other in a playful way. He had never been insulted so much and enjoyed it like he did with her. As she walked out of the spa, she stood halfway in the door and said, "Boy, my Mama said you'd be fun."

"Your Mama? She must be a hundred."

"Oh, she dead now."

David took a step back and said, "Are you sure you're not from New Orleans?"

Sister smiled and said, "I told you I been in New York all my life."

"Yeah, but what about Mama?"

Sister smiled showing all of her teeth. David was turning whiter than any white boy should. "What's your last name?" he asked.

"You know it, just like you know where Mama's buried. Ain't that right Mister Organism? You know I'm named Louisa after Louisiana, don't you boy. You knew that as soon as you saw me. I ain't been to no pelican state but Mama sure loved that swamp. She sure did."

She laughed, slipped out the door and was gone. Gisele looked at David who really looked like he needed to sit down. "What was that all about?" she asked.

David sat in one of the lobby chairs and said, "I'm not sure I'd be able to explain it."

Gisele started counting the money in the register. "Nasty old woman. That must have been so nasty. Such a skanky-ass old bitch."

"Remarkable old woman," David said under his breath. "Absolutely remarkable."

Chapter 73

A Big Decision

That night after walking Sophie in the park, he was sitting on the couch with his little dog in his lap. The TV was tuned to a baseball game that he didn't care anything about and he was eating a frozen Indian food dinner, palak paneer. It stunk up the whole apartment but it tasted pretty good.

He couldn't get his mind off that old woman. He kept thinking that her appearance was a sign or omen. Then he got all internal and started asking questions like, "Am I happy? If not, what would make me happy?"

He decided that he wasn't happy and then tried to figure out why. The "why" part was easy. He'd wasted his life running away from himself and everybody else. He was in New York, he liked New York but some how it slowly sucked the soul right out of him. He was working with Gisele and had been for a very long time, mainly because she was a lesbian and left him alone. She wasn't that personable especially since she took up with Andie. She had become greedy and hateful. He paid her a crap ton of money to do very little and showed almost no appreciation. She had somehow slipped into that category of people who felt like they are owed something more than what they have earned and she felt like it was David who owed her.

He didn't really like giving strange women orgasms for money. He was just good at it and he fell into doing what was easy and lucrative. He decided what he wanted to do was write, even though he had proven that he wasn't very good at it. He couldn't even write a one minute introduction for his Mister Orgasm performance. But that's what he would do, write a book. About what was the question. Well, of course, it would be about him. *Who would believe my story?* he thought. Analyzing it a little more, he decided that books didn't have to be believable. All they needed to do was create a desire to be read. *Who would read it?* was his next thought. His answer went from everybody to nobody. *Would Gisele read it?* He laughed to himself and spoke to Sophie, "If I put a twenty-dollar bill in it, she'd open it to the twenty, wouldn't she Sophie?" He rubbed the dog's ears.

He was excited about his new choice of careers. He finished up the ballgame on TV, somehow finding it interesting. The bowl of Pralines and Cream ice cream he ate for dessert seemed to taste better than it did the night before. He had a second helping. He looked up at the picture of three camels he had framed hanging above his mantel. They were the dumbest damn camels anyone had ever seen, Glutius, Maximus and Sphinxter. He thought about the good times instead of the bad and started to laugh. He laughed so hard that ice cream came out of his nose.

Sophie got concerned at his choking and wasn't sure if he was playing or experiencing apoplexy and the ice cream was his brain leaching from its cavity. The dog did what all dogs do, jumped up in his lap and tried to lick the ice cream off his face. David found this to be hilarious and snatched the dog up in his arms and spun around in his living room a few turns. For no explainable reason, he was actually happy.

Chapter 74

Action

When David arrived at the spa the next day, Gisele was sitting behind the counter being her grumpy self. She had made coffee but had drunk most of it and there wasn't enough left for even half a cup for David. While David started to make a second pot of coffee Gisele looked up from her magazine and said, "Make it strong. You always make it too weak. It's like you're trying to save money on coffee for Christ's sake."

The recipe called for four scoops, David dumped in eight. *I hope she gets the jitters.* When he finished, he sat in the lobby chair and asked her how many appointments he had today. She said that he had two and she wanted to talk to him. David thought, what a coincidence.

She started off, "Andie and I have done the math a thousand times..." David had an immediate sarcastic reaction: *Great, now Andie is going to run my business.* "...and we believe that you can afford to pay me more."

"How much more do you and Andie think is fair? Don't you make well over $100,000 a year?"

"That's with bonuses and the occasional tip sharing. My base salary is exactly $100,000. And you make three, four, sometimes ten or twenty times that."

"Okay, how much do you and Andie want?"

She hesitated for a long period as if she were searching for a fair sounding figure but David knew they had an exact number already rehearsed. Then she said it. "We think half would be fair."

"Half of what I make?" David wasn't sure if that is what she meant.

"Yes. Half of all revenue. It's fair since I do almost all of the work. I set up the appointments, balance the books, take the money to the bank, do the laundry, order supplies, clean up the place..."

"Don't forget, make coffee."

"That too," she said. David was just kidding but she took it seriously.

David sat quietly trying to regain the good feeling he had from last night. "You don't think the $50 or $60 an hour I pay you now is fair?" She shook her head slightly, indicating 'no'. Then David said it, "Okay, it's a deal."

"Really?" Gisele looked surprised.

"Really," David said. "Let me ask you, is Andie working right now?"

"Not right now. She hasn't worked in a while. It's hard you know, for actors and models." Gisele gave him that sad face but perked up to say, "She still goes to parties a lot, you know, trying to make contacts."

"Yeah that's got to be tough, party all the time and have someone else pay the bills."

David got up and walked over to her. "What would you have done if I said no to the raise?"

"Andie had a plan. She didn't tell me what it was but she said that she would make you so miserable that you'd finally agree."

"Miserable, huh? Sounds like blackmail."

Gisele shook her head, "Oh no, she didn't say anything about blackmail, just stuff about social media. You know, Facebook, Twitter, LinkedIn, Yelp, Snapchat, whatever, you know." David didn't really know but it sounded just like blackmail to him.

He reached out to shake her hand, "To seal the deal. I'll pay you half of everything that I make at the spa. Fair enough?"

She shook his hand in an exaggerated manner. "Fair enough," she said.

"But watch out what you ask for. Now, who's the first client?"

Chapter 75

The Clients

The first client in the queue was Mrs. Ambrose. She was a regular, or maybe it should be described as a semi-regular. She came in every two to three months or whenever she saved up enough mad money to afford a "treatment".

Mrs. Ambrose was in her mid-fifties and could be described as average but she thought she was something special. She didn't work for a living, her husband was some sort of executive, and she was a member of several social clubs. David heard about them every time she came in. What made her a special client was she asked David to turn the air conditioner down really low and fan her while she was cumming. She refused to allow herself to cum more than twice in any one session because she didn't want to sweat and smell like sex when she left the spa to attend her club meetings. David explained that she could shower before she left but she said it would take her at least an hour to get ready again and it would be a waste of her valuable time. She was the customer, she paid good money, so he gave her what she wanted.

When Mrs. Ambrose had gone, David sat at the counter and talked to Gisele. He asked her if they were to split that fee down the middle or if they should take out expenses first and then split what was left. He left it up to Gisele to decide. Being the greedy bitch that she had recently become, she opted for all the expenses to be paid out of David's half and she would get half of the revenue, not half of the profits. Sweet deal for her. She took $1,250 out of the register and stuffed it in her pocket.

The next customer came in early in the afternoon. Her name was Brooke Summerlin, another semi-regular. She was in her mid-thirties to early forties the best David could tell. She was slim, attractive and full of energy. She also had a well-to-do husband and didn't work but she volunteered at an organization that raised funds for St. Jude Children's Research Hospital. She always wore her identification badge when she came.

Brooke also had a peculiar routine. She was really friendly and talked a lot, maybe because she was nervous. She would disrobe, take out a pair of nipple clamps from her purse, lie on the bed and attach the them to her rather large nipples. Her breasts were relatively small but her nipples were large and poked out quite a bit after she played with them. When she was ready, she would put the soles of her feet together with her knees spread and start masturbating. Sometimes she would cum before David even got involved. Unlike Mrs. Ambrose, Brooke didn't give a tinker's damn about sweating. She just commenced using her fingers, then David started in on her and she would cum six or seven times before she began to wind down.

After she was done, David let her lie there a while. She told him that she loved her husband and he was a good husband but this was just for her. "You know, kind of like getting a massage," she said. When she was ready, she stood up to go the shower.

David said, "Aren't you going to take those off?" pointing to the clamps still attached to her nipples.

"I forgot about them," she said. She walked over close to him, put her hands on her hips saying, "Why don't you take them off?" She had her snatch right in front of his face and he couldn't help but notice a small scar to the left of her trimmed triangular bush.

David reached up and unclamped the devices. As he did, he could smell the richness of her womanhood. His little hard dick tingled when he did. He usually didn't get an erection during his routine sessions but he almost always got one with Brooke. She must have noticed in the past but she never said anything before. Today she did, "Who takes care of you? Your secretary?"

"No, she's a lesbian."

"Your wife then?"

"No, I'm not married. What woman could have a relationship with me knowing what I do for a living. I just endure or maybe take care of it at night."

"That's sad." She reached out and took the clamps from him and put them back in her purse. She strolled enticingly to the shower and gave him a quick look as she shut the door behind her. She stuck her head back out and said, "If you want to take care of that thing while I'm in here, knock yourself out. It's only fair. I'm going to do myself in the shower one more time anyway." She shut the door.

What the hell, David thought. He stood up, pulled his pants down to his knees and started jacking off with the intent of squirting on the sheets. They were going to get washed anyway. He was holding his shirt up with one hand and working his cock with the other.

About ready to cum, he noticed out of the corner of his eye that the bathroom door was cracked open and Brooke was peeking out. Fueled by her voyeurism, he got into it and quickly shot a knee buckling load all over the sheets. A second after he was done, he heard the shower door close again. It was a mutually satisfying, risk free, guilt free session.

Brooke left a $200 tip on the counter as she left. Gisele snatched it up and took one of the hundreds. Then she counted out another

$1,250 from the cash box. "This is great," she said. She just stuffed $2,600 in her pocket in four hours. "And to think, this is a slow day!" she said. "I'm going to be rich!"

David didn't expect any walk-ins so he told Gisele that he was going home and as soon as she finished cleaning up the spa, she could take off too. She was going to leave as fast as she possibly could anyway, just like she did every day no matter what David said.

If you divided her old salary by the number of hours she actually worked, she probably made $75 or $85 an hour. Today, based on their new deal, she made $433 per hour of actual worked time.

Chapter 76

The Next Day

Early the next morning David called the office and told Gisele to cancel all of his appointments. He was going to run some errands. He was actually going to an electronics store and buy a new computer, printer and trimmings with which to write his life story. It took him all day and a lot of help from the service team but the computer was finally ready to go. He took Sophie for her walk, watched an old movie on TV and went to bed thinking he had done enough for the day. Tomorrow he would start writing his best-selling novel or would it be the next great American novel, or maybe it would be just a pile of papers for recycling.

He slept in but as soon as he woke up he called Gisele and told her to cancel all appointments for the that day as well because he had some personal business which needed his attention. His personal business was walking Sophie and writing his book.

Gisele went back to her lavish apartment and sat down with Andie to figure out just how much they expected to make with Gisele's new financial arrangement. To be conservative, they decided they could count on a slam dunk $220,000 per year but really hoped for at least $350,000. Andie was ecstatic. She ran out of her apartment to go buy stuff. Lots of expensive stuff. Gisele just sat back in her lounge chair smugly satisfied at being such a great provider.

While Gisele and Andie mortgaged their souls for a new Lexus and the $5000 parking privilege that went along with it, David sat behind his computer and started to write:

Once upon a time.... nope, delete.

Call me David...nope, delete.

It was the best of times...nope, delete.

It was a dark and stormy night... fuck no, delete.

It was an affliction or maybe a blessing.... Okay, that's it.

Gisele and Andie, squealing with delight about their new purchases, went out to spend some more. They decided that they needed new wardrobes, a remodeled kitchen, a bigger bed, new purses, jewelry, ah! yes, lots of new jewelry, some art to hang on their walls, a bronze statue for the foyer and some additional enhancing surgery for Andie. They charged what they could on their six new credit cards, each having a limit of about $25,000. For the rest of the purchases they used "in-store" financing. Some of the local managers were encouraged to give credit by Andie's blow jobs. All the time she was sucking dick she was thinking a time was coming really soon when she would have so much money that they would all suck up to her. She couldn't wait.

The third day dawned since the deal. David told Gisele to cancel all appointments, he would be doing some more personal business. His day was the same as the previous, he walked Sophie and sat down to write. Gisele went to the office and made the cancellations and then went shopping with Andie, applying for credit cards at every store.

David got sidetracked that day because he was at a point in his life story that brought back a flood of emotions. He switched to a new Word document and started reworking his will. How depressing. He wrote in bullet points and got it done in two pages. He would take it to his lawyer the next day, which would necessitate another call-in to work. Gisele was happy to have the time off. Her shopping sprees with Andie were fun, plus she was reconnecting with her love even if she had to occasionally wait for Andie to give some stranger a blow job in the back room in exchange for financing.

Gisele was not usually jealous of Andie's method of securing financing because most of the people who arranged the credit were men. At Tiffany's, the financier was a gorgeous, lanky female. Gisele was fuming when Andie and the Tiffany's financier went to the back room to settle on an "interest rate". In an hour and a half, Andie came out of the show room wearing a diamond necklace, a platinum brace-let, a pair of pearl and London blue earrings and a new dinner ring.

Gisele ran up to her, "Did you eat her fucking pussy?"

Andie just said, "What do you think?" held out her wrist and admired her new jewelry.

"Fuck you!" was Gisele's response but Andie wasn't phased.

The weekend rolled around and David wrote while the girls shopped. Their capacity to want more was limitless and desire to get it was incessant.

Chapter 77

The Novel and the Deal

By the end of the month David hadn't been down to the spa a single day since he made the deal with Gisele but he had written nearly 90,000 words in his autobiography or was it a memoir. He made a mental note to look up the difference. On the first day of the month, after racking up nearly $450,000 of new debt, Gisele called David at home.

"Where's my check?" she asked. "It didn't hit my bank account."

David was at his computer and paused in the middle of what he thought was the most fascinating phase in his life, he was right up to the point where he and Gisele had made the deal. From this point on he would write the story as it unfolded.

David answered her, "Gisele, you made the deal remember? You're not on salary anymore. You share half the revenue."

"We didn't have any revenue because you didn't go to work."

"Precisely." David gave no other explanation.

There was a very long pause from the other end of the phone. "What am I supposed to do?"

Then a long pause from David's end. "Why don't you ask Andie?" She didn't say anything. "Or maybe you could go get a real job."

"I can't do anything that would make more than twenty bucks an hour."

David replied, "You should have thought of that when I was paying

$100,000 a year. Maybe if you and Andie both get real jobs you could make it together just fine."

"You don't understand; Andie will leave me if I'm not making any money."

"You'll be better off." David waited for a couple of seconds but heard no response. "Call me if she leaves you," and then he hung up.

In three days, Gisele called to tell him that Andie ran off with everything of value in the apartment, cleaned out the bank account and left her with all the debt. "She didn't even say good-bye."

David always knew that Andie was poison but he could never convince Gisele. He felt sorry for her and told her to meet him down at the office in two hours.

"We're going back to work!" she exclaimed, full of hope.

"No. I just want to meet you at the spa so I can give you some advice and do an errand."

When they met at the spa, a third person came in with David. He was the real estate agent for the property. David took Gisele's keys and gave them to the agent. "That's the last set," David said.

The agent started inspecting the property. Gisele asked, "It's over, isn't it?"

"I'm afraid so."

"I caused this, didn't I?" she asked.

"It was coming to an end anyway."

Gisele started to cry. David handed her an envelope. "What's this. A restraining order?"

David chuckled to himself. "No, you weren't that bad, you just listened to that mean lesbian bitch. It's a severance pay. I don't want you to be hurt over this too badly. Andie, on the other hand, can drown in the East River and I won't care."

Gisele opened the envelope to find a $100,000 check. She started to cry again. Slowly she walked over to David and hugged him for the longest time. The agent came back in the lobby and broke things up. David and the agent completed their business and all three went their separate ways.

Chapter 78

The Spirit

David went home that afternoon with a heavy heart, not just figuratively speaking but his remorse and loneliness actually put pressure on his chest. He could hardly breath. "I've got to snap out of this," he said to himself.

He walked Sophie in the park but had less enthusiasm than usual. When home, he cooked a sausage and hominy for supper. He gave most of it to Sophie because he didn't have an appetite either. He sat at his computer and typed in the latest chapter of his story, the closing of the spa and saying good-bye to Gisele. He just realized she had been in his life longer than just about any woman he had known. It was a sad chapter. He downloaded it to a flash drive and put it on his desk.

He next pulled out his Last Will and Testament. Feeling melancholy, he again changed things in his will. Finished with initialing, dating and signing all the changes, he put that away as well. David moved to the couch to watch a little TV. He settled in and Sophie joined him in her usual spot, lying on the couch with her head in his lap.

He had the remote control in his hand and was just about ready to turn on the TV, but for some reason, he laid it down to pet Sophie. As soon as he touched her head, she jumped up and barked once very loudly while looking past David to the corner of the room. David looked at her trying to say, "What's wrong, girl?" but the words never came out. Sophie barked again as if she were seeing something that wasn't there or maybe it was a thin, effeminate, dark shadow in the corner. The last thing David heard was two barks from his beloved little dog. He slumped to the side towards Sophie and died as peacefully as any one possibly could.

Chapter 79

Epilog

Sophie barked continuously all night or at least until the neighbors complained. The manager got a call and decided that he had to tell David to get rid of the animal. The manager hated to do this because David was paying him a $1,000 a month to bend the rules and look the other way, but Old Lady Tuttlewhite was complaining and he had to do something.

The manager knocked a dozen times with no response except the barking and scurrying of the little dog. The manager was joined by Mrs. Tuttlewhite wrapped in her housecoat and fuzzy slippers. She told him to open the door right now and shut that dog up or there would be holy heck to pay. The manager put his master key in the lock, turned the cylinder and pushed open the door. Before they entered, the dog went silent.

Creeping in slowly they first saw the dog sitting upright on the couch and then they saw Mr. Gideon, dead. Old Lady Tuttlewhite ran out screaming. The manager moved forward and examined the body, then called the police.

The manager had an emergency number for all of his residents and he called the number three hours later. To his surprise, it wasn't a spouse, sibling or child, it was a lawyer. By noon the next day the lawyer showed up and went to work executing the will.

After the lawyer had a long argument with the coroner, David's body was released without an autopsy and was cremated. The lawyer surreptitiously scattered David's ashes in Chelsea Park where he loved walking with Sophie. The furniture and all his other possessions, which didn't amount to much, were sold or donated. The lawyer made some phone calls, mailed some letters and wrote some checks and his work was done except for one small exchange.

Sophie was left in the bare apartment with a large bowl of water and an open bag of kibble. Every time there was movement in the hall, Sophie would alert, wag her tail and hope beyond all hope that her beloved master would walk through the door. On the third day of being alone in the apartment, Sophie heard another noise in the hall. Alerting for the hundredth time, she was rewarded with the door opening. The dog spun in circles, then sat waiting to see if it was David.

The person entered and turned to see the dog waiting in anticipation. It was not David. The person approached Sophie who was quivering with fear. Two large hands reached down and encircled the dog's chest, picked up the puppy and held her at eye level. "So, you're Dog's dog." It was Big Cindy. Sophie licked Cindy's face and a bond was formed forever.

Chapter 80

Big Cindy's Back Story

Big Cindy never moved more than thirty miles away from her hometown. She bought a few acres with a small two-story home and erected a warehouse where she started her candle company, Cindy's Scents. She married a guy she thought she loved but all he ever did was drink, be lazy, take from the till, have affairs, lose his hair, and get fat. She dumped him when she was in her fifties and he took everything he could get his hands on including the delivery van.

Once again, Big Cindy was on the brink of financial disaster. It wasn't the first time and it probably wouldn't be the last. She had four kids with this idiot and managed to put three of them through college. The oldest boy was an accountant in Dallas, the next son was a gay lawyer in San Francisco and the youngest boy was a geologist working for an oil company overseas. Her only girl chose to stay at home and help her mother in the candle factory. The daughter was a hard worker and gave her mother great comfort. Big Cindy's boys never came home and rarely called, texted, or emailed. Big Cindy kept up with them on Facebook.

One evening, while Big Cindy and her daughter were in the warehouse trying to decide if they had put too much lavender in the new French Swirl Bathroom Candle, they heard a knock on the front counter. Big Cindy went out to greet the customer. To her surprise, it was an attorney. Big Cindy's first thought was her ex-husband had dug up some excuse to sue her.

The lawyer told her that he represented the estate of David Gideon.

"Estate?" she said knowing exactly what that meant.

"Yes, I'm sorry to say that Mr. Gideon died peacefully in his apartment two nights ago in New York City. He had a little dog named...." The lawyer checked in a folder. "...Sophie." Big Cindy was crying for not a day had gone by in her life when she didn't think about David Othello Gideon. "Anyway, Mr. Gideon instructed me to ask if you would take care of the dog. You'd have to fly to New York to pick her up."

Big Cindy raced out of the warehouse to her home next door. She thundered up the stairs to her bedroom and threw some things in a tattered suitcase. She came down to the living room and found her daughter and the lawyer having coffee at their old beat up waxy kitchen table. "I'm ready."

"You understand that you are responsible for all of the expenses incurred for the retrieval and care of the dog?" the lawyer said in a courtroom tone.

"Okay," said Big Cindy as she and her daughter plotted how to afford the trip.

"Now Mom, take the company credit card, the only one with any room left on it, here's the money from the register, I have a few bucks in my purse." After gathering every penny they had, they hugged each other and Big Cindy was driving to Dallas.

Big Cindy had only been on a plane once before and that was when she went to a convention in Miami. The trip to New York was tiresome since it was just a one night trip. She flew on Southwest Airlines and it made three stops coming and going. When she arrived back at her house, she was exhausted and completely broke again. Gas to the airport, parking, the flight, cabs, the hotel, food and buying a crate and shipping Sophie was expensive.

Big Cindy was sitting with Sophie in her lap at the old, beat up, waxy kitchen table talking to her daughter about cutting back on a few things to make ends meet this month and maybe for the next few months, when someone knocked on the front door. It was the lawyer again.

"I trust your trip was a safe one?" He didn't wait for a response seeing the dog in Big Cindy's arms. "If you returned with the dog, I was instructed to give you this." He handed her an envelope and walked away.

Big Cindy, still carrying Sophie, walked back to the old beat up waxy kitchen table and sat down with her daughter. "What is it Mom?"

"I don't know. There's nothing on the envelope." Big Cindy flipped it back and forth a few times examining both sides.

"Well open it!" her daughter said with child-like excitement.

Big Cindy, arranged Sophie on her lap a little better so the dog wouldn't slide off and started opening the envelope. She was shaking. Her thick fingers couldn't get the envelope open without ripping it to pieces so that's what she did. She ripped the envelope to pieces. A flash drive fell out on the old beat up waxy kitchen table and then she pulled a single piece of paper out and unfolded it. When she did, a check fell face down on the table top. Big Cindy read the letter and handed it to her daughter. Her daughter eagerly scanned the short, handwritten paragraph.

Thanks for taking Sophie. She's a good dog.

I never forgot you. Ever.

Here's "looking" at you, Kid

David O Gideon

Big Cindy picked up the check and turned it over. Stunned, she handed it to her daughter.

Her daughter chuckled and asked, "Just how well did you know Mr. Gideon?"

The amount of the check was $4,200,000.

When they came to their senses, they ran out to the warehouse with Sophie nipping at their heels. They plugged the flash drive into their only working computer. Big Cindy fiddled with it a bit and then the contents popped up...and they began to read.

It was an affliction or maybe a blessing, a curse or a gift, the boy couldn't tell....

The End